The light faded. Rado froze. "Here I am," he said loudly. "What are you waiting for? You're a god, aren't you? Show me your divinity!"

He shuddered. His head slammed back against the cushions. Rado's arms slowly bent across his chest in deathlike rigor. His eyes rolled back until only white showed. Ripples of preternatural motion ran through him from head to toe, then ceased. Gradually every part of Rado's body relaxed. Only the cables on the headband kept him upright in the chair.

He was gone. The body remained, a living suit of flesh, but the mind and soul of Rado of Hapmark had departed from this world.

———

Other TSR® Books

STARSONG
Dan Parkinson

**ST. JOHN THE PURSUER:
VAMPIRE IN MOSCOW**
Richard Henrick

**BIMBOS OF THE
DEATH SUN**
Sharyn McCrumb

RED SANDS
*Paul Thompson and
Tonya Carter*

ILLEGAL ALIENS
*Nick Pollotta and
Phil Foglio*

THE JEWELS OF ELVISH
Nancy Varian Berberick

MONKEY STATION
*Ardath Mayhar and
Ron Fortier*

THE EYES HAVE IT
Rose Estes

TOO, TOO SOLID FLESH
Nick O'Donohoe

THE EARTH REMEMBERS
Susan Torian Olan

DARK HORSE
Mary H. Herbert

WARSPRITE
Jefferson P. Swycaffer

NIGHTWATCH
Robin Wayne Bailey

OUTBANKER
Timothy A. Madden

THE ROAD WEST
Gary Wright

THE ALIEN DARK
Diana G. Gallagher

WEB OF FUTURES
Jefferson P. Swycaffer

SORCERER'S STONE
L. Dean James

THE FALCON RISES
Michael C. Staudinger

**TOKEN OF
DRAGONSBLOOD**
Damaris Cole

THE CLOUD PEOPLE
Robert B. Kelly

**LIGHTNING'S
DAUGHTER**
Mary H. Herbert

THORN AND NEEDLE
Paul B. Thompson

KINGSLAYER
L. Dean James

THORN AND NEEDLE

Paul B. Thompson

THORN AND NEEDLE

Copyright ©1992 Paul B. Thompson
All Rights Reserved.

First printing: March 1992
Printed in the United States of America
Library of Congress Catalog Card Number: 91-67491

9 8 7 6 5 4 3 2

ISBN: 1-56076-397-3

TSR, Inc.
P.O. Box 756
Lake Geneva, WI 53147
U.S.A.

TSR Ltd.
120 Church End, Cherry Hinton
Cambridge CB1 3LB
United Kingdom

For Lib

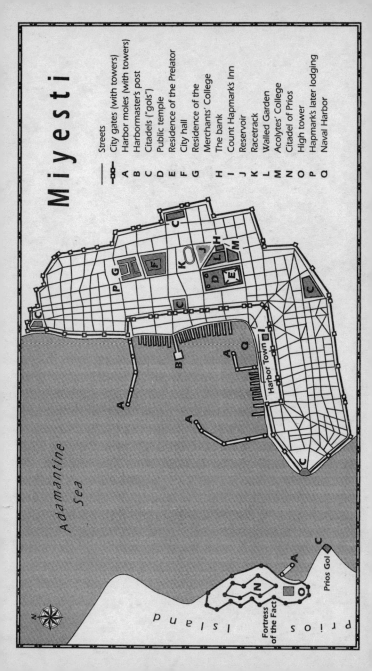

Miyesti

Streets
- City gates (with towers)

A Harbor moles (with towers)
B Harbormaster's post
C Citadels ("gols")
D Public temple
E Residence of the Prelator
F City hall
G Residence of the
H Merchants' College
I The bank
J Count Hapmark's Inn
K Reservoir
L Racetrack
M Walled Garden
N Acolytes' College
O Citadel of Prios
P High tower
Q Hapmark's later lodging
   Naval Harbor

Adamantine Sea

Harbor Town

Prios Island

Fortress of the Fact

Prios Gol

First: Two Nights in Harbor Town

But for Man's fault, then was the thorn.

Robert Herrick (1591-1674)
"The Rose"

I

"So this is Miyesti!"

The eight-oared barge rolled in the harbor swell, but the tall stranger kept his footing. He pushed the peak of his green leather hat farther back on his head for a clearer view. Rising above the wind-worn houses of the waterfront were the pearl gray walls of the city proper. Banners whipped from the high battlements, and bronze statues five times life-size stood atop each tower.

"My lord, please sit down. It would not do for you to be pitched overboard so close to landing." The thin, gray-clad figure who spoke thus tugged firmly on the tall man's coattail.

"I am the Count of Hapmark," the man replied. "I will go ashore standing, as befits a man of my station." The boy in gray, the count's valet, lapsed into prim silence.

The barge swung suddenly to port as the rowers on that side backed their oars. A low, lean galleot raked across the barge's course. A striking pennant crackled from the galleot's foremast: a red diamond edged in gold, set upon a white field. The count watched the galleot pass. The downswept ram cleaved the green water, pitching deeply with every swing of its oars. The count had to do some quick stepping to keep his feet under him when the barge wallowed in the galleot's wake.

The bargemaster cursed. The count turned to him. "Who were those impudent fellows, Master Firo?" he asked.

"That's the Brethren, my lord. We all must give way to the holy Brethren." Bargemaster Firo spat eloquently over the side.

"You sound bitter. Haven't the Brethren greatly enriched Miyesti in the past half century?"

"Oh, aye, that they have. But it's no life for a man to bow and fawn to a gaggle of priests with metal headbands. I was born a free man and I'm as good as any of 'em." Firo spat again, though with less vehemence.

"Do you hear that, Thorn? I would not have taken our good bargemaster for a republican," said the count. His valet, Thorn, only shrugged. "Do you not believe that some men are born more deserving than others?" he asked the bargemaster.

"We're all born the same way," said Firo. "Naked and bloody from our mother's womb. Bless the Mother!" He made the sign of the Mother Goddess on his forehead. Facing away from him, Thorn did likewise.

The count licked his lips and returned his gaze to the rapidly approaching docks. The waterfront teemed with activity. Lighters tied up at the end of the long piers, and stevedores kept an endless train of cargo flowing back to wagons waiting on shore to haul the goods away. The barge rowers lifted their oars high, and the square-bowed craft coasted in midway along one of the longest piers. Master Firo left his place in the stern and clambered forward. He tossed a mooring rope to a dockhand, who made it fast to a bronze cleat. One of the stern rowers threw the aft line, and the barge was secured.

The count stepped lightly over the seated men to a wooden ladder hanging down from the pier and climbed up. After adjusting the drape of his green velvet coat, he said, "Well, look alive, Thorn! Get my bags."

Thorn swayed up the ladder with a bulky travel case balanced on his narrow shoulder. He plunked the box down. The count hopped back. "You almost dropped that on my foot!" he said indignantly.

"Sorry, my lord. I don't see how I could have missed." Thorn descended to the barge again.

"Is that a jape about the size of my feet?" called the count.

A sailor hung a heavy canvas satchel on Thorn's back. "*Unh.* Of course not, my lord."

"Yes, well. Hmph."

Three bags and two crates later, all of the count's possessions were on the pier. Leaving Thorn to watch them, the count strolled down the dock to find a cart or wagon to hire. No sooner had he reached the street than he was engulfed by a swarm of yelling touts and barkers.

"Great one! Great one! You desire a guide?"

"I am Grovo, son of Grovo, purveyor of the finest smoking resins—"

"—women such as Your Excellency has never known! They do anything—"

"For only three ducats, as you are a foreigner and a guest—"

"Silence!" shouted the count. "Stand back, will you? Stand back!" It did no good. The touts fell to berating each other as thieves and charlatans. Some blows were exchanged, and the count feared he was in the center of a budding riot. His shout for order went unheeded. He reached for his sword.

A loud pealing scattered the scruffy crowd. Before the last ring faded, there wasn't a tout to be seen. Dazed, the count turned and saw a pair of soldiers coming toward him. They wore white quilted gambesons and burnished steel cabassets. Their coats bore the diamond insignia of the Brethren of the Fact.

"Good day, sir. I trust those ruffians did not harm you?" said the first soldier. He carried a stout pole, from the top of which swung a cylindrical iron bell.

"No, I'm quite all right," said the count.

"Have you just landed?" asked the second man.

"Why, yes, from the cromster *Bizon*."

"May we see your cachet?" said the bell holder. The count felt a warning bell of his own clanging inside his head. He opened his coat and took out a folded leather wallet. He handed the cachet to the second Miyestan.

"You are Count Rado of Hapmark?" the guardsman said, reading the slip of parchment inside the cachet. The count said he was. "Where exactly is Hapmark?"

"Nowhere certain," said Count Rado. He tried to laugh, but the soldiers did not find him amusing. "Actually Hapmark is our ancestral manor house in the province of Macerand."

"It says here you have a personal servant. Where is he?"

"Here," said Thorn, appearing noiselessly behind them. The two guardsmen started. The iron bell rang once before the surprised soldier stilled it.

The second soldier's eyes narrowed. "What is your name? What's written here is illegible."

"I call him Thorn," Count Rado said hastily. "An orphan, alas, with no real parents to name him. No doubt a bastard, too." Thorn looked his master in the eye and raised one brow ever so slightly.

The guardsman gave back the count's cachet. With a charcoal-tipped stylus, he wrote the appropriate information in his daily copybook. " 'One Count Rado, citizen of Macerand—' "

"I am a peer, not a citizen, if you please."

He dutifully made the correction. " 'And one Thorn, servant, illegitimate.' " He snapped the book shut. "Thank you for your cooperation, your lordship. Please have a pleasant stay in our city." The two men turned to go.

"Wait a moment. Could you tell me where I might hire an honest and reliable conveyance?" asked Rado.

The guardsmen exchanged glances. "We are not allowed to recommend anyone in particular," said the bell holder, "but any driver who displays the sign of the Fact should be everything your lordship desires. Good day and good morrow."

"Good morrow to you." The men marched away, shoulder to shoulder. Waterfront idlers gave them wide berth as they passed.

"What do you think of that, eh, Thorn?" asked the count.

"Are you asking a bastard's opinion?"

"Don't be testy. What do you think of these Brethren so far?"

"They seem well organized. And feared. Did you notice they dispersed a mob of twenty men simply by ringing a bell?"

Count Rado rubbed a finger across his narrow mustache. "Feared, yes," he said. "Dare one say even hated?"

* * * * *

It didn't take Thorn long to wave down a cart bearing the distinctive red and gold diamond. The driver very politely assisted Thorn in dragging the count's baggage from the dock. Rado seated himself in the driver's box and did nothing to help his valet with his burdens.

When Thorn finally heaved the last satchel into the cart, the driver said, "Where to, my lord?"

"Can you recommend a good inn in the city?"

"You may not go into Miyesti yet, my lord."

"Indeed! And why is that?" Rado demanded.

"You have only arrived on the morning tide, yes?" The count affirmed this. "Then you must wait in Harbor Town until the city prelates approve your entry," said the carter.

The count reddened. "I am a peer of the Homelands! Am I to be treated like any jetsam of the sea by the officials of a *colonial* town?"

The carter shrugged. "Pallo's Tavern has rooms, I'm told, at a very fair rate."

An idea made Rado smile. He worked a large Pazoan ducat loose from his money pouch. "Would this get me into Miyesti today?" he asked slyly. The carter lifted his blunt chin.

"My lord, I am a hard-working man. I could drive this cart for ten days and nights and not earn so much. But if you were found inside the city walls without the proper stamp on your cachet . . ." He let his listeners imagine the unhappy consequences. "I would not put you in danger of losing your freedom. The Fact teaches, 'Know how your brother feels, and feel that way for him.' "

"Come now, fellow, I'm not your brother."

"All men are brothers, my lord." The carter clucked his tongue. The mule jerked the cart forward, and Count Rado's gaping jaw snapped shut.

The cart wended its way along the cobbled street. The path was choked with pushcart vendors, wives laden with the day's victuals, pigs, chickens, dogs, and an occasional cripple or beggar. Sailors from ships anchored in the strait sauntered about in pairs and trios, sampling the local grog and eyeing the whores lingering in most of the second-story windows. Local law did not permit social commerce before noon, so all the mariners could do was look.

Rado was looking, too, though the carter piously kept his attention on the milling traffic around them. The count smiled at a yellow-haired creature in a white linen chemise who cunningly stood so that the late morning sun streamed in a window behind her. . . .

From the corner of one eye, Rado saw that someone was following the cart. He stole a look and saw a veiled woman trailing behind their right wheel. Thorn was sitting up, and the two were conversing so quietly that Rado couldn't hear a word they said. Before he could call out to his valet, the veiled woman melted into the crowd.

"Pallo's Tavern," said the carter. "Does this suit your lordship?"

Rado appraised the inn. The facade was clinker-built like a ship, with square ports and unpainted clapboards. Dirty strips of cloth hung over the empty windows. He snapped his fingers for Thorn. "Inquire within," he said. "I shall wait here."

Thorn jumped down. Rado watched the slight gray figure vanish into the dark doorway of the tavern. The count took out his barthwood pipe and cut a plug of smoking resin. The black gum was just beginning to bubble when Thorn emerged, flushed and grim.

"My lord," he began, "this tavern is the scene of wanton depravity and squalor. The landlord is a gross drunkard, his patrons are pimps and decadent sea vermin. The beverages served are tainted and foul. In short, my lord, it is a most suitable place for you."

Rado threw back his head and laughed. "You're an impudent prize, Thorn! Why I don't have you flogged I don't know." He stepped on the trace pole and lowered himself to the street. "This will do, good carter." He gave the man a Miyestan silver star.

"A moment, sir," said the carter. He deliberately counted out five coppers into Rado's hand. "Your change, my lord."

"Change? Hang me if a tradesman ever gave me *change* before!"

The carter drew the strings of his purse tight and tucked the twill bag inside his blouse. "As the Fact teaches us, 'Serve your brother as you would be served.' " Not only did he give change, but the carter helped Thorn unload as well. Then, with a wave of his hat, he slapped the reins over his mule's back and clattered away.

The count of Hapmark swept into the tavern's dim common room. Though not yet noon, the tables were thick with hard-looking men and women downing ale from tall clay mugs. At the bar, a line of seamen in rope shoes and leather kilts swilled evil-smelling liquor from thimble-sized cups. The patrons of Pallo's Tavern noted well the entrance of Count Rado. His fine clothes and jeweled rings marked him as a man of substance. But the cup-hilted sword on his left hip discouraged any notions they might have entertained about relieving the foreign stranger of his burdensome wealth. That, and the count's neatly-muscled physique.

"Proprietor! Proprietor!" Rado called. He rattled the hilt of his sword in its scabbard. "Proprietor!"

"Yah, yah, don' burst a vessel," rumbled a voice from under the bar. A vast white bulk rose out of the moldering shadows. In the bluish glow of a spirit lamp, a great misshapen head appeared. "I'm Bucker," said the lumpy face.

"Where's Pallo?" asked the count mildly.

"Dead and buried these forty year. You wan' something, you deal with me." One bloodshot eye showed a brow made of gristle and scars. The other eyelid was sunken and sewn shut.

"Very well. I shall need your best room for a few days," said Rado.

"How many days?"

"I don't know. Until your silly city prelates let me in the walls, however long that may be." Mention of the prelates stopped the steady hiss of talk in the room. Rado searched the room for trouble. "I hope it won't take more than a day or two."

"Yah, yah. You can have Room Six." Bucker slapped an iron latchkey on the counter. His dough-colored palm stayed open beside it. "Two silvers a night."

The count held up the same gold ducat he had tempted the carter with. "Is Six your best room?"

Bucker squirmed as the gleam of gold held him in its cold embrace. "Mostly best," he said vaguely.

"How about Number Four?" bawled a voice across the room. Bucker spat back a curse.

"What about this Room Four?" asked Rado. "Is it better than six?" He weaved the ducat through his long fingers. Bucker licked his fleshy lips.

"Yah. You wait . . . not long."

From under the bar, Bucker produced a black be-laying pin. He scrubbed his grimy sleeves up his arms, exposing a row of lewd tatoos. The floor trembled with his tread as Bucker disappeared up the twisting staircase. The count leaned his elbows on the bar and hooked one heel on the rutted footrail.

A knock resounded through the tavern. Muffled voices. A thud. A scream. The customers ignored it all, while Rado watched the ceiling in wonder.

Then a half-naked man landed at the foot of the steps with a crash. He groaned and lay still. Down in a clatter after him came a black-haired woman, frantically pulling the top of her dress over her bare shoulders.

"Pig!" she shrieked. "Fat swine-goat fornicator! You can't treat us like this! We paid—"

"He paid more!" Bucker bellowed, stomping down the stairs. "Now get out! Never liked having a cheap slut sleeping in my rooms anywhen."

"Slut! When have you ever had a real woman, you cattle raper?" The woman dragged her male companion off the steps in time to avoid Bucker's broad, booted foot. Thorn entered with the last of the count's bags. The woman tugged her man out by his heels, cursing Bucker all the while. Thorn held the door curtain for her. She kicked his shin as she passed, so he let the greasy leather flap fall in her face. With a final squeal, she fell backward out of Pallo's into the muck-filled gutter.

"Four is yours now," said Bucker. He grinned. It was not a pretty sight.

"You're too kind," said Rado. His thumb sprang up, and the gold coin flipped through the air. With surprising agility, Bucker snatched it with one meaty hand.

The count went upstairs. The upper hall was sparsely lit, but he found a door marked with four vertical lines of white. All the latch holes were shaped differently. Only the correct key would fit its matching door. Satisfied with the arrangement, Rado lifted the latch on Four and went in.

It was a big room; that was about all you could say for it. The fireplace filled the wall to the right of the door. Facing it was a triple-wide four-poster bed. Across from the door, the wall was pierced by a single window, but the shutter was closed and bolted. The count pushed them open. He heard the bump-bump-bump of Thorn hauling his belongings up the stairs.

"What a charming place," said Thorn.

"Tch, you're being impudent again. Our good Master Bucker isn't the sort to take kindly to insults paid to his establishment." Rado unhitched his sword belt and hung it on a bedpost. The humped feather mattress smelled as if it had been soaked in a tidal pool for at least a year. He muttered words to that effect.

"What?" said Thorn.

"Merely thinking, my boy. Get on with your unpacking."

"For a whole ducat, you'd think we would at least get clean sheets," Thorn said, throwing open the first travel case.

" 'We,' Thorn? What makes you think you'll be sleeping in this bed?" The valet did not reply. He stood and shook the wrinkles from the count's evening cloak. "At any rate, the ducat was not so much for the room as for the privacy it will buy."

"Do you think so?"

"I do. Who else would be able to pay so much for such a flea's nest?" Rado sank back on the bed. He loosened his trousers and scratched his stomach. "Thorn, what time do you make it?"

"Midday at least. Shall I find food and drink? I wouldn't trust any offering from Master Bucker's kitchen."

"I was thinking of another sort of need. Get a bag of coppers and go back to the waterfront. There's a certain lady in a certain house I want you to find."

Thorn sighed disapprovingly. "Now, my lord?"

"Of course now. I've just finished a very long and demanding sea voyage, have I not?"

* * * * *

Left on his own for the afternoon, Thorn kept to the tavern. In the common room, he found a seat with the fewest crude-looking customers. A mug of bitter ale was put in his hand without his asking for it as he sat.

"Good health to you all," said Thorn, lofting his mug. The others raised their own and drank. Thorn did not. He got just enough foam on his lip to feign that he had.

"Quite a city you have," he said. "One hears so many stories about the wonders of Miyesti. I hope to see some of them when my master and I enter the city."

"Hah!" said the sailor on his left. "Me, I been shipping out of this port for well on twenty year, and I never been beyond Harbor Town."

"That speaks well of the prelates, does it not?" responded the fellow on the sailor's left. He wore a long straight gown striped in varied colors. His face was bearded and swarthy. "They've enough sense not to let in wormy sea devils, yes?"

"There's a lying Kuruk for you," the man on Thorn's right said. "In the old days, nobody was too good or too bad to enter Miyesti."

"What's made the difference?" asked Thorn.

"The holy Brethren," said the gowned Kuruk.

"Hah!" The sailor made the sign of the Goddess and drank deep.

"Is it true the Brethren have suppressed the worship of the old gods?" Thorn queried.

"Suppressed ain't the true word for it," said the man by his right hand. "Lured folk away, that's what they've done, with their gentle words and fancy tricks. Left the shrines fair empty, and then the city claimed the buildings when the priests couldn't pay their taxes!"

"They are full of deceit," agreed the Kuruk.

"Do you avow the Brethren haven't kept their promises?" asked the fourth man at the table, who sat opposite Thorn. He was a young man, clean shaven and freckled. He wore a felt hat with a very wide brim.

"Magic, that's what they're about. There's no proper faith when a man can pray into a box and out pops anything he wants. The gods are like us; they don't do something for nothing. So what does this Fact god want?"

"I hear people go to the sanctuary on Prios Island and never come back," said the Kuruk darkly.

"Jealous slander," said the young man in the hat. "Prios is the Brethren's place of retreat. Is it sinister that new men should go to Prios for religious instruction?"

The sailor belched. "The Fact is there. On Prios."

Thorn's eyes widened. "Truly? *The* Fact?"

"True. The Fact was brought to the island fifty years ago by the great prelator, Ubarth. The elected ruler of Miyesti gave Prios to the Brethren as their sanctuary in perpetuity." The man in the hat slowly turned his mug until the handle was pointing at Thorn. "That was the most fortunate thing that ever happened to the city. Soon all the world will know the goodness of the Fact."

"Horse dung." The man on Thorn's right groped at his neck and fished out a length of silver chain. Dangling from the blackened links was a tiny statuette. "Here's a god for a man," he said. "Joder, god of storms. He speaks in thunder! He churns the sea with his little toe and pisses hurricanes! What can this gewgaw god of yours do compared to that? He can't even speak to his limp-rod followers unless they wear those pretty headbands!"

The man in the hat stood. "The god of the Fact is the only true god. All others are maunderings from the minds of suckling babes and drunkards."

The devotee of Joder let out a howl and flung his half-full mug. The man in the hat dodged the missile, which sailed on to strike with a splatter on a table beyond. The unintended target let out a roar.

"Who threw that?" An oarsman from the Isle of Jua, his hair braided in a hundred pigtails, loomed over them, ale dripping from the beaded tips.

"He did," said the Kuruk, pointing.

"Gutless barbarian!" the Joderite snarled. "I'll have your balls for bed warmers!"

The table went over with a bang. The sailor and the Kuruk fell backward off the bench. Thorn saved his ale and flung the stinging brew in the Joderite's face. The Juaan boxed the ears of the man in the hat, clearing him out of the way so he could get to the Joderite.

The commons erupted. Clay mugs flew, and a rain of sticky brown ale filled the air. Bucker banged his belaying pin on the wall and yelled for order. A three-legged stool hit him on the nose, and down he went. No wonder he looks the way he does, thought Thorn. He backed to the nearest wall and flattened himself against it.

The Juaan giant, twenty hands tall and muscled by his trade, made short work of the Joder worshiper by pounding his face mercilessly against a ceiling post. When the man was limp at his feet, the Juaan cast about for another victim. He spied Thorn alone by the wall and smiled. Every second tooth in his head had been deliberately knocked out and short brass fangs substituted in their place.

"I haven't eaten a foreigner in weeks," he said. "Hold still, little one—"

Thorn's hand flashed to his armpit. From under his left arm, he drew a steel stiletto two hands long. He pressed a stud on the handle and two tines snapped out, forming a hilt.

The Juaan only grinned wider. He passed a hand behind his back and brought out a broad, single-edged marlinspike.

A whooping sailor jumped from a nearby table on-to the Juaan's back. The big oarsman staggered but kept his feet. He reached over his shoulder with one hand, grabbed the sailor by the ear, and threw him off. The sailor hit the bench where the Joderite had been sitting, smashing it to flinders.

The marlinspike whispered by Thorn's throat. He'd been so intent on the flying sailor that he'd lost concentration on the Juaan for a moment. No longer! The Juaan swept the hook-bladed knife before him in wide arcs. The wall was to Thorn's back. He stepped forward . . .

. . . and caught the salt-blackened blade in the tines of his stiletto. The Juaan laughed and knotted the muscles of his thick arm. The hook turned in to-ward Thorn's chest. He couldn't repel the Juaan's thrust; the oarsman was far too strong. Instead, Thorn flung his wrist out. The stiletto rotated the knife out and away from Thorn.

Surprised, the Juaan watched his attack go awry. Thorn stepped back and punched him sharply in the throat. He extended the first joint of his middle fin-ger and jammed it in the oarsman's eye. The Juaan backpedaled, choking. The contempt evaporated from his face.

The Juaan bored in again, ignoring a barrage of mugs that bounced off his back. The marlinspike came down in a fast diagonal slash. Thorn caught the knife on his inside tine. He turned the stiletto outward this time, driving the short tine through the Juaan's hand. The big man roared like a gelded bull and stepped in, as Thorn knew he would. Rado's valet pushed the long tip of his weapon into the Juaan's forearm. The bright spike went through the hard muscle effortlessly. Blood welled from the wound in shocking quantity. The Juaan wobbled backward. Thorn followed hard, pushing him over the broken bench.

The stiletto was poised over the fallen man's jugular. Iron bells started clanging in the street. The brawl quickly dispersed. In less time than it takes to say "Brethren of the Fact," Pallo's common room was empty save for Thorn, the Juaan, and the unconscious Joderite.

Thorn straightened. He wiped the blood from his weapon with two fingers. "Begone," he said, "lest the guardsmen take you." The Juaan cradled his bleeding arm to his chest and blundered out the door. Thorn sheathed the stiletto and made for the stairs.

Count Rado's fancy girl chose that moment to descend. Frazzled but smiling, she jingled a pair of silver stars in her cupped palms. The two met at the sharpest turn, and Thorn found his nose pressed into the damp blouse of Rado's fancy girl.

"Find something you like?" she said brightly.

Thorn backed down a step and held out his arm. "By your leave, lady." The fancy girl laughed at him, her porcelain peals echoing down the stairs and out the door.

Thorn knocked discreetly on the count's door. "Enter," said Rado.

The count was propped on pillows against the headboard of the smelly bed. The corner of one of the flannel sheets covered his thighs. He puffed contentedly on his pipe. The smell of fine Kurukish resin swirled around the bedchamber.

"What was that commotion I heard?" asked Rado.

"I'm surprised your lordship paid it any attention," said Thorn. He saw his cuffs were edged with blood, black now on the soft gray fabric.

"It was not a lack of interest in the young lady's ample charms that prompted my question," Rado said loftily. "What happened?"

"I engaged some of the patrons of the tavern in a discussion on the state of religion hereabouts. A follower of the old gods wasn't feeling kindly toward the Brethren of the Fact. Someone rose to defend the new faith. An altercation followed. . . ." Thorn finished with a shrug.

Rado took the pipe stem from his teeth. "Did you kill anyone?"

"My lord!"

"Don't play the dissembling young man with me! I know that murderous instrument you carry tucked away. Did you kill anyone?"

"No, Rado. The fellow in question will not be rowing for some weeks, but he won't die if he finds a competent chirurgeon to bind the wound."

The count drew hard on the hissing resin. "Good, good. It wouldn't do for you to end up in prison our first day here, would it?"

"No, my lord. It would take some time to replace me." Rado breathed in too far and coughed.

Thorn went to the cold fireplace. His thin blanket was already unrolled on the brick hearth. The count gave him leave to rest, and Thorn stretched out his lean, tired body and relaxed with an audible sigh.

Rado watched him for a while as he sucked idly on his pipe. "Thorn," he said quietly. The boy didn't stir. "Thorn," he repeated, a bit more loudly.

"Yes, my lord?" was the weary reply.

"Here." The count flung a rag-stuffed pillow between the bedposts. Thorn gathered it in, burying his face in its knotty folds. "Thank you, Rado."

"*Count* Rado."

"Count Rado."

* * * * *

An open cabriolet, lacquered an elegant black, pulled up smartly before the door of Pallo's Tavern. Two guardsmen in Fact gambesons dropped off the rear rails and flanked the door. The driver leaned over and released the carriage's door. A silver-haired gentleman of proud bearing, clothed in white brocade and hose, stepped to the street.

The gloomy interior of the tavern reeked of sweat,

old ale, and urine. The well-dressed visitor held a small perfumed sachet to his nose. "Innkeeper!" he said in the rounded tones of an orator. "Where are you, innkeeper?"

"Yah, yah." Bucker got up from his usual place under the bar. He squinted at the newcomer. "By the bitch herself," he muttered. "Another nob come to Pallo's. I'll have to raise my rates, I will."

"Do you have a foreign gentleman staying here?" asked the man.

"Mebbe. What is it to you?"

The man parted his coat. A golden Fact emblem sparkled at his neck. "I am Harlic Vost, subprelate of the College of Peace. Do you have a foreign nobleman here or not?"

Bucker rubbed his nose—and swore; it was a swollen, purplish mass from the fight the afternoon before. "Yah, him and the boy's upstairs."

"Boy?"

"A servant. These well-born nobs, they can't wipe their own—"

"Yes, I see," said Vost. "Will you go up and ask the gentleman to come down here?" Bucker was reluctant until he glimpsed the guardsmen outside his door. Those pure-faced devils would keep his regulars away. There'd be damned little business until they were gone. So . . .

Bucker thumped the door with his fist. "Wake up, lordship! Wake up!" he called as tactfully as the memory of one gold ducat could make him. "Please, lordship, there's an important man here to see you."

Thorn's numb face and tousled hair appeared in a crack in the door. "Whossit?" he mumbled.

"One Vost, of the College of Peace. Very big nob . . . you know what I mean?"

"Oh, very well. Tell Master Vost the count of Hapmark will be with him shortly." Bucker twitched his face in a deformed sort of nod and left.

Thorn crept to the sleeping Rado's side. With great care and in perfect silence, the valet bent over until his lips were a hair's breadth from Rado's ear. He whispered two special words: "Remember Sasrel."

The count's eyes sprang open, and he catapulted from the bed. "How dare you say that to me!" he gasped. A painful spasm knotted in his chest.

"There is a Miyestan official downstairs, my lord," Thorn said evenly. "No doubt he wishes to interview you before he allows us to enter the city."

"Hunter's blood!" Rado said, sinking into the room's only chair. "I aged ten years from the scare you gave me!"

"If you will choose an outfit for the day, I will fetch a basin of water for your morning wash." Rado buried his face in his hands. Thorn turned on one heel and went in search of fresh water.

He returned with a copper bowl brimming with tepid water. Thorn pushed the door in with his toe and found himself staring down the length of the count's drawn sword.

"I ought to kill you. Then all this madness would

be over," said Rado.

"The water isn't the cleanest, my lord, but it is as good as can be had in Harbor Town."

"Damn you! How dare you stand there treating me like some drooling dotard! If you've no respect for me, I would think you'd at least fear nine hands of steel."

Thorn set the bowl gently on the bed. "I know what you are, Rado of Hapmark. The One Who Commands told me about you. There is *nothing* of your life and career I don't know." He folded his arms and looked Rado in the eye. "As for the sword, you may be skilled enough to kill me before I reach you, but in any case it would be extremely untimely for us to fight with Fact men below us. Is that not so?"

The sword declined to the floor. Rado leaned on the hilt. "How did I get to such a state? What curse cast you upon me?"

Thorn went to the largest trunk and unpacked a suit of blue brocade with pearls-in-wine smallclothes. "It wasn't a curse," he said. A pair of long black stockings came out in a tangle. "What you did, you did with a smile and a warm feeling for your own shocking cleverness. No one held a knife to your gullet. You did it for the benefit of your purse and your reputation."

Rado pulled the nightshirt over his head. He stood naked except for his breechnap. Seeing Thorn avert his eyes made Rado regain his arrogant composure. "Get me a new nap," he said with renewed haughtiness. Thorn rooted about in the box and found a clean breechnap. With his gaze fixed on the floorboards, he put the new nap in Rado's hand. The count whipped off his last stitch and flung it at Thorn. With his valet all but covering his face with his hands, Rado leisurely dressed.

* * * * *

Harlic Vost rapped his ring steadily on the arm of his chair. Bucker had found him a modestly clean seat and then had withdrawn to his hole behind the bar. The subprelate waited and waited. The watchbells in the city towers tolled six times—the sixth hour past midnight. He'd been waiting since the fifth bell, and still Count Rado hadn't come.

In the room upstairs, Rado held out his arms to Thorn. The latter stepped forward, encircling his master's waist. When the sword belt was buckled, Rado said, "The rabbit has stewed long enough, don't you agree?"

"As you say, my lord."

"Then lead on."

Vost leaned forward in his chair when he heard feet drumming on the worn treads. The first one down was a sprig of a youth, sixteen hands high, with an unruly crop of straw yellow hair. Three steps behind him came an older man, a good eighteen hands tall. His dark brown hair was gathered in a short queue. His eyes were also brown, and he wore a neatly trimmed mustache.

Vost stood. "Do I have the favor of addressing the count of Hapmark?"

"I am Rado of Hapmark, yes." The count crossed his hands behind his back. "And who are you, sir?"

Harlic Vost identified himself. "I am here to take your application for entry into Miyesti."

"Indeed. What must I do?"

"I will need to take your cachet for a while. That, and a report I make to the Prelate for Peace will determine our decision."

Rado waved to Thorn, who handed the cachet to Vost. The subprelate opened it and gave the contents a cursory glance.

"What is your business in the city, my lord?" Vost asked.

"I am making a tour of the eastern colonial cities. My estates are quite well managed by hired commoners, and that leaves me with the time and income to travel. My father, Duke Leadro of Macerand, suggested I broaden my experience by a tour." Rado felt in his coat pocket and brought out his favorite pipe.

"I see," said Vost. "Miyesti is not your first stop?"

"No, I spent eight days in Lykata. Dreadful place, Lykata—all that fish lying about, smelling awful." He stuffed a plug of resin in the shallow barthwood bowl. Thorn fetched a candle and held it down low so the count could light his pipe. "I called briefly at Cape Etro and the island of Oparos. From there I took ship to Miyesti."

"And where will you go next?"

"Ah . . ." Rado blew out a stream of tangy smoke. "Blood, what is the name of our next stop?"

"Tablish," said Thorn.

"Yes, that's it: Tablish. Marvelously heathen-sounding place, eh?"

Vost bowed. "It is named for a Kurukish chieftain who died there two centuries ago," he said. "The city is famed for its glass and pottery works." The subprelate tucked Rado's cachet into his breast pocket. "Thank you for your cooperation, my lord. I can't imagine there will be any difficulty approving your entry into Miyesti. Good day and good morrow."

"Wait. When may I expect to hear from you?"

"Tomorrow, my lord. A messenger will return your cachet here with validating stamps."

Vost departed briskly. The guardsmen mounted the cabriolet after him, and the subprelate hurried away. The black carriage was soon lost in the morning flow of humanity now filling the street.

II

The latch dropped. Thorn shook the door handle and found it secure. That done, he rejoined Count Rado in the common room.

"Shall we see the sights of Harbor Town?" said Rado. Thorn ran down a carter willing to carry them up the hill from the waterfront. With the count seated by the driver and the tireless Thorn deposited in back, they set off to expend a day of waiting.

Harbor Town was shaped like the joining of a thumb and forefinger. The long "forefinger" was the north-south section of docks and warehouses; the wider "thumb" was the east-west district of taverns, doss shops, whorehouses, and gaudily painted shrines. The latter did a heavy trade in protective amulets for sailors and travelers. Some shrines employed diviners of the sky or readers of entrails. As Rado and Thorn rode slowly along Mizzen Street, they could see by the size of the crowds that the old gods were not yet dead, even in the very shadow of the Fact.

At one corner, across from a garish shrine dedicated to the sea goddess Ludril, a man perched on a tall wooden crate. He wore a Fact symbol as wide as his chest on a string around his neck. A line of worshipers waiting to pay tribute to Ludril snaked by his stand. The man was addressing the devotees of the Mistress of the Tides. Count Rado tapped the carter on the arm. They creaked to a halt.

" . . . deceived by false gods, my brothers! Within that painted house, you will find not true divinity. No, you will find a carved statue, served by slatterns who take your hard-won money and give what in return?" The man gestured broadly. "*Nothing!* Empty promises, murmured words meant to comfort! Are you such children that you need soothing songs to make you brave? Do you doubt the evidence of your senses so completely that you give your worship unquestioningly to a woman-shaped block of wood?"

Someone in the line made a rude noise. Laughter rippled through the crowd, and a rowdy voice cried, "Who do you pray to, city man?"

"There is only one god, and that god has given us the Fact!"

"Nay! He has given us a jackass," sneered another Ludrilite.

"Laugh if you can! Mock if you will! From within this city will arise a host that will cover the world. Not an enemy, killing and destroying—no, not an army! A multitude of believers who have heard the word of the Fact will arise! From Miyesti, Lykata, Tablish, and Etro! From every city, every village, every heart in the world. God's word is the Fact; his voice is the Fact; the

Fact will transform the world!''

The Speaker was himself transformed. From a modest, tradesmanlike demeanor, he had achieved hysterical rapture. His face glowed, his eyes bulged, and sweat stood out on his balding head. The copper headband he wore glistened in the sun.

"How can I show you the truth? How can I make you know the wonder of the Fact? Tell me, brothers! Tell me, that I may prove the voice to you!"

He got plenty of wild and vulgar suggestions, which he chose to ignore. Finally a serious-looking young man with mason's tools hanging from his belt said something to him that Rado couldn't hear. The Fact Speaker stooped to listen. He heard the man's request, nodded, and smiled.

"Brothers! Here is a worthy request. This simple, honest workman has asked to wear my headband."

"Ho, ho! I'd like them shoes you're wearing. . . ."

The Speaker for the Fact stepped down. He embraced the mason and lifted the copper ring off his head. Count Rado was shocked to see raw skin under the band. The Speaker set the band gently around the man's head. It was too large and slipped down to the young mason's ears. The crowd made merry at that.

"I guess knowing this Fact gives you a big head!"

"You'd think a god would surely know everybody's hat size."

Rado and Thorn ignored the gibes of the crowd. They concentrated instead on the mason. His curious expression faded. He put his hands up to replace the

Speaker's, keeping the copper tight against his skull. The mason's jaw worked up and down, as though he were talking; his eyes lifted upward to gaze at unseen vistas. Slowly a smile of purest happiness spread across his face. He laughed like a baby, and tears flowed from his farseeing eyes.

The Ludril enthusiasts quieted. When they did, the faint sounds the mason was making reached Rado and Thorn.

"Ohwanwanohohwanohohwanwanwanwanoh; ohohwanwanohwanoh . . ."

"He's gibbering nonsense," said the count.

The crowd apparently thought otherwise. They listened in awe to the steady stream of patter flowing from the mason's mouth. The Speaker had to pry the man's fingers loose from the headband. The mason collapsed on his hands and knees. The Speaker replaced the copper ring on his own head.

"Stand up, brother," he said. The mason staggered to his feet. "Tell them. Tell them of the great presence of the god's voice."

"It—it spoke to me," the young man stammered. "I didn't understand what it said, but it was good—wonderful. I—I felt a thousand years away and saw a world where men live as gods and cities are built of everlasting jewels. . . ."

In a rush, the crowd swallowed the Speaker. "Follow me!" he cried. "Follow me to the goodness of the Fact!" He set off on Mizzen Street with at least forty men and women in tow.

"Drive on. Follow them—carefully," said Rado. The old mare leaned on her traces and followed in the wake of the converts.

They continued through the heart of Harbor Town, the Fact Speaker and the mason leading. The walls of Miyesti were nearer, a cliff of cloud made into stone. The whole street was submerged in shadow. Harbor Town's rough, unpainted houses butted right against the bottom of the street. Then, by the city gate, all the old dwellings were cleared away in a wide half-circle. A pair of soldiers manned the closed portal.

"Stand where you are! Who approaches?" challenged one of the guards.

"Varlan Churt, Speaker of the Fact!"

"Wait for recognition!"

The carter drew in his reins. Count Rado leaned forward expectantly. A hand rested lightly on his shoulder. Thorn stood behind him.

A dazzling light, brighter than the sun, burst from a cylinder mounted over the gate. The people shrank back in terror, but Varlan Churt reassured them. The light narrowed to a tight beam. It crossed Churt's face and came to rest on the Fact emblem he wore.

"Enter Varlan Churt, Speaker," boomed a strange and mighty voice.

"These good people would enter with me," Churt announced to the empty air. "They wish to know the goodness of the Fact."

"Let it be done. Open the gate."

The black iron doors parted along the center and

rolled back into slots in the wall. Varlan Churt shepherded the amazed band of converts inside. The gate closed, and the light went out. The guards resumed their bored postures on either side of the gate.

"I wonder what happens to them now," said Thorn.

The count brushed the valet's hand away. "They all become happy little Fact folk, I suppose."

"Na' tall o' them, my lord," said the carter.

"What do you mean?"

"Some's not fit to wear the band, you see. Them as not gets back to Harbor Town."

Thorn asked, "How do you know so much?" The carter held up the side flaps of his old cloth cap. Two long, straight scars showed on his temples.

"Tried it myself. I ne'er seen or hearn a thing."

* * * * *

Count Rado paid off the driver in Hogshead Lane, and he and Thorn got out to walk. It was late afternoon, the doldrums for Harbor Town. The busiest times in the streets were right after the change in tides, which is to say around sunrise and sundown.

The count strolled down the center of the lane. Thorn was at his side, half a step behind. The street inclined down to the docks, and Rado could see cromsters and tartanes anchored in the sun-reddened waters of Prios Strait.

"Seeking a ship?" asked Thorn.

"I was admiring the colors of the sea and sky," Rado said sharply. "You would do well to take an interest in the real world. A little worldly experience might give you a more tolerant view of life."

"My time with you has shown me more of 'real life' than I ever hoped to see. But the changed subject has not been forgotten. You were thinking of leaving, weren't you?"

"If I were?"

"You know, my lord, what that would mean."

The count stopped abruptly. "Refreshment is what I need. Refreshment and diversion. All this theology is too sobering." At any point on the compass was a tavern or a grog shop. Count Rado pointed to one of the larger houses, whose sign bore a vivid painting of an enraged bull. Instead of his usual equipment, the bull on the sign sported a large pair of dice. "That is the place!" declared the count.

They entered the House of the Wild Bull to the strains of a Kurukish pipe band. The pipers skirled a lively tune for a pair of men dancing in a circle of clapping patrons. The Kuruks didn't dance with each other; they performed a strenuous step-and-kick routine independently.

Through a gap in the curtain of people, Thorn spied the dancers' faces. "I know that one," he said. "He was at Pallo's last night when the fight started."

The Kuruk saw Thorn, too, and flashed a wide grin as he whirled around the circle. The music reached a wild crescendo and stopped. The onlookers hooted and whistled their satisfaction with the show. Some threw coppers to the bowing dancers.

The Kuruk worked through the crowd, gathering gratuities. He steered over to Thorn and the count. Mopping his face with one voluminous sleeve, he presented himself.

"Greetings, my friend! The events of the past night prevented us from being introduced properly. Now I must make amends." The Kuruk pressed a palm to his chest. "Ishaf Indolel, at your service." Thorn presented the count and himself. "Ah, great one, your servant is indeed a warrior of the street. How coolly he dealt with that veritable giant of a Juaan! It made my heart glad to see it."

"You seem to have come through the fray intact," Rado observed dryly.

"Ompy favored me, I assure you." Ompy was the Kuruks' god of luck. "Seeing I was outmatched, I did as the sage teaches and 'lived to be a better man tomorrow.' Of course, I was not the only one to depart," Indolel added hastily. "The Miyestan in the broad hat was the first fellow out the door."

"How do you know the man was a Miyestan?" asked Thorn.

"He wore the symbol, the diamond." Seeing their puzzlement, Indolel said, "The sign of the Fact. You have seen it?"

"Yes, yes. Now, what was a city man and Fact worshiper doing in a dross shop like Pallo's?" mused the count. "Backsliding?"

"He seemed to be a man of stout convictions," said Thorn.

"No matter." Rado surveyed the crowded room. "The sign out front promised gaming. Where might this be, Master Indolel?"

"Does the great one wish to try his fortune at the tables? Allow Ishaf to be your guide."

The Kuruk weaved a winding path through the throng. The band resumed playing, and the shrill notes of Kurukish music added a sharp counterpoint to the loud hum of conversation. Wine flowed freely—the House of the Wild Bull served only local vintages—and more than a little was spilled on the count and Thorn as they trailed Indolel.

The dancer paused by a mosaic-covered wall. "Know, great one, that the masters of the Wild Bull do not care to share their commerce with the foreign gaming houses in Harbor Town. Therefore a price must be paid by those who enter here."

Thorn's hand strayed under his arm. He smelled treachery. The count merely looked bored. "How much?" he said.

"The usual tithe to Ompy is a twentieth part of your purse." Indolel shrank away after saying this, as if he expected the count to strike. No doubt many of the Wild Bull's players did just that. Rado fixed his eyes on the Kuruk and extracted a gold coin from his belt pouch. Wordlessly he gave it to Indolel. The Kuruk bit it and tapped twice on the wall. A panel popped open, revealing a peephole. Indolel dropped

the ducat through, and the panel snapped shut. With
much creaking and grinding of dry gears, the entire
section of mosaic wall pivoted outward. Thorn
stepped into the gap. When he was certain it was safe,
he stood back and let the count proceed.

"May Ompy guide your hand!" Indolel said. As
soon as Thorn followed Count Rado through the
space, a bare-chested lackey on the other side cranked
the hidden door closed.

They had entered another realm. The wide, low-
ceilinged gaming room glittered with precious furnishings. Rich tapestries covered the walls. Carpets
deep and soft spread over the floor. Candle-decked
chandeliers hung above the gilt wood tables where
several hundred men and women wagered stacks of
gold and silver on the whims of chance.

A robed Kuruk bowed before them. "What is your
pleasure, great one?" he inquired in mellow tones.
Even his smile was full of gold.

"Is it permitted for one to browse?" asked the
count.

"One may browse, taste, and sample," replied the
Kuruk. "There is only one commandment here, great
one: have joy."

"Thank you, ah—?"

"Afrez Mirora, at your beck and call, great one."
Rado slipped Mirora a silver star and strolled on.
Thorn kept close to him and tried not to gawk at the
opulent decorations and the richly dressed players.

Rado passed the usual sports: beroq, five-and-

seven, dice. The games he didn't recognize he
guessed were Kuruk specialties. One odd game was
played out at a circular table where a man sat in the
center. The surface of the table was inset with scores
of clay cups, colored and numbered. When the bets
were down, the man in the center tossed a wooden
ball in the air. Where it landed determined who won
and who lost. It seemed just an elaborate version of
the fate wheel, until Rado realized the man control-
ling the ball was blind. . . .

Thorn said something under his breath. "Speak
up, boy, I can't hear you," said the count.

"I said, it is a sin to see so much wealth squandered
for mere pleasure."

"Sin? I expected more subtlety from you, my dear
Thorn. Haven't I taught you anything? What does
sin have to do with pleasure? Isn't sin that which of-
fends the gods?"

"You know it is, my lord."

"And do the gods disdain pleasure?"

"Of course not, my lord."

"And doesn't pleasure bring happiness?" Rado
continued remorselessly.

"Not in every case, my lord. One man's pleasure
may be another man's pain."

"Exactly! So where does the sin lie, virtuous
Thorn? The man who feels pleasure is happy, and the
man who has pain is not. Do the gods therefore de-
spise the suffering man for not feeling happy?"

Thorn didn't answer. A serving girl passed, bearing

a tray full of brass goblets. Rado plucked two from the tray and offered one to his valet.

"Drink, Thorn. Drink and deny pain, if only for the moment." The count drained his wine goblet in one long gulp. Thorn stared into the dark red liquid. When Rado lowered his goblet, the valet poured his portion into the count's cup.

"I am pledged not to forget, my lord. That, it seems, is your task." Rado frowned and finished the second draft as quickly as the first.

Near the rear of the gaming room, the count found what he'd been seeking. Around a six-sided table covered in green satin, a game of towers was being played. There were two empty chairs. Rado stood behind one and said, "May I sit, gentlemen?"

The dealer, an Oparan sea captain by his coat, replied, "Do you have the stake?" The count's answer was to drop his weighty belt pouch on the table. The solid clank of metal assured everyone of his right to play.

"What about him?" asked another player, a Tablishite with skullcap and beard.

"My servant," explained Rado. "I do not pay him enough to game at this table."

"Very well, then, send him away," said the dealer. "I don't like men standing over me while I play."

"A wise policy," said the count. "However, since he carries my real purse, I insist he stay. Will it disturb you, captain, if my man kneels beside me?" The Oparan grunted his grudging permission.

The other two men were a westerner who called himself Geffrin and a shipowner from Tarabina named Yoteza. The stakes were one star per play, which was high; the sea captain was doing well. Geffrin had a fair pile in front of him, while Yoteza and Nishom, the Tablishite, were obvious losers.

Towers is played with a pool of sixty engraved tiles. The five colors didn't matter in this game, only the ranks. The dealer gave each man three tiles, which remained facedown on the table. The player placed a wager on each tile. Then the dealer turned two tiles faceup in the middle of the table. These were the Towers. The players bet that they could play one of their down tiles between the Towers in one of three possible positions: lower than the lowest tile showing (this was called a tunnel); equal or between the two up tiles (called a bridge); or higher than the higher tile (called an arch). Everyone played against the dealer in turn. It was a nervy game, requiring constant attention to what was being played and what had already been shown. Rado loved towers more than any other game.

He placed a star over each of his tiles, the lowest possible bet. The first towers were four lions and nine serfs, a good spread. Nishom played first. "Bridge," he said, turning up the twain of torches. Too low. Cursing, he swept the lost silver coin to the dealer.

Rado was next. "Bridge," he said, and the Oparan turned up eight lions for him. The sea captain paid him one star. Rado left it on the table to build his wager.

"Tunnel," said Geffrin. He displayed an eight and also lost. Yoteza called arch, a risky play, and turned over king fool, the highest tile in the suit of serfs. Yoteza was pleased and clapped his hands with delight.

Nishom studied the spent tiles intently. "Tunnel," he said. The Inferno appeared—highest tile in torches. "By the bitch!" he choked. "I cannot win to save my own life!"

Rado tunneled easily with a three. Geffrin tunneled again with a lone lion. Yoteza missed his bridge, and Nishom lost yet again. He scraped his last pair of silver stars off the green satin. "Alas, my friends, I must bow out. I have to pay my night's lodging, and the way fortune has deserted me, if I continued I should sleep in the street tonight." He clasped his hands in front of his chin and bowed good night.

They played on for a time, until the sea captain ran out of tiles. The box passed to Geffrin. The players stood and stretched their idle limbs while Geffrin stirred the box of tiles. Rado was modestly ahead. He'd wagered very conservatively, weighing his opponents with care and measuring the fragile luck of the table. Thorn was bored. He yawned at his master's elbow.

A man dressed in a somber redingote approached the table. Without a word, he dropped a silk bag of coins in front of one of the empty chairs.

"For a mute, you speak quite loudly," said Rado. "Please join us."

The man sat and threw back his hood. He wore a mask of brown felt that covered his eyes and nose. As he drew his tight gloves off finger by finger, Geffrin remarked, "It is usual in a game of gentlemen to allow one's identity to be known, sir."

"Then I am at the wrong table, for I did not come to play with gentlemen," said the stranger. The others took offense and dropped their hands off the table. "Be at ease. I don't care whom I play with, truly. Rogues and princes are all the same to me, so long as they have money to lose."

The count laughed. "Very good, Master Mask. This will not be the first time I have played with a rogue either!"

"That is certainly true, Count," the stranger said.

"You know me?"

"It is possible."

The masked man poured out a generous pile of Miyestan gold. The money's place of minting wasn't significant; any trader in the room would have local coins. The noteworthy thing about the stranger's gold was the large size of the coins. He had fifty double crowns, equal to two hundred Pazoan ducats.

"Is it too much?" said the stranger. The whole table was staring at his horde.

"No, indeed," said the Oparan. "We were just payin' homage."

Thorn squinted over Count Rado's arm. Something about the masked man was familiar. His voice? He had heard so many new voices in the past two days. The face under the mask was youthful and clean shaven; that somehow was familiar, too. Thorn scrutinized the masked man so hard that sweat popped out on his face.

Wine was brought at the count's request, and the game restarted. Geffrin shook the box a final time. Rado's luck ran hot and cold, so that by the time four rounds were done, he was no better off than when he began. Not so Geffrin. Normally the deal is a sure time to gain money, but the new player bet so oddly and so heavily that Geffrin began to lose. The stranger's style was uncanny. He would lose three small bets in a row, then win an impossible gamble for five double crowns at once. He did this several times, and Geffrin's tidy stack of winnings evaporated.

"Sir," said Geffrin coldly, "you are the most peculiar towers player I've ever met."

"Thank you. I have only recently learned the game."

Temper, thought Rado as the dealer flushed red around his tight silk collar. Geffrin smoothed back his wiry brown hair and dealt the last round in his turn. Without the towers built, the masked man bet ten double crowns on the first tile, fifteen on the second, and twenty-five on the last.

"I cannot cover those," Geffrin said.

"Then I'd better not win," said the stranger. A faint smile appeared beneath the soft felt.

Geffrin built the towers: a six and a seven.

"Tunnel," said Yoteza. His first tile was a ten, and he lost his stars.

"Tunnel," said the sea captain. He turned a six, a bridge, and forfeited five Oparan marks.

"Arch," said Rado. An eight won him a single star.

"Bridge," said the stranger. Rado bit his lip. The man was mad! The odds greatly favored high or low. To bet on having a six or a seven exactly was bolder than brains could allow.

The seven of lions roared, and Geffrin had to pay off ten double crowns.

Sweating, Geffrin gathered in the spent tiles and set two new towers. King fool leered out at the players. The nine of suns stood next to him. Yoteza toyed with his last few coins. "Tunnel," he whispered. The beggar queen bridged him and he was wiped out. He lowered his head to the table with a soft thump.

The Oparan captain called bridge. He showed a twain. Lost.

Rado kept track of the tiles already played in his head. Less than half remained. A large proportion of low tiles had been used already. The most likely call to make would be bridge. For some reason, he glanced at the masked man and said, "Tunnel."

The tile was four torches. Geffrin paid him two stars.

All eyes came to rest on the stranger's tile. If he won, he'd break Geffrin. All the silver the dealer had wouldn't amount to more than six or seven double crowns. The stranger sat straight, his hands in his lap. Thorn noticed his eyes inside the mask. They were green.

Him?

"Tunnel," the masked man said.

"May I?" said the count, reaching for the tile.

"I would be honored, my lord." Rado flipped the clay plaque. The single serf, hands out begging for alms, took every bit of Geffrin's money.

Silence covered the table. "I'm ruined," Geffrin said flatly. He shoved the pile of silver forward in disgust. "Take it all. I have no more."

"I will accept your debt," said the stranger.

"You'll get nothing!" Geffrin's rising voice carried in the room. A pair of large Kuruks, well-muscled and not smiling, drifted toward the towers table. Geffrin saw them. The taut constriction of his shoulders relaxed. "Give me your residence, and I will send the difference to you tomorrow," he said.

"I would prefer to call on you."

Geffrin's hand went inside his coat, and Thorn's, by reflex, went for his stiletto. If Geffrin came out with a throwing knife, Thorn could pin his hand to his chest before Geffrin could fling his weapon. But all the dealer brought out was a folded slip of parchment, upon which he scribbled the name of the inn he was staying at. The charcoal stick snapped halfway through writing. Geffrin swept the black bits to the floor. He tossed the parchment on top of his lost silver. Then, without a word, but with an eloquently hateful glare, he strode away.

"I am done, too," said Yoteza. "My wife will not speak to me for a month for losing so badly." He managed a weak smile. "That is the only advantage to this night I see. And now, if you will excuse me, I must find the water closet."

The sea captain had money left but decided to save it for something more worthwhile. "Wine," he said, shaking his flabby, depleted purse.

Only Count Rado, Thorn, and the stranger were left. "I seem to have won myself out of the game," said the masked man.

"Betting and winning with double crowns will usually do that," Rado observed. He rose and cracked his knuckles. "I feel like a walk. Don't you, Thorn?"

"Whatever my lord wishes."

"A valuable man," said the stranger. "Be careful, Count. Someone may hire him away from you."

"I couldn't let him go," Rado said. "The boy's been like a son to me." He slapped Thorn on the back. The two of them pushed through the crowd toward the exit. The masked man called after them.

"Count Rado! Count!" He shouldered past the wealthy gamblers. "I have a favor to ask you, my lord."

"I hasten to grant favors to rich young men."

"Since you are armed, could you escort me out of the building? I carry enough metal to cast a statue."

"Certainly, if you will favor me with your name," said Rado.

"I am Ferengasso."

The count put out a hand. "Lead on, Master Ferengasso."

The outer rooms of the Wild Bull were even more full than before. Men and women danced around wine vats that had been dragged out onto the main floor to speed the consumption of the Kurukish vintage. Wild, purple-faced wantons howled through the hall, their clothing reduced to dripping rags. As Rado and company eased by, they witnessed the birth of another maenad. A tangle-haired woman erupted from a vat, spewing sweet red wine from her lips. The spray splashed on Thorn. He started after the drunken female, but Rado caught him by the waist and pulled him back.

Outside, the sky was fully night. The moon had not yet risen over the sea. Even so, far out in the strait, a white glow tinged the night sky.

"Is that a ship on fire?" asked the count.

"White fire?" said Thorn doubtfully.

"No, no, that is the light of Prios," Ferengasso said. "The sanctuary of the Fact on Prios burns with the divine light of the true god. It can be seen on any clear night." When he said that, Thorn was certain his hunch was right. He knew now where he'd seen Ferengasso before.

They walked Mizzen Street toward Pallo's Tavern. The way was mostly free of other pedestrians. Ahead, town watchmen were lighting the lampposts from muleback.

"Where do you go?" asked the count.

"I have a private carriage waiting by Drom's tannery," Ferengasso said. "It's only a few houses beyond Pallo's."

"I don't recall saying we were staying at Pallo's," said Thorn.

Ferengasso laughed disarmingly. "Ah, but you did. How else could I know?" Thorn was still pondering an answer to that when the first flanking figure emerged from shadows on the harbor side of the street. Three more appeared behind Thorn.

"Well, Master Ferengasso, you were right to ask us along," said the count. He drew his sword. "These fellows don't look like kindly Brethren to me."

Thorn had his stiletto out. He and Rado closed together back to back. Ferengasso stepped in with them. The four men, armed with knobby staffs, stood in a circle waiting for some sign of their own.

Leather heels clacked on the cobbles. A lone man walked into the sphere of light around a lamppost.

"Good evening," said Geffrin. A honed dueling estoc glittered in his hand. "I've come to settle my debt, Master Mask."

"You needn't have brought a crowd," said Ferengasso. "I haven't even tallied up the amount you owe me."

"Oh, but it is you who owe *me*, and I am ready to take payment." The thugs closed in, tapping their clubs on the heels of their hands.

"Shall I give it to him?" asked Ferengasso under

his breath.

"Blood, no! One can't go around encouraging this sort of behavior," said Rado. To Thorn, he added, "Can you keep the bullies off my back?"

"There are only four of them, my lord."

"I know it's not fair, but they're asking for a lesson."

The count yelled and lunged at Geffrin. The latter parried sharply and whipped off a riposte. The tip of his sword skidded off the cupped hilt of Rado's weapon. The count stepped back and assumed formal fencing stance. Geffrin did likewise.

"What school are you?" asked Rado.

"The Emerald," said Geffrin.

"Excellent! I am Moonstone." They closed together with a jarring scrape of steel.

Thorn and Ferengasso were surrounded by thugs. Rado's valet displayed the point of his stiletto, but the hired bullies were not discouraged.

"Take the one with the scar," said Thorn.

"Which scar?"

"That one, on the chin." The bullies moved in. "Now!"

Ferengasso grappled with the indicated man. Thorn sidestepped a club swing, turned in, and thrust the stiletto through his assailant's gut. The tip drove up, piercing the heart, and when Thorn withdrew it, the man fell dead. A sidewise blow he caught in his left hand. It stung all the way up his arm, and he jabbed at the second thug's face. The man flinched and lost hold of his stick. The third bully attacked, and Thorn warded off his strike with the second man's club. The disarmed fellow didn't hang back; instead, he dove at Thorn's legs. The three of them went down in a knot. The squirming heap broke apart, and the hireling who had dared attack Thorn bare-handed rolled aside with a tine buried in his spine.

Ferengasso and his opponent rolled over and over, in and out of the muck in the gutter. Though young and agile, Ferengasso was not a fighter. The bully got on top of him and wedged his stick against the masked man's windpipe.

Count Rado and Geffrin made four tight circles in the street. Their swords danced back and forth, seeking flesh to pierce. Were it not for this deadly intent, they might have been artists performing a ritual dance. Both men panted, the count more so for his heavier blade.

"You are skilled for an Emerald," said Rado, tasting sweat on his lips.

"And you are not so limp-wristed as most Moonstones I've killed," Geffrin replied. Their blades rang off each other like the Brethren's iron bells.

Thorn couldn't free his stiletto. Empty-handed, he retreated before the savage swings of the third man's club. This one knew his business. Thorn tried to grapple and got a smashing clout on the neck. He tried to kick the street fighter's kneecap, but the man stuck the butt of his stick into Thorn's belly. Thorn hit the pavement and rolled, avoiding killing strokes aimed at his skull.

Ferengasso was at his opponent's mercy. The black night was getting blacker and blacker as his life's breath was choked off. In another few seconds, it would be finished.

Thorn snapped to his feet. His foe hadn't expected him to recover so fast. They were side by side in a flash, and Thorn threw his right arm around the man's neck. Grabbing his left ear, Thorn braced against the bully's left arm and twisted. The man bellowed once and went limp. Thorn had wrung his neck.

Light returned to Ferengasso. The pressure on his throat vanished. As the roar in his ears faded, he saw Thorn pulling the stiletto out of the man who'd been strangling him.

"Can you breathe?" asked Thorn, peering under his mask. Ferengasso coughed and shook his head up and down feebly. Thorn ran to help his master.

The duel up to now had been dead even. Thorn halted between the swordsmen. Both men lowered their blades.

"You bested them all?" Geffrin said in astonishment.

"Thorn is an invaluable servant," Rado said. His arm ached, and blood pounded in his temples. "More capable than any number of bullyboys." Ferengasso staggered into view. "The odds have gone against you, Emerald."

"So I see. The debt may yet fall to me." Geffrin saluted his blade. "I concede, Moonstone. For now." He sheathed his sword.

Count Rado slid his own weapon back into its scabbard. Thorn was confused. "You're letting him live?" he asked.

"Gentlemen of the sword fight with honor," said the count. "Master Geffrin has conceded. He may live, but he must bear the shame of his concession."

"Shame! Is that all? He and his men tried to kill us!" Thorn took a step toward Geffrin. The Emerald school duelist went to his hip.

"Stop!" said Rado. "The fight is over. Restrain yourself, my boy. Remember your training. Do you really want to kill a man so hotly?"

The stiletto's tines closed with a click. Thorn put the deadly spike away. Geffrin quickly melted into the shadows.

Ferengasso joined them. "Many thanks, my lord . . . Master Thorn. You were both magnificent," he said hoarsely.

"Tosh, old fellow. I enjoyed it immensely." The count looked around at the four dead men. "Still, we ought to put some distance between ourselves and Master Geffrin's bullies. I daresay the Brethren's guards would chasten us for littering the street with such trash."

They finally came to the alley where Ferengasso's carriage stood. The driver, likewise masked, helped his master into the closed compartment. Ferengasso parted the curtains from inside. He said, "Again, my thanks. Count, I know that you cannot accept largess for a good deed, but permit me to show my gratitude to your valet." Ferengasso gave Thorn a double crown. "I am glad of your skill."

Thorn bowed. "My joy is to serve."

The carriage, drawn by matched black geldings, sped away up Mizzen Street. When it slipped below the crest of the hill, Rado pried Thorn's hand open and took the double crown from him. "What a night!" he said. "Wine, games, and swordplay. You know, I could get to like it here."

"Yes, he played the game well," said Thorn.

"Eh? What do you mean?"

He pointed after the departed carriage. "Our friend Ferengasso. He's the same fellow I met in Pallo's the other day wearing the big hat. He started the fight there with his overly staunch defense of Fact worship."

"Are you certain?"

"His voice and his eyes I recognized at the gaming table. After I removed the robber from his throat, I peeked under the mask. Ferengasso is Master Big Hat."

"An interesting coincidence," said Rado, "but hardly sinister. I mean, the fellow obviously likes to play the devout Fact Brother by day, then prowl Harbor Town at night seeking diversion."

"With a purse full of double crowns? I hope your lordship is right."

"Of course I'm right." He smoothed out his coat and snugged his blue silk cravat. "Only one thing is needed to make this night complete."

"What's that, my lord?"

"I think you know, Thorn."

All expression left the valet's face. "If your lordship persists . . ." he said rigidly.

"It needn't be such a dire duty. You could enjoy it if you wanted to."

"You know how I feel, Rado."

"Your feelings scarcely matter, do they?"

They descended the hill to Pallo's, passing from lamppost to lamppost, shadow to shadow. The waxing moon rose out of the sea, its silver halo jealous of the distant glow of Prios Island.

III

Even the debauched of Pallo's Tavern slept. The watcher waited in the gloom outside until the tavern's common room grew dark and still. Then he entered the door noiselessly, his softly matted slippers padding on the worn, sticky boards.

Up the steps he went, keeping to the wall lest the treads creak under his weight. The stairs topped out in a second-floor corridor. The watcher became the listener, creeping along the hall with his ear to every door. He caught snores and wheezes, dreams and nightmares. There really is no quiet when people sleep. Only the cessation of speech makes it seem so.

He paused by a door marked with four lines of paint. He pressed his head to the dry panel. Breathing. They were in. With a length of bent wire, he groped in the latch hole for the door release. His hands grew damp and his lip trembled as the wire bumped over the mechanism, seeking the latch. There! He balled his free hand in triumph. The latch rose, the door opened, and the listener slipped carefully inside.

The occupants of the room paid him no attention.
They were attending to a more elemental need. As
the listener crouched in the darkness by the fireplace,
he heard the rhythm of limbs, the quick breathing of
passion. His eyes adjusted and he could see them in
the ancient bed, coupling with great urgency. Odd,
he thought. Having watched the tavern for several
hours, he hadn't seen any women go up to the
count's room. The only other person he knew to be
with Rado of Hapmark was his valet, Thorn. His *valet?* So Count Rado could add that vice to his list of
many others!

The listener put out his hand and felt the side of a
heavy wooden travel case. The lock was away from
him, so he slowly enfolded the box in his arms. The
wire went into the keyhole. Blindly, deftly, it found
the secret workings of the lock—

Click.

"Rado . . . Rado, stop!"

"Stop? Are you crazed? I can't!"

"Rado, there's someone in the room with us!"

Curse the luck! Why did the blasted lock have to be
so noisy? The man left the box. He didn't go for the
obvious way out, the door. Instead he went toward
the window. A silver stream of moonlight showed
through the closed shutters.

A shout—strong hands grabbing—something fell
on him. He shoved the person off and gathered himself to hurtle through the shutters. Hands around his
ankles tripped him. Reluctantly he reached for his

dagger. It wasn't in his belt.

A voice said, "Looking for this?" Someone dealt the intruder a stunning crack across the face. Next thing he knew, he was pinned to the floor on his stomach, the cold iron of his own dagger poking his kidney. The same strong fingers twined in his hair and wrenched his head back hard.

A lamp flared. The smoky yellow light grew until it was bright enough to see in the room.

"Who is it?" asked the count. He was in bed, holding the lamp.

"Turn over," said the other voice, who must be the valet. The intruder rolled onto his back. The wild creature astride his waist with the dagger poised at his throat was no valet. A wedge of tan skin formed around the neck led his eyes down to two small but unquestionably female breasts. Farther down, an even darker wedge confirmed his startling discovery. Thorn was a woman.

"Master Ferengasso," Rado said. "What are you doing down there?"

"He's a spy!" said Thorn. "I knew it! It was too coincidental that he kept turning up wherever we went."

"Are you a spy?" asked the count. He sat up, gathering the sheet around his waist. The tip of the dagger was so tight against Ferengasso's throat he dared not open his mouth. "Oh, let him speak," said Rado.

"I have nothing to say," gasped the spy.

"We shall see. You realize, don't you, the awkward

position you've put us in. Having discovered Thorn's secret, we shall have to find some way to keep you quiet."

"Who employs you?" asked Thorn. "Is it the Brethren? Is it?"

"I say nothing."

The count got up, sheet trailing after him. He drew his sword from its belt and ordered Thorn off the prostrate intruder. She got off reluctantly. Rado handed her a white chemise.

"She's not what you'd call a woman of ample charms," he said, "but she is learned in ways you cannot imagine." Thorn blushed and retreated to the bed. Rado leaned over Ferengasso. He held the sword loosely, not threateningly, and said in a confidential tone, "She knows a great many nasty ways to cause pain, my boy, so if I were you, I'd start talking before she starts cutting."

"I do not fear evil," Ferengasso said. "The Fact is my strength. The Fact is with me."

Rado poked the spy's hat off with the tip of his sword. A ring of abraded skin showed where Ferengasso's headband had been. "I understand now the hat and mask. Where's your band now?" asked Rado.

"I was told to leave it—" He stopped, shutting his mouth firmly.

"Will you get on with it?" Thorn said angrily. The stiletto was out. "We know who sent him."

"Be still!" Rado tapped Ferengasso on the head to

get his attention. "You wouldn't take her for a religious woman, would you? She is, you know—a fully consecrated priestess. Her order is trained in hand-to-hand combat. She can trounce a dozen ordinary men."

Ferengasso said faintly, "The Sentinels of the Temple."

"Yes, you've heard of them? Good, good. I'm glad you understand." The spy understood only too well. His youthful face went waxen in the lamplight. "They are a relentless corps," the count went on, "raised inside the temple precinct from babes abandoned to the priestess. Only one girl-child in ten has the strength and skill to enter the prefectory, but once there, they are trained in every type of violent hand combat known. Isn't that true, Thorn?" She stood back against the bedpost, her boyish countenance hard and immobile.

"The sentinels not only guard the temple, protecting its secrets and treasures, but they are also responsible for the safety of the priestess. Sometimes, in very special circumstances, a sentinel may be ordered to protect someone else."

"How did you rate that honor?" asked Ferengasso.

"Oh, I worked very hard for it, never fear. I—"

"Enough of this! The spy must be dealt with," Thorn said. Ferengasso opened his mouth. Rado swung his blade around till the cold, sharp edge rested under the spy's ear.

"I wouldn't shout if I were you. No one in this fine

old inn would pay the slightest heed." Ferengasso
closed his mouth. He waited for the steel tongue to
plunge into his neck. Rado held the tip steady, but he
didn't move.

"Do it," said Thorn.

Rado dropped the point. "Why should I? This is
your sort of deed, not mine."

"You've slain more men than I have."

"In duels, mind you. Affairs of honor. My opponents were on their feet and armed."

She snorted in disgust. "And that makes it right?
What do you propose, arming the spy? Shall I lend
him my stiletto so your male sense of honor will allow
you to kill him?"

"What do women know about honor? Nothing. Is
that what your mistress taught you? 'The only proper
end of combat is death.' Ha! That's a savage's thinking!"

As they argued, Ferengasso sized up his chances. If
he could snuff out the lamp, he might have an opportunity to escape. The fingers of his left hand closed
over a mound of soft cloth. Velvet. One of the count's
fine waistcoats.

Thorn stalked between Rado and the spy. Her
movement forced Ferengasso's attention back to his
captors' debate.

" . . . no knowing what they've found out about us
already. If we kill him and dispose of the corpse discreetly, there will be no way the Brethren can tie his
disappearance to us."

Rado replied, "Who else could they suspect? He's been following us for two days."

Thorn halted in midpace by the fireplace. She spied the travel case with Ferengasso's lockpick wire still protruding from the keyhole. She made the sign of the Goddess.

"He was in the box!" she said. "He was in it!"

Rado swore. "Hunter's blood! Did he see it, do you think?"

"Can we take the chance?"

Thorn and the count stood over the box. Ferengasso got to his feet and sprang for the closed window. In the blink of an eye, Thorn whirled and threw the dagger. It sank up to the hilt in the small of the spy's back. He uttered a brief cry and reached for the sash bolt. The shutters parted, and he plunged headfirst to the street below.

Fog had crept in from the sea. It filled the street, coating the lampposts in amber mist. Rado and Thorn burst out the front door of Pallo's. They hunted in the murk until they found Ferengasso. He had crawled a few paces from below the window.

The count turned him onto his side. Blood ran from the spy's lips. He coughed wetly. "Doesn't make sense," he gasped.

"What?" asked Rado.

"The two—you. Like enemies . . . why?"

"Neither of us are here by choice," said Rado. "Thorn's along to ensure that I do what I am to do." The dying man's eyes asked the question his voice would never utter. "I have come to kill your god," said Rado.

They carried the body to the harbor and dumped it in. Thorn stooped and washed the blood from her hands. She flung the dagger into the water, and the two of them walked back to the tavern.

"Sordid business," muttered the count.

"But necessary," Thorn countered. "Had he lived to escape, you and I would have met the hangman together."

"I hear the Brethren don't execute their enemies."

"Nonsense. That's just a story they tell to pacify the gullible."

The bells in the city towers rang twice. As Thorn and Rado mounted the slope from the harbor to Mizzen Street, wrapped in balmy fog, a steady drone filled the sky above them.

"What's that?" asked Thorn, craning her neck.

"It's coming from Miyesti." The count strained his eyes to pierce the mist, but night and fog were too thick. The droning grew louder and nearer. It passed directly over their heads and then on over the harbor. They followed the invisible presence by its sound. The noise grew fainter. Thorn started up the hill again, but Rado grabbed her arm.

"See?" he said breathlessly.

Far out over the strait, a brilliant beam of light stabbed down from the clouds. It raked the sea from side to side like a blind monster groping for guidance in the fog. And then, a more remarkable thing:

Above the lance of light, blurred by the white mist, was a dark shape. Long and curved, it suggested a ship's hull sailing through the sky.

Ships in the sky?

"What can it be?" asked the count as the light and droning disappeared over the horizon.

"More magic," said Thorn grimly. "Did you notice where the apparition was going? No? You really must learn to pay closer attention to things besides gaming and women. Whatever that thing was, it was heading directly for Prios Island." She knotted one hand into a fist. "We must go there, too."

Second: The Perfect City

Do you not know, my charming lady, that the law is good, that all rules, all exact standards are good?

Hanns Heinz Ewers,
Alraune (1911)

IV

Harlic Vost returned the next day with Count Rado's cachet. He arrived in the same carriage, with the same guards, wearing the same clothes. Thorn, haggard from lack of sleep, received the subprelate in the common room. She poured hot water from an earthen pot into a cup of Juaan tea bark. The fastidious Vost firmed his lips when Thorn gulped the resulting brew without bothering to strain out the floating bits of bark.

"As I expected, there was no problem in approving Count Rado's entry," Vost said. He placed the cachet on the table in front of Thorn. "There was some concern about you."

"Me?" asked Thorn.

"Yes. It is not usual for us to admit persons of unspecified lineage or allegiance. So many rogues are attracted by the wealth of Miyesti." Thorn raised an eyebrow. Vost added hastily, "However, in view of your close association with Count Rado, your entry was also approved."

"Glad to hear it!"

Rado, posing dramatically against the stair rail, cloaked, hooded, and wearing his sword, stepped down with exaggerated weight to the floor. "I couldn't survive without my faithful valet. Please express my gratitude to the College of Peace."

"As you wish, my lord." Vost stood and handed Rado a Fact medallion. "There are a few other matters I must explain to you, Count."

He took the metal diamond and chain. "Such as?"

"Within the walls of Miyesti, it will be necessary for you to wear this at all times."

"And if my lord doesn't wish to?" asked Thorn bluntly.

"He will be subject to arrest and summary expulsion," said Vost. "You, Master Thorn, are not being provided with an emblem; therefore, you must remain in the count's company at all times. The guardsmen are strict on this point, so I urge you not to test them."

"Never fear, Master Vost. I will certainly wear my emblem." Rado shot a worried look at Thorn. "Anything else, Subprelate?"

"There are a number of laws within Miyesti instituted for the purpose of public order. You will encounter them as needed, but you should know of three of them in particular. You will come under their jurisdiction immediately."

"And they are—?"

"Firstly, the city curfew. No one may be on the streets after eight bells or before five bells in the morning. Secondly, women are barred from public houses—"

"Really? Sounds terribly dull," said Rado.

"Why do that?" asked Thorn.

"We Brethren have been taught by the Fact that woman's place is at home, managing the household and caring for children. Allowing them in public houses, theaters, and so on encourages them to neglect their duties."

"Very sound, I'm sure, but it still sounds awfully dull," said the count. Vost cleared his throat.

"Thirdly, no matter what you see in Miyesti, you mustn't interfere with any marvelous event. I know that sounds vague, but the Fact's great goodness is manifest every day in the city. The consequences could be grave if you don't observe this law."

"I wouldn't dream of interfering, nor would Thorn." Rado hung his emblem around his neck. It was made of some cheap metal, tin perhaps, painted in the usual red-and-gold scheme. He noticed it was rather thick to be as light as it was, and this made him suspect it was hollow. The subprelate's medallion was even thicker and handsomely cloissonéd.

"So when do we go?" Rado queried.

"You may enter by any Harbor Town gate this morning between eight bells and ten," said Vost. He buttoned the flap of his official pouch and straightened the seams of his tunic. "Good day, my lord, and may your stay in Miyesti be most enlightening." He bowed. "Good morrow, Master Thorn."

When Vost was gone, Thorn said, "Insufferable prig."

"Agreed," said the count. "But you ought to cultivate an air of indifference when these Fact folk inflict their beliefs on you. Failing that, you will only arouse their suspicion."

The eighth bell of morning had already rung, so they decided to make for the nearest gate right away. Thorn awakened Bucker. Rado gave him five coppers to help Thorn bring his baggage down to the street. While the cases and bags piled up on the stoop, the count managed to catch a half-empty wagon. The driver was willing to carry them to a gate for the right price.

Bucker heaved the last crate into the back of the wagon. Thorn wedged them in place among the rest of the freight, called to the driver, and flopped onto a heap of soft drygoods. Then they pulled away from Pallo's Tavern, leaving the ugly proprietor in the street. The wagon dipped out of sight as it topped the hill. Bucker wiped his hands on his filthy apron and went back inside.

* * * * *

Whether by chance or by the whim of the gods, Count Rado and Thorn found themselves at the very same gate that Varlan Churt, the Fact Speaker, had used to enter the city with his new converts. There was a line of men and women waiting to pass through the

gate. The wagoner reined in and stopped close behind a cart laden with vegetables.

"Blood, this is intolerable," said the count.
"Would it be any faster at another gate?"

"Mebbe, lordship, an' mebbe not," said the wagoner. "There's always lines of one size or t'other."

Rado fumed at the delay. "Thorn, go to the guards
and tell them to let us through immediately."

She regarded him dubiously. "How am I to do
that, my lord?"

"Tell them who I am," Rado declared imperiously.

With no great conviction, Thorn hopped down
from the rear of the wagon and went to the head of
the line. The guard she spoke to waved her off with
vigorous hand motions and loud but indistinct re-
proaches.

Thorn came back, shading her eyes from the morning sun. "He said all visitors were equal, and that the
count of Hapmark was no more equal than anyone
else," she said.

"Impudent rascal! Did he really say that?"

"He expressed it more forcefully. His exact words
were—"

"Never mind."

It was after nine bells before they reached the gate.
The guard recognized Thorn, and so made a special
effort to find a flaw in Rado's cachet. In the end, he
couldn't, so he passed them through.

"Here we go!" said Rado.

No magic lights or divine voices manifested themselves as they passed into the gate. The passage was remarkably deep, twice as deep as the wagon and team combined. The walls were as smooth and hard as marble. No seams showed between the blocks. It was as if the wall had been laid down in a continuous liquid mass.

Inside the gate was an open, paved circle. The wagoner steered around the curve and stopped. "Here is where I leave you, my lord," he said.

"But why?"

"I han't got a pass for me, and if I did, I still couldna drive you." He pointed to a white wooden sign fixed on a post opposite the gate. In black Homeland script, the sign read, "NO DRAFT ANIMALS BEYOND THIS CIRCLE BY ORDER OF THE COLLEGE OF HEALTH."

"That's ridiculous! How can one move about so large a city without horses? Do they expect Thorn to carry all my belongings on his back?"

"I hope not, my lord," she answered.

The wagon was unloaded and the driver paid. Thorn and the count were left with a dozen other newcomers, some of whom had brought large piles of goods to sell. When the last team of horses disappeared into the gate tunnel, the tenth bell of morning sounded. All around Harbor Town, the city gates were closed.

"Well, don't just stand there," Rado snapped. "We need transport, my lad. Go and find some."

Thorn pulled a rolled-up felt hat from her pocket

and put it on. She joined the band of seekers with similar intent, and together they walked up a short, wide street to see what they could find.

A broad avenue lay beyond the first row of houses that paralleled the city wall. The houses Thorn saw were not like the weathered wood and terra-cotta of Harbor Town. Regular white blocks of dwellings rose in ordered rows as far as her eyes could see. Three, four, and five stories were common, and all of them had blue slate roofs and glass windows. Far away, across the hills where the city climbed higher, were even greater things: huge domes, mighty spires, tiered edifices with columns taller than a ship's mast. Thorn took all this in, in a rush. Amazed, she stepped off the low curb into the avenue. Around her, the other newcomers were equally stunned.

A scream brought her back to earth. Thorn looked to the source of the cry and saw a runaway wagon bearing down on them. "Get back!" she shouted. "A wagon's broken loose!"

She ran toward the runaway, thinking she could climb aboard and help the terrified driver set the brake. As she braced herself to leap, the wagon swerved away from her. It rattled past, and Thorn saw the driver was *steering* the horseless vehicle by means of a curved pole, like the tiller on a boat. The man seemed unconcerned by his situation, and the wagon sped on. Thorn watched openmouthed as the wagon rolled up the incline of the street and vanished around a corner.

"What was *that?*" asked someone behind her.

Her fellow visitors were transfixed with wonder, terror, or both. Some fell to their knees and prayed to the gods for protection. Thorn barely had time to digest the first wonder when another horseless vehicle, this one a three-wheeled cart, approached from the other direction.

She waved both arms at the man in the cart. The uncanny thing slowed and stopped. The driver wore a helmet like an old-time jouster. He pushed up the visor and said, "Is something wrong? Is someone hurt?" He had to repeat himself twice before Thorn could answer.

"What is that thing?" she asked, indicating the self-moving cart.

"This? The go-about?" He looked past the cringing strangers and saw the gate. "Oh, I see! You're new here. You've never seen a go-about, have you?" Thorn shook her head. "You must get used to them. They are very common in Miyesti." He pushed a lever down with his foot. The cart started to roll. "Good morrow to you, brother!" said the man.

Thorn ran back to Count Rado. Stammering, she told him what she had seen. He scoffed. "Enchanted cart? What do you take me for? Rot!"

"See for yourself!"

Leaving her to mind the luggage, Rado went forth to see for himself. At the junction of the great avenue and the gate road, he saw a vast wagon, as big as a six-horse dray, taking on bales of cloth, pressed parchment, hides, and other drygoods. Across the side of the wagon was a sign proclaiming, "FORG MINYASIC—MERCHANT OF FINE CLOTH AND LEATHER."

There were no draft animals in front of the wagon. Rado hailed one of the yeoman at work loading. "I say, fellow, where could a gentleman obtain a ride in this city?"

" 'Spect he'd have to hire a go-about," grunted the husky fellow. He and a helper heaved the last bale of Homeland linen into the wagon. "That's it," he called. "Come lads, push!"

Six yeoman planted their feet on the paving and leaned into the wagon. The high wooden wheels groaned. The driver, sitting high up front, hauled back on a long lever. Somewhere underneath the frame of the wagon, metal scraped on metal. The vehicle pulled away from the pushing men, and they ran after it, jumping onto the open bed one by one.

"Apologies," Rado said to Thorn when he had returned. "You were no more than truthful."

"I am always truthful. Haven't you noticed?"

The sun crept over the pearl gray walls. In twos and threes, the other folk who had entered with the count and Thorn set off on foot or were taken by the great self-moving wagons dispatched to get the mercantile goods that had been brought in from Harbor Town. No one had room for two passengers, and by the eleventh hour, Thorn and Rado were alone in the gate road.

"Time to walk," said the count, slapping his knees.

"What about the baggage?"

"You'll have to manage, won't you?"

In the end, Rado agreed to carry one travel case and onc leather satchel. Thorn was saddled with the rest. She couldn't possibly carry them all, so she tied them together and dragged them by a harness strap. They bore left on the avenue, downhill, not knowing where to go or whom to see. Go-abouts whisked past them, but despite the count's shouted offers of gold, no one stopped to help them.

It was sultry in the street, with the sun glaring off so many light-colored houses. Sweat soaked through Thorn's jacket, so she draped it over one of the crates she was dragging. Rado clucked his tongue. "You'd better put that back on," he said. "The dew of labor has stripped away your masculine pose."

Regrettably, it was true. Thorn's homespun shirt was damp enough to reveal what she had to conceal. Grudgingly she donned the hot corduroy again.

The hill bottomed out and started rising. Thorn endured the slope for a time, but she couldn't keep going. She threw down the towing strap and said, "Enough! That's it, Rado! I'm not pulling your foul wardrobe any farther!"

"Fine talk from a servant," he replied. "Have you forgotten our pact? Your high priestess commanded you to serve me in anything I require, so long as I carry out the task she gave me. Have you forgotten that, Thorn, my lad?"

"Blast you, no!" She pushed her streaming face a whisker's width from Rado's. "I have borne your using my body to gratify your lust. I have stood for your arrogant pretensions of nobility. The Goddess has heard me suffer in silence at your gloating over my boyish disguise, but I will not be worked to death like a worthless slave!"

He smiled in his careless, irritating way. "Let it never be said that Rado of Hapmark was inflexible. If you wish to be released from our pact, I am willing to do so now. At this very moment, in fact. What do you say?"

Thorn's shoulders sagged under the burden of duty. "You know I cannot agree. Only my mistress can negate our charge." She shouldered the strap. "But hear me, Rado: When our task is done, I shall make you pay for your liberties."

"*Count* Rado."

The avenue seemed to go on forever. It was a shade before noon when they encountered the guardsman. He was fitted out like the ones they had seen in Harbor Town, only this city guard wore a cloth hat instead of a steel cabasset.

"Could you assist us, fellow?" asked Rado. Thorn all but collapsed on the road at his feet.

"By the holy Fact, what is the problem here?" asked the guard.

"We are strangers in Miyesti, and lacking horse and carriage, we have walked ten bowshot from the gate we entered by. The sun has been strenuous, and my poor servant is done in."

The guardsman asked for the count's cachet. He perused it briefly, then examined Rado's medallion. "A hundred pardons, my lord. Did not the Brethren by the gate tell you they could arrange for a public go-about to carry you whither in Miyesti you cared to go? No?"

"The man on the gate was extremely rude—ask my servant. If he were my man, I should have him punished."

The guard took out his pad and marker. "Give me the hour and the gate, and it shall be done, my lord."

Rado felt a flush of pleasure. He gave the guard the information. It was noted, and the Miyestan said, "Please rest here, my lord, and I will call you a conveyance."

He went to a nearby lamppost. Like most features of Miyesti, this post was grander than ordinary. It was twice the height of a man and as thick as Rado's thigh. At face level, a funnel was set into the post, wide mouth out. A turn crank, such as are used on spice mills, was mounted next to the funnel. The guard did an odd thing. He spun the crank rapidly and spoke into the gaping funnel.

"This is Peace Brother Smert, on Prince Tem's Way. I have a foreign noble, a Count Rado, and his valet in urgent need of a go-about. Please send one at once." He stopped cranking and came back to Rado. "If you remain here, a cart will arrive shortly." He turned to go.

"Wait," said the count. "Do you mean someone far away heard your request? How is that possible?"

"The Fact, my lord. The Fact has made all things possible to those who believe. Now I must continue my rounds. Good day and good morrow."

Thorn raised herself to a sitting position. "This is the maddest city I've ever heard of. Carts without horses! Talking to lampposts! We'll likely be here when night falls."

"I think not," Rado said. "Here comes a go-about now."

A four-wheeled cart veered over to them. The wooden side slats and bed were painted white, and a Fact banner waved from the tip of a spring pole stuck in the obsolete whip socket. A smiling, mustached fellow with a big Fact emblem around his neck let the tiller spring forward from his hands. The cart stopped.

"Day and morrow to you! Are you Count Rado of Hapmark and valet?" he asked.

"We are."

The man bowed. "Suvin Haynarc at your service. My regrets for not arriving sooner."

"How did you know where to find us?" asked Thorn.

"The guardsman called, did he not? Come! Let us set your boxes in the machine." Rado set the bags he carried in the cart and took his seat by the driver's spot. Thorn dragged herself and nothing else to the go-about. The hearty Haynarc slung case after case in-

to the back of the cart. The last box was the same case
Ferengasso had tried to pick open. Haynarc couldn't
lift it the first time he tried. He spat on his hands and
tried again. Neck veins bulging, he heaved the heavy
case off the pavement.

"What's in this one?" he asked bluntly.

"Gold," said the count. "That's my coin box."

"You must have a prince's pension in there!"

Rado fingered his sword hilt absently. "You might
say that."

Haynarc climbed behind the tiller. "Where shall
we go, lordship?"

Rado confessed his ignorance of Miyesti.

"Perhaps an inn or hostel?" suggested Haynarc.

"Yes, that will do."

"I know an inn fit for a prince," Haynarc said. He
pulled the tiller down to his lap. The cart gave a small
lurch. Thorn gripped the side of the cart bed tightly.

"Ready? Here we go." Haynarc lifted his foot off a
lever that protruded through the floorboard, and the
cart leapt forward like a startled deer. Rado managed
to retain his composure as the vehicle gained speed.
Haynarc smiled the smile of a happy child and turned
the tiller to the left. The front wheels canted, and the
go-about rolled around a street corner. Haynarc
pushed the tiller farther down, and their speed increased.

"A remarkable apparatus," said the count over the
rush of air. "How is it moved?"

"Only the Brethren know," said Haynarc. "The

prelates of the College of Peace have given us many wonders in the past few years. I used to drive a two-horse dray, but I learned to steer a go-about after the College of Health banned animals in the city."

"Why did they do that?" called Thorn from behind.

"Manure," Haynarc said over his shoulder.

"I beg your pardon!" exclaimed Rado.

The Miyestan laughed. "No disrespect intended, lordship. I meant, the prelates banned horses, mules, and oxen from the streets so's not to have manure underfoot. Now Miyesti looks and smells cleaner than any city in the world."

He twisted the tiller sharply right, and they careened around another turn. A three-wheeler flashed past them going the other way. Wheel hubs scraped for an instant, and the other driver shouted something vulgar. Haynarc went serenely on.

"Did you hear what he said?" asked Thorn.

"It matters little," answered Haynarc. "He was an unbeliever. I can only wish him luck in finding the Fact someday."

"Are there many unbelievers in Miyesti?" Rado asked innocently.

"Not many. The Speakers have been active here for a long time."

"How many would you say?"

Haynarc closed one eye to guess. The go-about swerved and nearly rammed one of the stout metal lampposts. Thorn inhaled sharply but said not a word.

"Perhaps one man in seven, eight? I'm not good with ciphers," said Haynarc.

"Well, do the women of Miyesti believe in equal proportion?"

"That I cannot say, lordship. Since women may not hear the voice of the Fact, it is hard to tell by sight if they believe or not." Rado glanced past the driver. Thorn ran a finger across her forehead. Neither of them had seen or heard of a woman wearing a Fact headband.

Haynarc stomped on the floor lever. The go-about skidded to a halt, almost throwing Rado out of his seat. "Here we are . . . the Inn of the Red Frog."

Red Frog indeed! Rado and Thorn stared with unabashed amazement at the crystal clear glass. There were no fewer than eight floors. Above the double bronze doors was the Red Frog itself, just as with any inn sign, only this frog was outlined in glowing matchcord. It shone bright red even in the full light of day. The entire front of the inn was faced with polished white stone fit for the interior of any palace or temple.

Haynarc's mulberry face seemed about to split from smiling. "It's not the best inn in Miyesti, but I think your lordship will find it acceptable," he said. Rado nodded dumbly. He stepped down and walked around the front of the go-about. Thorn was already off and pulling out their baggage. Haynarc helped her. The count paid Haynarc a ducat for his trouble, to which the Miyestan promptly gave four stars change. The magic cart snapped away, its iron-rimmed wheels hissing over the clean brick street.

"What have we gotten ourselves into?" Rado murmured. "That a city can have such a place for travelers . . . what must their official buildings look like?"

"Fine stone doesn't build the truth," Thorn countered. "Nor do fancy tricks make a true religion." She grabbed the harness strap and dragged the train of cases to the inn door. When she was still five steps away, the massive bronze portals swung open. No lackey held them apart; they stood open without any mortal hands upon them. "More tricks," Thorn said disgustedly. "Are there no end to them?"

They entered the common room and found a closed octagonal counter in the center of the room. A man in cream and gold livery stood inside the octagon. His Fact emblem glittered with inset jewels. A second emblem was tattooed in colored ink on his forehead.

"Welcome, honored guests. I am Claren Sarstic, keeper of the Red Frog Inn. How may I assist you?" he asked.

Rado assumed his most arrogant expression. "First you may have my belongings brought in from the street. Do you expect my poor valet to carry them all in?"

Claren Sarstic smiled and leaned over the counter. He spoke into a slim funnel mounted on the dark wooden top. Within seconds, a pair of robust yeoman appeared with a small trolley. Sarstic dispatched them to fetch Count Rado's baggage.

"That's better. Now, may I have a room with a fireplace and bathtub, and with an adjoining closet for my valet?"

Sarstic consulted a thick ledger. "Yes, the Dolphin Suite is available. That will be fifteen stars per night, or five ducats, five stars for a week." Rado snapped his fingers. Thorn hoisted the coin box onto the counter and let it land heavily on the polished wood. Using the key on the thong around his neck, Rado unlocked the strongbox and counted out six gold ducats. The fifteen stars change he received he swept contemptuously into the coffer and slammed the lid.

"Now, if you please, may I see your cachet?" asked Sarstic.

"For what purpose?"

"City law requires that foreign guests leave their cachets with the inn's keeper while they are staying on the premises." The count produced the wallet reluctantly. "As long as you wear your visitor's emblem, you may go about the city as you choose," Sarstic explained. "Should you desire to leave the inn, or the city, we will, of course, return your cachet to you."

"How kind," Rado said sourly.

"Count Rado of Hapmark," the Miyestan read. "I hope you will be comfortable at the Red Frog."

Rado sniffed. "Hmm, can't say I care for this cachet foolery."

"Regrettable, my lord. But it is the law."

The yeomen pushed the creaking trolley past the octagon. Thorn looked around the bright but sparsely furnished common and said, "Where are the stairs?"

" 'Tween the columns, there. But we has a faster way," said one of the men. "Follow us."

They manhandled the trolley across the common, carefully staying on the granite path not covered by the check-patterned carpet. The porters stopped at a single metal door. The man in front of the trolley pushed a brass stud on the wall. The door slid aside into the wall, revealing a tiny room.

"Follow us," repeated the porter at the rear of the trolley. They trundled the load through the door and beckoned Rado and Thorn to join them. Once Thorn had crossed the threshold, the door slid shut.

The room quivered, and Rado distinctly felt the soles of his boots pressing into the floor. A bell rang once, twice, four times. On the fifth chime, the little room ceased moving. The door rolled back. A long carpeted hall, lit by the same sort of bright, unflickering lamps they had seen in the common room, stretched away from the tiny closet.

"Ev'rybody out." Thorn sprang out and flattened against the wall. The porters got the trolley out and rumbled past her. Count Rado sauntered after them, hands on hips. This weird business was not going to get the better of *him!*

The porter unlocked the door of the Dolphin Suite—there was a mosaic of a leaping dolphin on the

blue enamel door—and gave the key to the count.
The Miyestans unloaded the baggage then departed
with smiles and bows. Thorn threw the door shut behind them. "I'm going mad!" she declared.

"Really, my boy, I thought you were trained to be
serene in the face of adversity."

Thorn scowled, her bottom lip sticking out like a
schoolboy's. "Give me a sneak thief, and I'll be serene. Face me with a drunken blacksmith with rape
on his mind, and I'll be the calmest of women. Send
a crazed bull after me in a blind alley, and I'll cope—
but this! What kind of place is this where carts and
rooms move on their own and inns are built of marble
and bronze?"

"A very powerful place, I'd say," said Rado. He
made a quick tour of their rooms. The suite had four
chambers: a main bedroom, a smaller bedroom, a
closet, and a room with nothing in it but a porcelain
chamberpot and an enormous bathtub. "A very rich
place, too. The Adamant Palace in Pazoa has no
apartments the equal of this."

Thorn sat in a plush chair. "That's what weighs
upon me. If wealth such as this can be squandered on
a mere inn, what resources must the Brethren have
already at their disposal? I never imagined Miyesti
would be like this. I don't think the One Who Commands did, either." Voicing that thought gave Thorn
pause. For the first time, she wondered if their mission were truly feasible.

"Be of good cheer, Thorn-in-my-side," said Rado.

"If our efforts fail, consider what tasteful decorations a Miyestan dungeon must have." He unbuttoned his coat and threw it over another chair. "I'm for a nap. Wake me by the fourth hour."

He lay down on the wide bed. His boots made black smudges on the crisp white counterpane. Pig, thought Thorn. He never gives a thought to the drudgery of others. . . .

She rose wearily to her feet. A nap would have suited her as well, but she had more pressing duties. From the smallest travel case, she withdrew a slim leather-bound folio. She retreated to the smaller bedchamber and spread the book open on the floor. An onlooker wouldn't have recognized the writing on the leaves. Instead of the cursive Homeland script, Thorn's book was block-printed in the ancient pictographs known only to the initiates of the temple. She puzzled through the pages her mistress had marked for this moment. When the meaning of her instructions was finally clear, Thorn bowed her head.

Why must it be so hard? Was this her ultimate purpose—to fulfill the ancient orders set down in the temple's Millennium Book? Thorn had pledged her life to the Mother Goddess and her obedience to the high priestess of the temple. She could not, would not shrink from her charge simply because her compliance now bore a heavy price.

But for the first time in her life, she considered disobedience.

V

Thorn stood over the sleeping Rado. He'd rolled over in his dreams and buried his face in the soft nap of the counterpane. She bent down and pinched the relaxed muscle in his midriff between her thumb and forefinger. The count gave a yelp and bolted from the bed.

"What's the meaning of this?" His smooth hair was splayed across his face, and his shirt was twisted around his neck. "How dare you!" he said, rubbing his abused side.

"It is the fourth hour," Thorn said. "My lord wished to arise at this time."

"You didn't have to gouge me. A simple tap on the shoulder would suffice. You really do have a mean streak, Thorn." He noticed she held an ornate envelope in her hand. "What's that?"

"It came while you slept." She gave Rado the missive. The wax seal was impressed with a noble coat of arms that he didn't recognize. Rado broke the red disc and lifted the flap. Inside was a single sheet of vellum, folded once. Rado read the elegant hand aloud:

*"House of Vostig, 16th Day of the Month of the Crow
4th Year of the Prince-Prelate Rhom*

"To the Noble Rado, Count of Hapmark, Greetings:

"Having received word that your lordship was visiting our city, I have taken the liberty of sending this invitation to dine with us tonight in the House of Vostig. We seldom enjoy visitors from the great noble houses of the Homelands, and we look forward to your honoring us with your presence. If you would come at the sixth hour to Cormoring Way, the House of Vostig is the third house sunwise around the Princes' Plaza. You will know it by the sign of the Thistle.

*"With fraternal regards,
Sverna, Princess of Vostig"*

"What do you make of that?" asked Rado.

"I take it for a good sign," said Thorn. "Princess Sverna is one of us."

"One of us, as in well-born, or one of us as in one of you?"

"Both," said Thorn. "I will draw your lordship's bath and chose a suit for your evening out."

"I suppose I have to go." The invitation sounded boring and formal.

Thorn went to the door of the chamber with the bathtub. Steam billowed out the door, streaking the cold tile floor with sweat.

"You amaze me, Thorn. Tired as you were, you still toiled up all those floors with buckets of hot water for my bath!"

"I did not, my lord."

"Eh?"

Thorn went over to the tub. She worked some decorations on the wall, and water gushed from a spout into the tub. "No more effort than that was required," she said.

Rado beamed like a child. He unpinned his cuffs and stepped through the door. When his shirt was free, he tossed it carelessly over his shoulder and loosened the drawstring of his trousers. Thorn lowered her eyes and made to leave.

"Stay where you are," he said. "I expect you to assist me."

"What assistance could you possibly need?"

"Do you think I can scrub my own back?" Rado's pants fell in a heap at his ankles. He lifted one foot for Thorn to tug his boot off. She grasped the heel and levered the calf-high boot loose. The other followed, and Rado kicked his velvet trousers aside. He dipped a hand in the water. It was pleasantly hot, leaving a blush on his skin. He slipped his breechnap down over his narrow hips and plunged his foot into the tub. Thorn was at the door, looking out to the main chamber.

Rado lowered himself into the water. "Come here," he said. Thorn came toward him like a sleep-walker, sliding her feet across the tiles, her eyes tightly closed. "Take this," he said, tossing a fat sea sponge at her. Sightless as Thorn was, she easily caught the sponge with one hand. Rado leaned forward, resting his chin on his knees. "Well, what are you waiting for? Scrub my back, there's a good fellow."

Thorn knelt. She let the sponge soak for a moment, then lifted it out. Water cascaded down Rado's pale back.

"Is this Sverna the one you've been waiting to contact?" he asked.

"I have been in contact with my sisters from the hour we landed in Harbor Town," Thorn replied. She worked diligently, pausing often to refresh the water wrung out of the sponge.

"How many of you are there in Miyesti?"

She pressed hard on his shoulders. "It is better you do not know."

"Afraid I'll tell the Brethren?" he asked. "They could never break me."

"If you say so, my lord, though I suspect it would require little more than the right fancy girl and a steady flow of wine to make you talk."

He reached back and caught her hand. "Why do you think so poorly of me? If I'm such a worthless scoundrel, why did your mistress choose me for this job?"

"I judge by what I see. As to choice, you owe a

large debt to us, and that debt will be paid. One way or another."

The count stood up and jerked Thorn to her feet. Drops pattered on the floor and in the tub. He held her wrists close to his chest and glared into her passive face. "Look at me," he hissed. "Hunter's blood! Open your damned eyes and *look* at me!" She paid no heed. Rado let go and struck Thorn's face with his open palm. She staggered back against the wall but never opened her eyes.

"Because of my oath, I may not strike you back," she said. "Because of my faith, I will not look at your unclothed body. Until the hour comes when you do what you must do, I am your serf." She groped backward for the door. "But I am planning a time and type of death for you, Rado. With every humiliation you heap upon me, you make your own death more unpleasant and more sure."

Thorn slipped out of the bathing room. A chill crept over Rado, a chill not caused by cool air on his wet skin.

* * * * *

Claren Sarstic arranged for a go-about to carry Count Rado and his valet to the House of Vostig. The streets of Miyesti would remain busy until dark. When the sun went to rest behind the tallest buildings, the great metal street lamps cast a dazzling light from the glass globes at their tops. It was half-past the fifth hour when they left the Red Frog. Rado was resplendent in his black cutaway coat and scarlet hose, matching his dark hair and red ribbon tying it into a queue. His leather cape was lined with Homeland red wool, and a curled-brim hat completed his ensemble. The straight estoc stood between his knees as they rode, and a small dirk fitted invisibly inside the folds of his cape. Thorn was plainly clothed in taupe, her only concession to male fashion being the white silk ruff at her neck. She had trimmed her pale yellow hair before dressing and more than ever resembled a boy of eighteen years.

Cormoring Way ended on a grand plaza five bowshot across. The center of the square was dominated by a complex group of bronze statues. Facing the plaza were the largest, most elaborate villas Rado had ever seen. There were eight in all, two to each side of the square.

The House of Vostig was dark. At first Rado wondered if the invitation was wrong and no one was home; he then saw that, unlike the other mansions, the House of Vostig was not illuminated from within by dazzle lamps. Pale, shifting light showed in the windows, a sure sign of candles and oil lamps in use. Thorn saw this, too, and expressed her satisfaction.

A footman met them at the door. He took Rado's hat, cape, and sword, and Thorn's woolen cloak. Compared to the inn, Princess Sverna's home was old and dim. The interior was paneled in dark wood, and what metal fixtures there were had a soft patina from years of loving polish.

"This way," said the footman. Rado strode ahead, squaring his chest like an actor preparing to declaim a heroic soliloquy. The salon door curtains drew apart, drawn by an alert lackey with a pullcord, and Count Rado entered into the presence of the princess wife of the House of Vostig.

Sverna was a handsome woman, at least ten years older than Rado. Her full figure was swathed in many turns of pearlescent satin, and her whitening hair was piled atop her head. The princess's face bore the immobile veneer of nobility, gained from a lifetime of ceremonies and protocol.

Rado bowed. "Your Highness," he said. An elderly servant tardily puffed past the deeply bowed count and announced him to his mistress.

Sverna extended a hand. "Count Rado," she said, "it is good of you to come."

"The honor is mine, Highness." He straightened. "May I present my devoted valet, Thorn?"

She did not bow. Instead, she made a swift gesture with her left hand from her face to her heart. Princess Sverna's aristocratic glaze cracked. Her blue eyes widened, and a clenched fist rose to her lips.

"Master Thorn," she said with difficulty. "I am pleased Count Rado brought you along." With a harsh wave, she dismissed the aged butler. When they were alone, Sverna rushed to Thorn and knelt at her feet.

"Sentinel! I knew you would come someday! I am

at your service!" As Rado watched in astonishment, Thorn bade the princess rise.

"It is good to be with a sister again," Thorn said. "I have traveled a long and winding path to reach you."

"There is much to tell, only—" Sverna glanced around. They were completely alone.

Rado said, "What is it, Highness?"

"In Miyesti, it is impossible to speak so that the Brethren do not hear. Even in my own house, they have ears." Her voice was barely a whisper.

"The Brethren have spies in your household?" asked Thorn.

"No, it is not mortal ears that listen. . . ."

"If you have news to tell, do so," said Thorn. The authority in her tone surprised Rado.

Sverna said, "I shall, Sentinel. Hear what I do not say." She pulled a bell cord and the old butler appeared. "We will dine now, Latz."

"Very good, Your Highness."

The princess led them from the salon down a long corridor to a small dining room. A great house like this would have a hall for formal dinners. This elegant chamber was probably designed for more intimate occasions, or for when the prince and princess dined alone.

The blackwood tabletop was a mirror. Rado waited until Sverna was seated by the butler before seating himself. The plate and service were wrought in solid gold. A silver goblet stood by the plate, and sterling finger bowls were conveniently placed on either hand. Rado noticed there were only two settings, for himself and the princess. Of course, Thorn being thought a servant, she wouldn't be expected to dine with her betters.

Latz withdrew to bring the first course. Sverna said, "I apologize for the arrangements, Sentinel. If you wish it, I will have a place set for you."

"No," Thorn said. "I must play the role given me."

"Begging your pardon, Highness, but why do you defer to this person?" asked Rado.

The cold face of command returned. "Don't you know? She is a Sentinel of the First Flow. Among those who revere the Mother, she is considered worthy of great respect."

"The count has little respect for women, regardless of their station," said Thorn. Latz returned with a trio of servers. Wine was poured, the finger bowls were filled with lilac water, and fragrant chowder was served in shallow golden bowls.

The servants remained, hovering in a neat row along the wall. Stirring his soup casually, Rado said, "Highness, I couldn't help but notice you don't have any of the magic lamps that seem so plentiful in Miyesti."

"I won't allow them in the House of Vostig," she replied.

"Why, pray? They seem to work admirably well."

"Dazzling lamps are just one more trifle with which the Brethren of the Fact seduce the people of Miyesti," Sverna said. "Their pretty toys have lured the people away from the old gods. The Brethren will not be satisfied until all the world serves their god."

"Would that really be so terrible?" said Rado. "There would be a lot less friction in the world if all men worshiped the same deity."

Both women looked at him as if he'd grown a second head. "You miss the point completely, my lord," Thorn said. "To turn our backs on the whole of heaven would surely bring the wrath of the gods upon us. And no number of magic lamps or go-abouts would save us then."

Yes, and what would happen to all the priesthoods and temples? Rado thought. They'd have to find real work! He kept this to himself but asked, "Highness, if you so oppose the Brethren, how did they manage to become so dominant? Their control of Miyesti seems complete."

"It is, Count; it is. Their ascendance broke the heart of my dear husband, the late prince." Sverna looked away, remembering. "To understand the present, you have to know something of the past. Do you know how Miyesti was formerly governed?"

"No."

"Eight families shared rule—eight houses descended from the captains of the first eight colony ships that founded Miyesti. My own ancestor by marriage was Gallo ti Vostig. He and the other captains established a system in which every three years an election was held. A prince of one of the eight houses was elected First Prince of Miyesti and ruled with a

Privy Council of Seven. Oh, those were wild, tumul-
tuous days! The candidates vied with each other to
win favor with the voting citizens—"

"The *people* chose their ruler? How very odd," said
Rado.

"It worked very well, and both men and women
could vote, provided they had sufficient property to
qualify," said the princess. "Fifty years ago, the seed
of our present despair arrived. It was during the
fourth reign of Prince Ceven of the House of Latorx.
The Prelator of the Fact, one Ubarth, came and converted the First Prince to the way of the Fact. Ceven
gave the Brethren the island of Prios for their sanctuary."

"Where was the Fact before then?" asked Thorn.

"It was carried about in a large caravan, they say,"
Sverna said. "Ubarth brought the Fact to the shore
outside the city wall. An enormous barge was con-
structed, and the Fact was floated to Prios."

"Did anyone see it? What did it look like?"

The princess glanced at the servants. "Bring the
second course," she said. Latz shooed the waiters out.
Sverna lowered her voice. "My father paid a guard ten
crowns to let him see the Fact. It was shielded by partitions and veils, but my father crawled under them
and saw it." She paused dramatically. "He said it was
twice the size of an ox and golden."

Anticipation fell from Rado like shards of glass. "Is
that all?" he said incredulously.

Sverna lifted her chin. "He only had a moment to

peek at it. There were many guards."

"And after that the Fact went to Prios, where it remains to this day?" asked Thorn, trying to keep the conversation focused.

"Yes, Sentinel. There was an old castle on the east coast of the island built a century ago by Kurukish corsairs. The Brethren occupied and greatly enlarged it. They say—" Latz returned with cold carrots and peas seasoned with oil and vinegar. The vegetable course was eaten with unseemly haste. The flesh course—rabbit basted with spiced honey—was likewise dispatched. The princess's anxiety built to the bursting point as the elderly butler entered with fruit and cheese. He sliced and served with glacial slowness.

"Latz!" she said tautly. "It is too warm here for dessert. Prepare three cordials and bring them to the veranda. We will take them there."

"Three?" said Latz. Thorn, of course, had not dined at all.

"Three, yes, three! Count Rado is very thirsty!" Latz paled and withdrew, bowing as he retreated.

Sverna pressed fingers to her lips and inhaled deeply. "Come, let us retire to the garden."

The veranda was in fact more like a balcony, as it stood on pillars overlooking a deep wooded ravine. The princess explained that the garden below was the last vestige of the old forest preserve where the princely families had once hawked and run their hounds after deer and rabbit.

"Even this small greenwood will pass away," Sverna said sadly. "The Brethren teach that hunting is a barbarous pastime."

A mild breeze stirred, smelling faintly of the sea. Sverna sat in a folding leather chair. Rado positioned himself opposite her. The table between them was a short, fat cylinder of blue-streaked marble. Thorn went to the iron rail and stared into the umber trees. Her fingers gripped the chiseled ivy leaves hard.

"Deny the Mother and deny the Hunter," she said. "What will be left of the rhythm of life if the Brethren overthrow the great Goddess and her consort?"

Latz set a heavy tray on the marble table. Three tall cones of cut crystal, brimming with golden liqueur, formed an equilateral triangle. Sverna dismissed Latz and lifted the nearest cordial.

"We may speak more freely here," she said. "Under the open sky, in our Mother's sight, the Fact cannot hear us." Rado raised his goblet. "Will you take mead with us, Sentinel?"

Thorn turned her back to the ravine. She took up the third glass. "Hail, Goddess, Mother of bounty!" said the princess. Rado mumbled some similar sentiment.

Thorn merely raised her portion high and said, "Death to the Fact! Death to the monotheists!" She poured the silken mead onto the ground below.

* * * * *

Princess Sverna poured out the history of how the Brethren had subverted and taken control of Miyesti. As the evening went on, she spun the story against a steady counterpoint of hedge crickets.

"In the beginning, the Fact folk were confined to their island. Oh, some came to Harbor Town to buy food for their fellows, and others came to accept cargoes shipped in from around the Adamantine Sea. Odd cargoes, too—ingots of copper, lead, and tin; nitre and vitriol and soda ash. The Brethren filled barges with sand scraped from the beaches north and south of Miyesti and rowed them back to Prios. The night sky was filled with strange flashes of lightning as the Fact was encased in a fortress of stone and glass. The people wondered, and many were afraid.

"Then one night, two years after the coming of the Fact, the lightning did not play on the horizon. The next morning a galleot docked in Harbor Town. Ten men disembarked, ten Speakers of the Fact. They were the first of many Speakers who would come to tell the people of the new god. Among them was the man who is now their leader, Prelator Rhom.

"It was difficult to see the progress the Brethren made. The Speakers were jeered and assaulted. Where the gods of sea and air were strongest, the Fact Speakers were treated with a dagger in the gullet." Sverna flushed at the rude image she'd called up. "But the city was open in those days, and before long the Speakers won admittance to the finest houses, where they converted the wealthy and the well-born.

The House of Latorx was the first to succumb. Prince Ceven himself appeared in the council rotunda wearing the headband of the Brethren. The moneylender Gurdasic converted, and the society of metal workers joined in a body. Every week brought news of another conversion. The low and the mighty, the poor and the rich alike heard the words of the Fact and believed. And to my knowledge, no one has ever abandoned the Fact once he has joined."

"You omit an important bit of information," Thorn said. "All these converts were men, were they not?"

"Yes, Sentinel. The Speakers declared in the streets that women could not hear the words of the Fact, but many women are nonetheless believers. Truth be told, the Fact has such a reputation that now thousands believe who have never worn a headband."

"Where the bull leads, the herd will follow," Rado quipped.

Thorn ignored him. "When their numbers were strong enough, the Brethren seized control?" she asked.

"Oh, no. It was done lawfully. Believing citizens voted for Brethren as candidates. Soon the only way to win was to worship the Fact. Now I am the only head of a princely family who has not converted, and I am powerless in the Privy Council. The old laws of property have been cast aside. Only men who are citizens of Miyesti and who reside within the city walls may vote. Women and all the folk in Harbor Town have lost their voice." Sverna balled a smooth, white fist. "They gave away their power and their rights, just gave them away!"

The crickets sang their corrugated song. From the watchtowers far away, the city bells rang eight times.

"We must go inside," said the princess. "The curfew."

"Surely the guardsmen cannot object to our sitting outdoors at your own house," said the count.

"My lord, no one is to be out from under his roof after eight bells have rung!" Sverna fidgeted in her chair. Her elaborate coiffure was beginning to fall. Faint rings of perspiration darkened the fine fabric of her gown.

"What are you afraid of?" asked Thorn.

"Sentinel, I am ashamed to be so fearful in your presence, but—" Sverna looked up into the sky. "The Brethren hear and see things no mortal could ever discover. Why, only last week a temple sister and her husband were taken to the College of Peace. The man came home two days later, but of Ajilla we've had no sign!"

The three retired from the veranda. Faithful Latz promptly appeared in the corridor with a candelabra. "Highness, I have taken the liberty of preparing accommodations for his lordship and Master Thorn," said the butler.

"Very good, Latz. You may go now." He handed the candles to Thorn and left.

Princess Sverna stood back from the waving flames.

She whispered, "We who are loyal to the Goddess are almost spent. No one dares take action against the Fact. The guardsmen of the College of Peace are everywhere, and we are left only to pray and invoke the Mother's divine intervention."

"Be of sure heart, Highness," Thorn replied. "Count Rado and I *are* the Mother's intervention."

"But what can the two of you do?"

"We have the means. In our possession is a weapon of such power no mortal has ever dreamed of. It was made in the Inner Temple according to instructions set down a thousand years ago. With it, we will kill this Fact and destroy its usurping faith forever."

Sverna looked from Thorn to Rado and back to Thorn. She could believe almost anything of a Sentinel of the First Flow, but the cynical, self-indulgent count was another matter. What was his part in all this?

VI

Rado, his hands tied behind his back, was shoved to his knees. The vast hall was lit by fitful fires burning at the top of short pillars of red sandstone. The silent ranks of priestesses flanked him on three sides. Two Sentinels of the Temple, his none-too-gentle escorts, stood close behind him.

The fires flared. Between the sheets of flame came the One Who Commands, the high priestess herself. She wore the mask of a tormentor. Emerging from the flames, she flung a still-smoking flail to the floor before him. Rado lifted his sagging head to her. The black mask frowned down at him. No living eyes showed through the lacquered bronze mask.

"Vile man, I throw down the instrument of punishment. Shall I take it up again, or will you do as I bid?" the priestess intoned.

"What must I do?" asked Rado hoarsely.

"Kill the false god."

"How can I kill a god?"

"Take the Goddess's weapon to the sanctuary of the False One and place it in her enemy's heart. Will you do it?"

What choice do I have? Rado thought bitterly. He knew his torment would go on if he declined. At least by agreeing, I might gain some time. . . .

"I will do it, Lady," he said.

The high priestess raised her hand. From the shadows on her left, a slim figure emerged, dressed in a polished cuirass and leather kilt. Another Sentinel, more grandly dressed than most. Her eyes were fixed entirely on the high priestess.

"Sentinel Eridé," said the priestess, "I give you charge of this malefactor. It will be your sacred duty to go with him, protect him, and obey him in every degree that affects your mission. If he attempts to flee, if he deviates from the goal I give, if he fails my charge in any way, you will strike him down and feed his body to the birds. Do you swear it?"

Eridé held her silver stiletto point against her heart and swore. The high priestess removed her mask. Her face and Thorn's were the same.

"No!" shouted Rado.

The room was black and still. Thorn said, "You were dreaming."

"A nightmare is more like it. What are you doing?"

"I'm going out."

He sat up. "The Brethren will take you."

"They can try." Rado heard the snick of the stiletto tines snapping out.

"Why are you going? What do you hope to do?"

"There is a local shrine I have to visit. There are things I must discuss with my sisters."

Rado couldn't see at all. The room Princess Sverna had provided was an interior one, with no window. He heard Thorn cross the foot of the bed. He said, "What happens to me if you don't come back?"

"You will complete the task on your own," she said.

"Would I do that?"

The door handle rattled. He faced toward the sound. Thorn was framed in the light rectangle of the open door. "You wouldn't continue," she said. "I know that. But remember, my lord, that I am not the only Sentinel in the world. I have sisters everywhere, even in Miyesti." Her profile vanished from the gray aperture, leaving Rado alone with that unsettling reminder.

* * * * *

She didn't go out by the front door. Instead, she left by a window on the second story, tying a rope of woven black silk to the balcony rail and lowering herself to the ground. The great house next door made a wide alley between itself and the House of Vostig. The alley was as quiet and dark as an empty coal mine. Even the crickets had gone to sleep.

She skirted the square, keeping close to the mansions all the way around to Cormoring Way. The street was deserted. The dazzle lamps were out.

The princess had given Thorn directions to the last shrine of the Mother Goddess in Miyesti: four corners down the hill on Cormoring, then turn right. Two corners, turn left, and find the low house faced with white stucco. In the alley behind the house would be a set of steps leading down to a cellar. The shrine was there.

A fine thing, Thorn mused. The creator of the world worshiped in a cellar.

Thorn skipped along on her toes, ready to spring in any direction. At the second street corner, a go-about, moving without its lamps burning, scuttled into sight. She threw herself to the pavement and waited. In the absolute stillness, she heard every sound the machine made—the scrape of its iron-rimmed wheels on the brick road, the creak of the axles, and something she hadn't noticed before, even when she had ridden in one. A hum, faint and steady, coming from the rear underside of the thing. Thorn realized she was hearing the captive spirit that made the go-about move.

The vehicle turned away from her and continued on its way. Thorn pushed up with her hands and tucked her feet under her. She crouched, waiting, listening.

A brilliant shaft of light lanced down Cormoring Way, right where she would have been had she immediately gone on. The go-about had dropped a guardsman, who swept the street with his powerful lamp. The window above her was deep, and the lamp cast

wide shadows from the sill. She was completely submerged in a wedge of black. The guardsman put out
the dazzler and rejoined his comrades in the go-
about.

The near miss sent a surge of energy through
Thorn. She was in her element now, fighting the enemies of the Goddess. The months of training behind
that wastrel Rado, playing his drudge and his whore,
had worn her down. Not now! She was a Sentinel of
the Temple once more.

She made the turn at the fourth corner. The sign-
post said "Prelator Joth Street." Even streets weren't
safe from conversion. At the second turn, where she
was to go left, another—or the same?—go-about was
moving along the route she was supposed to take.
Thorn froze against a wall and waited for the machine
to pass.

A dazzle lamp burst on behind her. In the glare,
Thorn saw a Fact guardsman in breastplate and helmet wielding the lamp. He had a crossbow slung on
one shoulder. The Miyestan advanced on Prelator
Joth Street, swinging his lamp from side to side. A
quick glance revealed the go-about was proceeding
slowly away from her. Much too slowly. Inevitably the
guardsman on foot would spy her. She might take
him, but there was no knowing how many more
armed men were riding the go-about.

The lamp flashed across the street from Thorn. Out
came the stiletto. By the time the Miyestan brought
his light over to where she had been, Thorn was al-

ready halfway to him.

He dropped the lamp. It was a long metal cylinder, closed on the end, and it dangled by a cord from his belt. The guardsman reached over his shoulder for the bow. Thorn saw him backpedal in the splash of light from his dazzler. The steel cuirass extended down to his hips. Thorn closed the stiletto's tines and rammed the single point through the man's throat. She clapped a hand behind his neck and pushed until the stiletto tip broke through the base of his skull. Thorn lowered the dead man silently to the ground.

A second light appeared. The go-about had reversed and was coming back. She unbuckled the bloody chin strap and slipped the dead man's cabasset on. With that, the lamp, and the crossbow, she stood up and walked toward the cart.

The beam hit her in the eyes. She returned the favor and the men in the cart couldn't see who she was.

"Sholly?" called a voice. "Is anything wrong?"

"Not a thing," Thorn answered. "Put out that light, will you?"

That was a mistake. The go-about lowered its lamp. When Thorn did the same, they instantly saw she was an imposter. A chorus of shouts erupted. Thorn heard three distinct voices. She shouldered the crossbow and squeezed the trigger bar.

The flash and roar that followed blew Thorn backward off her feet. She landed heavily and lay too long stunned. By the time she recovered, the go-about was blazing. A man with his cloak in flames fell from the

cart. She ran to him. He was dead. The second Miyestan was scattered over the street, utterly destroyed.
The third, the driver, was impaled on his own tiller.

There were shouts in the distance. Thorn had a
quick notion. She dragged the body of the first man
she'd slain and pushed him into the flames. The helmet and lamp were also consigned to the fire. Though
the wooden sides of the go-about were rapidly being
consumed, Thorn crawled under the high-wheeled
contraption and planted her feet on the smoking underside. She flexed her legs, and the three-wheeled
cart careened over on its side.

She ran from the scene lightly, on her toes, as her
fighting instructor had taught her. Faster and lighter
she ran, until only the very tips of her toes touched
the ground. Few were the trackers who could follow so
scant a trail. By the time she stopped in the alley behind the white stucco house, her heart was hammering in her ribs. The crossbow was still in her hands.

Thorn tapped on the cellar door. A wicket fell
open. "Who calls in the night?" whispered a woman
through the peephole.

"A messenger from the Mother," said Thorn.

"What do you bring?"

"Her blessing and her strength."

The formula satisfied, the door was unbolted.
Thorn squeezed in, mindful not to let any stray light
escape.

Two women were in the small cellar. The younger
one, who'd opened the door, stood vigilantly beside a

ceiling post. A flanged mace hung from her hand.
The other, older woman, robed and veiled, sat at a
simple table a few steps away. Flame licked around
the rim of the brass brazier in the center of the table.
The elder priestess's features seemed to move and
change with the firelight.

"Good health to you, sister," Thorn said. She
crossed her arms and bowed from the waist.

"Kapthys has been blessed with the dream
tongue," said the younger woman. "If she speaks, I
will interpret for you." She set the mace in the corner.
Thorn kissed her on either check. "Oriath, Sentinel
of the Sixth Flow. We have been waiting for you since
midnight. We feared you had been caught."

Thorn introduced herself as Thorn and told the
young Sentinel of her battle in the street. "I don't
know why the cart should have burst," she said.

Oriath put a hand on the crossbow. "May I?" Thorn
let her have it. "You see, lady, this slot in the stock?"
Oriath pressed the smooth metal plate with her finger.
A blue steel quarrel head popped out. Oriath withdrew the quarrel and displayed it to Thorn. It was half
the length of a regular quarrel and wrought entirely in
metal. She laid it on Thorn's palm.

"It's heavy," said Thorn.

"There's a captive spirit in the head which, if
struck hard, bursts out and destroys what it touches.
The guardsmen call these 'thunderbolts.' They're only allowed to carry them on night patrols." Oriath
pushed the quarrel nock-first back into the slot. "An-

other gift of the Fact," she sneered.

"A company of men armed with these could destroy—anything!"

Oriath nodded solemnly. " 'Tis said a pair of the Brethren's galleots wiped out a whole squadron of corsairs who had the temerity to try to waylay them." From the table, the old priestess mumbled something. Oriath hurried to her. She knelt, one ear cocked to the blessed Kapthys.

"She says you are the First Flow. She says we are to give you anything you ask for, even our lives. She says you bring with you a terrible thing not seen since the gods were young and the world was still wrapped by the fogs of Chaos." Oriath looked to Thorn. "It's true, isn't it? Everything she said." Kapthys muttered a long string of unintelligible words. Oriath interpreted, " 'Read the bluelines, canto 74, lines 36-39.' Does that make sense to you?"

A heavy fist pounded on the door. "Open! We are guardsmen of the peace!"

"They followed you," Oriath whispered.

"Impossible! No man could—"

"No man could, but what of the Fact?"

"Open now! This is the order of the Subprelate Ferstratis!"

Thorn looked around quickly. "Is there another way out?"

"A trapdoor . . . there." Oriath gestured to the far corner of the cellar. "It leads into the city drains."

Thorn ran to the corner. She groped through the

muck on the floor for some sign of the trapdoor. Under a thick rime of mold, she felt a metal ring. With great effort, she freed the encrusted panel. The drain's rank odor assailed her nose.

"Come quickly!" she said. "Bring the old sister with you!"

The guardsmen were already battering on the door. "No," said Oriath. She put down her mace and took up the crossbow.

"I order you!"

"No, sister. Only you must escape. I will stay and hold the enemy off. They will attribute your deeds in the street above to me. Once we are taken, they will not search further for you."

"You'll be killed, Oriath." The center plank in the door broke and flew inward. Oriath cocked the bow and pushed the trigger bar.

The blast in the confined cellar was even worse than it had been in the street. The door vanished, leaving only a few burning splinters imbedded in the jam. Thorn felt the searing heat on her cheek, then she dropped through the hole. The trap banged down.

Oriath must have survived the first bolt, or else the Miyestans were using their own, for two more thunderclaps rocked the house to its foundations. Thorn lost her footing in the slime-filled tunnel and fell. Shouts and screams filtered down from above. Oriath had sold her and Kapthys's lives dearly.

Thorn scrambled to her feet and started down the drain. The round tunnel was just slightly smaller than she was tall, and as black as a moneylender's heart. In her neophyte days, Thorn had often been expected to run for miles through the forest with a thick blindfold on. The drain was nothing compared to that. Her only worry was that she had no idea where she might emerge.

Several times she heard go-abouts rattle over her, rushing through the streets in pursuit of foes of the Fact. The drain branched in four directions, and Thorn took the tunnel that led back to the Princes' Plaza.

Much time and many streets later, Thorn came to another trapdoor. It was actually a slab of bricks mortared together, but she was able to force it up enough to peek out. She was in a short, wide street. As she climbed out, the chiming of the city bells startled her half to death. Five bells. Dawn was coming.

Thorn ran for the distant House of Vostig. Breathing began to hurt. She dropped her hands to her sides and refused to falter. *My strength is your strength, my duty your will.* The pledge came back to her, the pledge every Sentinel made when her flow began.

She burst upon the Princes' Plaza from the west, away from Cormoring Way. Though visible from every window, Thorn ran straight across the square to the House of Vostig. The black rope still hung from the second floor railing. Hand over hand, she dragged herself up. Thorn rolled over the rail and collapsed, pulling the rope in after her.

There were lights in the sky—two pairs of them,

swinging to and fro over the city, searching for her. The air had lightened a touch with the imminence of dawn. Thorn saw silhouettes, long, dark shapes moving against the wind.

She staggered into Rado's room. He wasn't in bed. Wrapped in a dark red dressing gown, he stood by the cold hearth, mindlessly poking a charred log. A row of candles were lit on the mantel.

"Thorn," he said. "You're a sight." He sniffed. "And a smell."

She was indeed. The sleeves of her blue coat were stained darker still with blood. Fire, smoke, sweat, and slime marked her from head to toe.

"I found the way," she said.

"What way? Where?" Rado asked, but Thorn could say no more. Her knees folded, and she sank to the floor.

Rado walked slowly around the end of the bed. He picked up the limp woman and laid her on Sverna's elegant guest bed. She might have been dead for all the movement she made.

He put a hand to her throat and applied the slightest pressure. Thorn's face reddened. She coughed, and Rado took his hand away. "Not yet," he said softly, "not until your eyes are open."

VII

Young Eridé shifted nervously on the hard bench. She would have much preferred to be gathering apples in the temple orchard or combing the goats for burrs instead of waiting in the prefectory. She'd been cross to Lualu, another foundling girl, hitting her in the eye with her fist because Lualu had taken Eridé's bread pudding at supper the night before. Now she was going to be punished. The sisters didn't understand. Was she to let that greedy pig Lualu eat all her bread pudding? This wasn't the first time she'd stolen it.

The prefectory was dusty and quiet. Massive leather-bound tomes lay on their sides on the shelves. Gray- and brown- and black-ridged spines. Eridé ran a dirty finger over the bumpy edges. Faded gold leaf letters told what was in the books, but Eridé couldn't read.

"What am I to do with you?" The girl spun and saw one of the priestesses standing in the shadowed doorway. "You blackened Lualu's eye, you know."

"She ate my pudding," Eridé said, her voice faint but stubborn.

"Lualu's family came from Vendrollo. She saw them starve to death there. She still hasn't learned she doesn't have to steal food here to stay alive." The priestess stayed where she was, shrouded and indistinct. "What am I to do with you, Eridé?" she asked.

Her small hand closed over the spine of one of the books. "Teach me to read," said the girl.

"What could a stripling like you want to read?"

Eridé dragged the great tome from the shelf. The cover was as wide as her chest, and she could only hold it by wrapping both arms around it. "I want to read this," she declared.

"The Millennium Book. Yes, that is a fit remedy for truculence. Sit down."

And so Eridé learned to read. She read no other book in the rest of her life but that first one. The Millennium Book was made up of admonitions from the Goddess to her mortal daughters. The text was written in two columns, two languages, and two colors of ink. The left column of text was written in the secret tongue of the Inner Temple. The right-hand blue text was written in ordinary Homeland speech. It was this part Eridé learned first.

* * * * *

Count Rado broke fast alone. It was past nine, and the princess was an early riser. Latz lingered for him in the great dining hall, where he served Rado in the midst of vacant splendor. The oak table could have seated a hundred.

A smooth pallet of clouds hid the morning sun. Rado sipped buttered tea and counted birds as they dashed across the expanse of tall windows lining the east side of the hall. By the tenth hour Thorn had still not appeared. He called the old butler.

"My lord?" asked Latz.

"You have bathing facilities?" asked Rado.

"Indeed we do, my lord."

"Draw a hot tub, would you? My man Thorn will be needing a bath."

"I'll have the tub set up in the kitchen, my lord."

"No," said Rado before Latz could scurry on his way. "Have the bath prepared in my chambers. Poor lad, Thorn. He is very shy about his deformity." Latz gave a wise nod and departed.

He waited till the last of the long train of servants returned with empty buckets before going upstairs. Rado flung the door back, letting it bang hard against the paneling.

"I knew you'd come," said Thorn. She was seated in the wooden tub with her back to the door.

He grinned. "You knew, did you?"

"It's your nature to intrude. Shut the door, my lord."

A small fire burned in the grate. Rado thrust the poker into the smoky flames and found a wad of charred cloth. Thorn was burning the evidence of her nocturnal adventures.

"How many did you kill?" he asked.

"Does it matter? They are with the gods now. What does matter is the information that Kapthys gave me." He didn't ask her to explain. Thorn let her head go back to the tub rim. She closed her eyes and recited:

"A ship with oars and no men to row them,
With clouds so firm a windmill can throw them,
In gold the poison firmly will plant them,
A man in their midst the needle will break them."

"The Fact is on Prios Island in the heart of a fortress. We must go there by ship," Thorn said.

"Only ships of the Brethren are allowed to go there," Rado observed.

She scooped warm water into the hollows of her neck. "Exactly."

"Do you think we can just board one of their galleots and say, 'Ah, look alive there, fellow; to the Fact as quick as you can'?" Rado asked.

Thorn said nothing. She eased down in the water, letting it lap over her shoulders. Rado watched the ripples from her sinking form hit the tub's sides in weaker and weaker waves.

After a long time, Thorn said, "Are you afraid to die, Rado?"

"It's not something I often think about," he answered. "I know I shall die someday, and I would hate to lose all the things in life I enjoy. On the other hand, the notion of choosing my own time and place to die appeals to my vanity."

"The poetry I quoted is from a sacred book known only to priestesses of the temple. It sets me a pretty problem. Not only does it tell us how to reach the Fact, it says a man will be the one to administer the death blow. Do you see? You swore to the One Who Commands to carry out her order, as I swore to serve and protect you in the execution of that order. But knowing your importance to our mission, why should you continue? You have only to refuse, and the charge is futile."

"And if I balk, you will kill me."

"Yes."

"You hate me enough to kill me now." She let this declaration go unchallenged. "What you've failed to include in your neat little formula, my dear Thorn, is that I might want to continue."

She grabbed the sides of the tub and sat up. "Why?" she asked.

"Having been in Miyesti a day and a night, I've gotten a pretty good idea of what the Brethren have to offer the world. Prosperity, order, magic—quite a tray of goods in all. But I confess to you, Thorn-in-my-side, these people scare me. Yes, scare. Have you thought about the way they live? No taverns, no gaming, no willing ladies for company . . . no horses! Hunter's blood! Piety is an admirable trait in priests and old folks, but rampant as it is here—ugh! Can you imagine the whole world governed as Miyesti is governed? What joy would there be in being a man?"

"You favor a world like Harbor Town."

"Blood, I do! A man, or a woman for that matter, ought to be able to live and love with every choice that's available—root in garbage or dine off golden plates! Fight for money or fight for honor! Manure may stink, but it grows better flowers than all the fine marble there ever was."

Thorn picked a towel off the stool next to the tub. She wrapped herself in it. "In every way you are a worthless rogue, Rado of Hapmark, but I believe what you say. I have hope again."

He scratched his chin on his knuckle and said, "What's our next ploy?"

"We should return to the Red Frog. After last night, our presence is a danger to Princess Sverna. If we stay out of the hands of the College of Peace, we should be able to figure out how to stow away to Prios."

Rado went to the door. "I will beg leave of the princess." His hand hovered over the door handle. "You are quite a remarkable person," he said quickly. Before Thorn could respond, the embarrassed Rado was out the door.

* * * * *

Sverna saw them off. She generously offered Rado gold to ease the burden of the stay in Miyesti on his own purse. The count graciously declined. "The price of this expedition has already been underwritten by the great temple in Pazoa," he said.

The ride to the Red Frog was uneventful. The streets were the same as before, go-abouts dodging each other at every corner, pushcarts and pedestrians hugging the walls of the high, spotless buildings. All was busy and humdrum, save for one disturbing feature: On every corner, pairs of Fact guardsmen stood watch. The day before, they hadn't seen five in all the time they had spent in the streets. The guardsmen were armed, too, whereas earlier they hadn't carried anything more serious than a hardwood baton. Now, in each pair, one man shouldered a halberd, while his partner carried a crossbow. As the go-about passed, Thorn wondered if the bows shot the terrible thunderbolts.

They entered the Red Frog just at noon. Claren Sarstic flinched when Rado rapped on the counter with his balled fist.

"Count Rado, it's you!" he said too loudly. Out of the corner of her eye, Thorn spied a man seated across the room on a divan. When Sarstic made his arch declaration, the man rose and approached. Thorn flexed her hand and felt the hard length of the stiletto under her arm. . . .

"Count Rado of Hapmark?" asked the man politely. His voice was resonant and deep.

"I am he."

"My lord, my name is Goss. I am with the College of Peace. Might I have a word with you?"

"Oh, is it necessary? I've had an abysmal breakfast

this morning, and if I don't find a decent mug of ale soon, I shall expire!"

"This will only take a moment, my lord."

"Very well," Rado said sourly. He slapped his hat on Thorn's chest. "Make yourself useful, boy. Hold that, and mind you don't crumple it."

The count and the stranger strolled away from the counter. "My lord, there was an incident last night, an act of brigandage in a street not far from here," Goss said quietly.

"Oh? What of it? A city street at night often sees acts of mayhem."

"Not in Miyesti, my lord. The college was concerned for your safety. A rich foreigner, unfamiliar with the city, could easily lose his way in the streets and stumble into trouble."

Rado stopped short. "What are you saying, Master Goss?"

"As I said, my lord, our concern is for you. The innkeeper tells me you did not return to your room last night."

"We did not. I'm just now returning from the House of Vostig, where I spent a pleasant evening in the company of the Princess Sverna. Delightful woman, the princess—a bit willful, I'll admit, but all in all, quite delightful. Wonderful hostess, too. Widows always are. She's a relative of mine. Did you know that?"

"No, I didn't." Goss looked at his shoes. "I don't wish to pry, but I take it your lordship stayed the entire night at the House of Vostig?"

"Dusk to dawn. I might have left sooner, but this curfew of yours is damned inconvenient." He winked broadly. "Still, as confinements go, it wasn't entirely unbearable."

"Ah, yes." Goss fingered the collar of his white tunic. "May I beg one last indulgence from your lordship?"

"What is it?"

"May I see your hands?"

"My—?" Wide-eyed, Rado held out his hands. He flipped them palms up. His lightly tanned skin was smooth and unblemished.

"Many thanks, my lord. Good day and good morrow." Goss walked briskly away without acknowledging either Thorn or Claren Sarstic. Rado ambled over to the counter.

"Master Sarstic," he said, "would it be possible for me to obtain a map of Miyesti?"

"A map, my lord?"

"Yes, with streets named and major buildings labeled, if possible. There was some nasty business last night, and Master Goss thought it best I not wander about finding trouble. If I had a map, I could plan my routes ahead of time. There are so many fine things to see, I shouldn't want my tour of the city to be incomplete."

"An engraver might have such a map," Sarstic said. He was plainly bothered and confused by foreign troublemakers and city officials lingering in his inn.

"Shall I send a boy to find one for you?"

"Right away, there's a good fellow." To Thorn, he barked, "Well, don't just stand there, lad! Summon the moving room for me."

In their rooms, Thorn said, "It was clever of you to ask Sarstic for a map. Now we'll be able to trace the Brethren's boatyard, wherever it is."

"Shut up!" Rado unbuckled his sword belt and hurled it on the bed. "He *knew*, damn your eyes! That fellow Goss knew I was connected to your bloody escapades last night. He thought I was the culprit!" He related Goss's odd desire to see his hands. "He was looking for marks of a fight!"

"Did you notice he wore no Fact emblem?" Thorn asked.

"He did—no, wait a hair—he didn't, did he? What was he, an imposter?"

"No, he was a genuine brother, I'm sure. Did he say what rank he was?"

"I assumed he was at least a subprelate."

Thorn walked over to the window. The first specks of rain dotted the spotless pane. Her breath silvered the glass. She reached up and rubbed one finger absently through the mist.

"Suppose he were not a subprelate, but a higher rank. Rather than display his importance, he removed his emblem before he came. Sarstic was upset; that was obvious." Her finger traced a diamond on the glass. "Sverna was right," she said.

"What are you gibbering about?"

"The Brethren are always aware of our activities, here and in Harbor Town. We've been watched since we first set foot on Miyestan soil, since the guards read your cachet in the street. The spy Ferengasso, the men who almost caught me last night . . . The princess is right. The Fact is somehow watching us."

"Rubbish," Rado snorted. "If they know so much, why aren't we under arrest?"

"They can't know exactly what our purpose is. They can't imagine our true goal. For all they know, we might be spies for a Homeland warlord, or even for the Kuruks."

"So where does that leave us?"

Thorn twisted slightly. The stiletto appeared in her fist. She spread the tines and lowered it point first onto the small table by the window. She took her hand away. It stood.

"Balanced," she said softly. "Very delicately balanced."

* * * * *

Tepid rain ran in fat rivulets down the sides of the glass pyramid. Beneath the skylight, ten subprelates of the College of Peace were assembled. With them was their chief, Wivon Forgani. At his side was the man who called himself Goss.

"And that, my brothers, is the state of affairs regarding Count Rado of Hapmark," Subprelate Vost said. He closed the parchment folder before him and looked toward his superior.

Forgani said, "The count and his man have been made aware of our interest?"

Goss cleared his throat. "I couldn't have been more obvious about it. Whatever the count's purpose is in Miyesti, he must either abandon it or hurry it to fruition."

"I don't like it," Vost said quietly.

"You spoke, brother?" prompted Forgani.

"I don't like it!" Vost repeated more strongly. "We should have this man in our hands, not let him roam the city at will. He's dangerous—see how many guardsmen died last night!"

A lesser subprelate shuffled through a stack of crisp vellum. He read, "There were six killed, three grievously wounded, one eye put out, one leg severed above the knee—"

"Yes, yes, Brix, that's enough. Vost, you have heard Goss's argument. Do you wish to refute it?"

"Only to say this: The Prelate of the Guardians is gaming with very high stakes. What does he hope to accomplish by allowing this Hapmark fellow to go his own way?"

Goss leaned forward, resting his entwined hands on the table. "Does the subprelate recall the story of the farmer and the fox?"

"Are you proposing to tell us nursery tales?" asked Voss.

"Do you recall it?"

"No."

"The farmer was losing chickens every night to the marauding fox. The farmer hid in the roost one night to catch the beast. When the fox showed up, it killed two fat hens and dragged them away."

Vost blinked. "Why didn't the farmer bag the fox before it killed again?"

"He stayed his hand because he knew one fox wasn't eating all that meat. So he allowed the fox to carry off two hens. The farmer followed the bloody trail to the fox's den. He broke it open and found two kits. Then he slew all the foxes, thus ending his problem for once and all."

The room was still. Brix, the scribe, held his quill poised for Vost's next words.

"I concede the point," Vost said. "But I still say too many risks are involved. We are not guarding chickens here."

"I tell you what I was told," said Goss. "I have communed, my brothers, and the Fact has told me what to do. Count Rado is to have a free hand until the last moment. Then he will be ours."

The meeting dissolved. The subprelates dispersed to other duties, leaving Forgani and Goss alone.

"Who is he, Goss, this Rado of Hapmark? Just who is he?" asked Forgani.

"An adventurer and libertine of no great substance. An unbeliever, too, and not only in the Fact. Men such as he don't believe in anything. He's here for gold or glory, that's all." He clapped the elder prelate on the shoulder and smiled. "We have his measure, old friend. Never fear."

"And the valet?"

"The valet is merely a valet. Ferengasso noted some frightening fighting ability of his in a tavern brawl, but Hapmark doesn't even allow his man to wear a sword."

"I wish we would hear from the spy again. He is overdue."

"Spies by their nature are unreliable." Goss yawned. "I think the College of Peace is becoming ingrown. Fear and suspicion among the subprelates is generating phantom menaces where only a single sly man exists. Your men ought to go by turns to Prios and have close communion with the Fact. That would put an end to their fears."

"Is that an official opinion from the Prelate of the Guardians of the Fact?" asked Forgani.

"All my opinions are official." Goss rose to leave. "There is only one God—"

"—and he has given us the Fact." Forgani completed the benediction. "Do you plan to return to Prios tonight?"

"Yes, late. The College of Light is crying for more spirit to be sent by the underwater cable. As more and more citizens learn to use the magic lamps, the demand for spirit increases daily. Once I find out their projected requirements, I'll be off to the sanctuary. The *Promicon* has been dispatched for me and will arrive shortly."

Forgani embraced him. Goss said, "May the Fact

guide you, brother."

"And you, excellent Goss."

The rain fell harder. The clouds closed in until it seemed to Forgani they would crack the diamond panes of the pyramid skylight.

Third: Sanctuary

When the crow on the tower made of brick
For seven hours will continue to scream:
Death foretold, the statue stained with blood,
Tyrant murdered, people praying to their Gods.

Nostradamus
Centuries, IV-55

VIII

"Hold the candle still!"

Thorn braced her wrist with her free hand and tilted the fat tallow stick toward Rado. A blob of molten wax lipped over the edge of the candle and dribbled over the back of his hand.

"Ow! Miserable—! You did that on purpose!"

"A hundred pardons, my lord. I didn't want to drip wax on the map," she said.

Sarstic had found a city map in less than an hour. Medric the engraver had no less than eight in stock, which he eagerly offered to sell to Sarstic for a mere ten stars each. The innkeeper stiffly responded that only one was required, and he wouldn't pay more than five silver pieces for it. Sarstic repeated this tale of virtue in tiresome detail until Count Rado tossed him a gold ducat and bade him vanish.

"And if you come back with change, I'll take a stick to you!" Rado had said. Two hours passed, and Claren Sarstic did not return.

Rado sat cross-legged on the carpet, the map scroll spread from knee to knee. According to the date in the legend, the chart had been engraved three years ago, but for their purpose, it was new enough.

Miyesti, like Harbor Town, was shaped like the joint of a thumb and forefinger. The wall surrounded the city, landward and seaward. There were six major gates on the land side, plus a dozen posterns. Ten gates connected Miyesti with the harbor. All these were tightly regulated. The posterns were sealed except to city officials—which is to say, to the Brethren.

West of Harbor Town, the wall extended right down to the beach. It encompassed a blunt, wedge-shaped headland that protruded into the strait. To the north, the wall followed the shore to a dry riverbed. From there, it turned inland in a series of staggered insets, with plenty of towers to prevent besiegers from tunneling under the defense.

"What's that?" asked Thorn, tapping the parchment with the butt end of the candle.

Rado squinted at the wispy script. "Yestigol. Whatever that is."

Thorn consulted the legend, a box of text in the lower right corner of the map. " 'Yestigol is one of two ancient citadels built by the Kurukish kings five centuries ago. The city of Miyesti derives its name from the old Kuruk stronghold, which has been incorporated within the wall of the present city.' " Her thumb raced through uninteresting details. "The companion fortress of Yestigol is called Priongol. Guess where it was located."

"Prios?"

"My lord, your wisdom increases daily. Priongol must be the old citadel Prince Ceven ceded to the Brethren."

They bent over the map again. Yestigol was atop the western cliffs. The sea lapped at its very foundation.

"What are you thinking?" asked Thorn.

"I am thinking I would like a bottle of brandy." Rado rolled up the map. "That, and how convenient it would be to have a dock set in the rocks below Yestigol. One could come and go as one pleased, without disturbing the merchant shipping in Harbor Town. Also, the strait is narrowest between the headland and the island."

"How do you know that?"

"The captain of the *Bizon* said so when we first entered these waters." He unbent his knees and rubbed them. "I wasn't joking about the brandy. Go and see if Sarstic has any to sell."

"By the bucket or barrel?"

"Go!" he thundered. She went.

Thorn returned with a dusty clay bottle. "This is the only strong drink he had," she said. "I think it's been here longer than the Brethren."

"Ah, aged in the bottle," said the count. "Did you overpay him?"

"By half again as much as needed. Why do you insist on throwing gold at these people?"

He pried the cork out with his dirk. It went *pop!* and a potent aroma invaded the room. "It pleases me to spend money that's not my own," said Rado. "And I love the anxious faces the Fact folk make when generosity rears its ugly head."

Rado poured a cup of brandy. He sniffed it, touched the tip of his tongue to it, stirred it with his little finger. These tests done, he expressed his satisfaction by draining the cup dry.

"Ah!" he gasped. "Sarstic doesn't know what he gave up!" He poured another measure. "Do you suppose the highest men in the Brethren secretly indulge in forbidden pleasures? I'd bet they do. Drink like sailors, whore like waterfront fancies, and stick those emblems up each other's—"

"Moderation, my lord, is a universal virtue," Thorn said, sliding the bottle away from him.

He grabbed the brandy belligerently. "What do you know of moderation? Denial, that's your game. You've lived all your life with a gaggle of weird women, learning how to walk and to fight like a man."

"I don't have to have the pox to know how one gets it." A faint but urgent alarm was sounding within Thorn. It was not good for Rado to drink like this. The air between them practically sparkled with tension.

By the fourth drink, he was insulting priesthood in general and the Temple of the Mother Goddess in particular. Thorn tried not to listen. She blanked him out and concentrated instead on the route she'd memorized that they could take to Yestigol. The turns and sidetracks to make, the dead ends to avoid . . .

Rado said, "Come here."

"You require something, my lord?"

"Huh. You. I acquire you." The liquor tricked his tongue. "Take off your damn clothes and come here."

"No, Rado. I'm busy."

He made a vulgar sound. He was drinking from the bottle now. "As long as you are mine to command, you will do what I say to please me."

No! Thorn thought angrily. Fight back! He's no match for me, drunk or sober. I could crush his gullet with one punch. A twist and his neck would break. Then the words her mistress had written for her came to Thorn's angry mind: *There is a greater purpose in your service, a purpose only the next generation will understand.*

She went to him dumbly. The rheumy light of alcohol lit his tired eyes. Rado watched intently as Thorn discarded her doublet, trousers, and shoes. Only her yellowed chemise remained.

He hooked a finger under the lacings, intending to tear them apart, but his balance was bad and they fell to the floor together. Rado struggled with brandy and Thorn's inertness, trying to free both Thorn and himself of clothing. He took her there, on the floor, without a word or any pretense of gentleness. Thorn reached up to the short table and cupped her hand over the stub candle.

Oriath was right. Pain did turn the mind to other planes, other places.

* * * * *

"Eridé? Eridé, where are you child?"

Imadin, mistress of the temple kitchen, shouted up the stairwell. The serving girls had long since emptied out their communal bedchamber. Only Eridé, a stormy eleven-year-old, remained. She huddled under her horsehair blanket and shivered.

"Eridé? You wicked girl, you get to the kitchen at once. The day's bread is lying there with no one to knead it. Do you hear me?" The steps groaned under Imadin's ponderous feet. Why were cooks always fat? Eridé wondered. It must come from working with food all day.

"Eridé?" The cook's puffy face appeared around the doorjamb. "Still in bed, you lazy cat? I'll change that!" She waddled through the aisles to where the girl lay. Imadin snatched a corner of the blanket. Wheezing with effort, she whipped the brown cover away.

Eridé turned listlessly onto her back. Imadin gasped. "The Mother save me! Child, you're bleeding!"

"I know," the girl said feebly. "I'm dying, cook. I can't stop it."

"Nonsense, girl. The time is right for the coming of your blood. I'd best get one of the sisters." She draped the blanket over the girl's thin frame. "Rest easily, child. You han't going to die."

First to come was Alind—grave, solemn Alind, not

yet thirty, but whose hair had gone ash white. She glided soundlessly to Eridé's bed and knelt beside her. In her hand, she held a sprig of evergreen. Alind's cool hand caressed Eridé's cheek. She never spoke, but peeled a bit of bark from the sprig and put it in Eridé's mouth. With gentle pressure, she indicated the girl should chew the woody pith. Eridé did, and the gnawing pain eased. She and Alind exchanged a secret smile.

Next to arrive was Bretya, the weaver. She sized Eridé up and down with the blanket removed. From a sack she carried slung on her back, Bretya produced several rolls of colorful fabric. These she laid over the girl. Eridé was grateful for the warmth, but in her present state, she cared little about the rich brocade fabric dyed in dark blue and vivid crimson.

Sherdy joined them. Sherdy was Imadin's mistress, the jolly keeper of the kitchen hearth. Happiness seemed to radiate from her, and she always smelled of good things: rising bread and spices, butter, honey, fruit. She brought Eridé a small platter heaped high with the finest viands the temple could offer. Eridé's nose twitched when she detected spice cookies. They were her favorite. But when Sherdy lowered the platter to eye level, a wave of nausea overcame the girl, and she turned her face away. Saddened, Sherdy stood back with her sisters.

Last to come was Nandra. As usual, her temple robe was drawn up between her thighs and tied, giving her the freedom to move swiftly. Unlike Alind,

Bretya, or Sherdy, Nandra was bareheaded. Her glossy black hair was cut close to her head, exposing her ears and the nape of her neck. Her sleeves were rolled back to her shoulders. She was red-faced and sweating. She looked angry. Eridé was afraid of her.

Nandra held a weapon in her right hand. It was a long, slender spike. She made sure Eridé saw it, turning it this way and that, letting the light glint over its whole length. Shifting it to an overhand grasp, Nandra brought the point down toward Eridé's belly. If Alind had wielded the stiletto, Eridé would not have been afraid. Alind was a healer. Had Bretya brandished it, she would have known it was a carpetmaker's needle. In Sherdy's hands, such a thing would serve as a spit for roasting squab.

Nandra was none of these. In her hands, the stiletto would kill.

Eridé sat up and threw out her hands. She caught Nandra's wrist and held off the deadly spike, though the pain in her belly almost burned her in two. Nandra pushed harder and harder. Eridé grasped the shaft of the stiletto itself and tried to wrest it from the woman's hand.

She did it. The sharp steel rod slipped from Nandra's hand to Eridé's.

"She has chosen," said Alind. "She is yours, Nandra."

"What have I chosen?" asked Eridé.

"Today you become a woman," said Bretya. "To stay in the temple, you have to choose an order in which to be trained. The homely arts of medicine, weaving, and cooking would keep you here a few more years, until you wanted a husband and children. By wresting the stiletto from Nandra, you may enter the Prefectory as a Sentinel of the First Flow."

"The choice is a final one," added Sherdy. "Once committed, you must remain forever loyal to the rigor of the Sentinels, even unto death."

Eridé knew of the Sentinels. They guarded the temple and its precincts from thieves and rivals, and served as protectors of the priestesses in the world beyond the holy ground.

Nandra said, "Do you stand by your choice?"

Eridé looked to Nandra. The Prefect of the Sentinels stood, hands on hips, waiting. Her strength was palpable. And something more, something Eridé had never had in her short life: confidence.

"I stand by it," she said.

* * * * *

The count snored like a pig. Thorn pushed him aside. What Nandra would think of her if she could see this scene! Nandra was in the Inner Temple now and thus was spared the knowledge that her best pupil had submitted to the embrace of a drunken lout.

The water from the ewer was cold. Thorn welcomed its bite. She poured it over her thighs and washed herself clean.

IX

Rain settled over the city like an old hound on a warm hearth. The count and Thorn rode down a broad avenue in a four-place go-about landau with only a narrow strip of canvas to keep the slow drip off their heads. Rado was in the grip of a caustic hangover. He slumped in his seat, collar turned up around his cheeks. His pipe was clenched tightly in his teeth, and a wad of black Nom resin did its best to smoke in the bowl despite the random droplets that fell in.

He'd not said a word since Thorn awakened him. She insisted they hire a conveyance and see the city as they had told Sarstic and Goss they would. Thorn bundled the inert Rado into foul weather clothes and pushed him out the door of the Red Frog.

"Banner Street," she told the landau driver. Dry and warm in his glass booth, the Miyestan shoved the tiller over. They rolled off Eaglet Way onto Banner Street, the avenue that ran the length of Miyesti's municipal district.

The scenery immediately began to change. The blocks between the inn and Banner had been filled with nearly identical houses, cubic stone buildings of four to eight stories that housed families, workshops, and storehouses with no distinction between tenants. The east side of Banner Street was different. Set back from the road by slate promenades were some of the largest structures Thorn had ever seen. Slabs of stone and colored glass rose ten, fifteen, twenty floors above the ground. The lower parts showed obvious pre-Fact influence: Kurukish-style windows that were high narrow slits, keyhole doorways, and terra-cotta tile sheathing. Growing out of these native styles were the amazing Fact-inspired buildings of seamless stone.

"How do they stand so high?" Thorn wondered aloud. "Why, I should think the sheer weight of the upper walls would crush the lower stories to rubble."

The count sucked on his pipe. The resin had gone out.

Thorn consulted the map. She held it close to her face, so as not to let raindrops spoil the spidery ink lines. It proved easier to read the tiny letters of the legend when they were just off the tip of her nose.

"The first one there is the College of Health," Thorn read. "The citizens of Miyesti who are ill go there for healing. The subprelates of health are also responsible for keeping the streets clean and the water supply pure."

A three-wheeler dashed around them, flinging spouts of water from its rear wheels. The spouts broke over the left side of the landau, soaking Rado. He blinked and rubbed the water from his face.

They passed the College of Works, Light, and Metals. There was an interval of trees and grass twice as wide as the street, then the central plaza began. Here were the towers they had glimpsed in the clouds ever since their ship first entered the harbor. Rado slowly leaned forward. He tapped on the driver's booth and motioned for him to stop the carriage.

Three square towers reared into the murky sky, sleek, tapering obelisks, striped from base to apex with continuous windows. The north and south towers were equal in height; the west tower was shorter by a third. At the bottom, all three merged into a massive block base, so monstrously big that the figures walking around it at street level were mere mites by comparison.

"Hunter's blood." Those were Rado's first words that day.

According to the map, this tripartite structure was the combined home of the Colleges of Peace and Speech.

"Go to the worship hall," said the count. The driver nodded and released his foot lever. The last hundred steps to the entry pylon were clogged with pedestrians. Despite the steady drizzle, the day's worshipers were assembling for the morning service.

"Stop here," Rado told the driver. "I want to go with these people."

"We can't," Thorn objected. "We're not Brethren."

"Neither are they. This is a public ceremony." The landau slowed at the outer edge of the throng. "Come, aren't you curious? Or are you afraid?"

Thorn tossed her head scornfully and jumped down, splattering muddy water. Rado foppishly adjusted his cape and gloves and descended to the street with all the aplomb the count of Hapmark could muster with a hangover.

The Miyestan crowd was made up of common folk, dressed in workaday attire. Bakers rubbed elbows with woodcarvers; leather tanners vied with tinsmiths for the better places in line; laundresses stood with carpenters, charcoal burners, weavers, and cobblers. Thorn saw not one beggar in the crowd. Rado noted almost half the eager worshipers were women.

A quartet of Brethren descended a shallow set of steps flanked by guardsmen. They braced themselves with ceremonial halberds that bore wooden Fact symbols at the tops instead of steel blades. The first pair of Brethren rang their iron bells. The gabbling crowd fell silent. The trailing pair of Brethren stepped forward. In unison, they declared, "The hour of the Fact is come. All who would hear, follow and be humble. There is only one god, and he has given us the Fact!"

"We hear the Fact and know god," the worshipers replied. The Brethren turned and went inside. The crowd sorted itself into a neat line, four abreast, and followed them.

Rado grasped Thorn's arm. "Stay by me," he said. An odd inflection colored his voice. Thorn cast a probing eye his way. It was hard to see past the gray mask of the brandy hangover.

They passed through an antechamber under the watchful gaze of guardsmen. Rado's visitor's emblem got him by, but the guard reached out and stopped Thorn. "Where is your emblem?" he demanded.

"This boy is my servant," Rado said smoothly. He dangled his emblem at the guard. "I was told he was covered by this one."

"No one enters without an emblem." The guard dipped into a rattan basket behind his feet and came out with a cheap Fact symbol on a long loop of string. He held this out to Thorn. She regarded it as if were an aroused viper.

"Take it," said Rado. "We're impeding the line."

"I don't want it!"

"Take it, or by the blood, I'll let them take you!"

Thorn accepted the emblem numbly and they moved on. She closed the string in her fist and let the Fact symbol hang free, not touching her in any way.

The worship hall opened outward and upward as one vast chamber. Broad arches of gray stone support-ed the roof. The floor was polished black basalt. All around them were signs of the Fact's gifts—dazzle lamps, moving rooms carrying people to the high balconies, and those odd posts men spoke into to make themselves heard far away. The far end of the chamber was dominated by a high platform. On this stood the biggest Fact symbol yet, rendered in three dimensions instead of two. The Fact wasn't a flat diamond; the object on the platform was shaped like two pyramids joined base to base. The flat sides glistened greenish black, like beetles' wings. The edges and apexes were gilded. The golden borders reflected the rays of the dazzle lamps so brightly that the entire Fact symbol was surrounded by a gentle halo.

The line disintegrated a few steps into the chamber. The worshipers fanned out to find favorable places to sit while the ceremony was conducted. Ranks of banded Brethren sat on either side of the platform, facing it. As the people filed in, none of these men— there were at least two hundred of them—paid the least attention to the commotion below. To a man, they gazed unflinchingly at the Fact symbol.

The crowd hushed when bells jangled. The guardsmen struck the stone floor with the butts of their halberds, the signal for the congregation to sit. Rado and Thorn dropped on their haunches. Out of reflex, Thorn surveyed the room for alternate exits. She saw no obvious ones. They sat on the cold basalt in the midst of thousands of Fact worshipers, and for the first time since entering Miyesti, Thorn was truly afraid.

The outer portals were closed. A dull boom reverberated through the hall.

A single brother, quite young, appeared at the base of the Fact platform. He carried the usual bell staff, only his bell was made of bronze. He stood poised at the base of the platform, itself taller than a man. The end of the staff was hard against his right toes. His arm was straight and rigid. The young brother, whose clear and handsome face plainly displayed the exaltation he felt, rang the bell once.

"Oh!" he sang in a bright tenor.

"Oh!" echoed the crowd in an indifferent bass.

The bell clanged twice. "Oh-wan!" sang the brother. The worshipers repeated that, too. Three rings. "Wan-oh!" And so it went, up to ten, at which the young Brother sang "Wan-oh-oh-wan!"

"That's the same rubbish the fellow in Harbor Town spouted. Do you remember?" whispered Thorn.

"Yes. Be quiet!"

The brother muted the bell with his hand. Stillness radiated from him as loudly as any peal of his bell. With everyone's attention focused entirely on the bell ringer, it was a shock when words filled the chamber from above.

Another brother was standing on the platform, just in front of the Fact symbol. His shoulders were draped with a heavy white mantle that fell to his feet. The brother wore no insignia other than a very elaborate headband. It was gold, and short, stiff lengths of wire stuck out like rays all around the man's head.

He said, "There is only one god, and he has given us the Fact."

"*We believe*," replied the crowd with fervor.

"The Prelate of Speech?" Thorn muttered.

"Or the prelator himself. Shh!"

"The Fact speaks to me, and I speak to you. The

words it gives are truth and light made solid. If you would know the truth, stand and listen."

The worshipers rose en masse. Thorn was momentarily lost in a forest of legs until the count kicked her to her feet.

"Before there was a world, there was heaven; and before there was heaven, there were two spirits. They were the eternal opposites: Light and Dark, Full and Empty, Substance and Void. The spirits were everything that was, but they were blind, unknowing forces until they combined into a third thing. This was god. God is the sum of the two spirits, yet he is neither, for the spirits exist even today, even in this sacred hall.

"God made the world from himself, with Life and Death to govern it. Men lived and men died in ignorance and brutality, for they had no knowledge. God tried to speak to men and guide them, but men could not hear god's voice. It was then that god made the Fact. He cast the Fact to the world in our fathers' lifetimes, and through the Fact, the voice of god is now heard."

The prelator raised his hands. "My words are empty compared to the Fact's. I will speak no more. Those among you who would hear the Fact may come forward and put on the holy band. May the Fact fill you and bring you peace." He lowered his arms. The assembled Brethren who had been communing with the Fact stood and came down in moving rooms to the main hall floor. The worshipers surged toward them, eager to be granted a few moments with the Fact.

The press pushed the count and Thorn along. Thorn dug in her heels. "My lord, can we go now?" she asked.

"No. I want to try it myself," said Rado.

"No! My lord, don't—"

He tore his arm free of her grasp. A strange delight filled him, and he joined the push for the Brethren. Thorn held her place, unwilling to go on but unable to back out and leave the count behind.

Rado used his height and presence to cleave through the crowd. In short order, he was facing a gray-haired brother who had removed his headband and was holding it for the next man to try on, for only men were allowed to do it, however briefly; guardsmen politely removed any women from the line. The Miyestan lowered the copper ring to Rado's head. It slipped on, and the old brother raised Rado's hands to hold the band in place.

Thorn hopped on her toes to see. Only the top of the count's head was visible, and she saw the red metal ring on him. To her own surprise, Thorn said a brief silent prayer to the Goddess for Rado.

Then it was over. The Brother lifted the band, smiled benignly at Rado, and gently pushed him aside.

Thorn cut through the onlookers to where the hearers of the Fact drifted. She snagged Rado's slack hand and yanked him after her. She weaved in and out, dodging knots of unqualified believers. In the antechamber, she flung the borrowed emblem back to the guard who had given it to her. Thorn burst out the doors and gasped loudly, like a drowning swimmer desperate for breath.

The rain had ended. Spears of sunlight sheared through the cloud cover, pointing shafts of gold into the green harbor. Thorn forced the drying air into her chest in deep, measured drafts.

Rado said, "Let go, will you? You're breaking my hand."

She dropped his hand. He rubbed it to make the cramp go away. "The landau is waiting," said Thorn. They got in. She lowered the canvas top, and Rado told the driver to take them back to the inn.

"We will not succeed," he said in a low voice.

"What do you mean?"

"I heard it, Thorn. I—felt it. It spoke to me, and I sensed it was right there with me, all around. . . ."

"Illusion, my lord. You were alone. I saw you. More magical tricks."

"It was as real as you are!" he said vehemently. "More than that, the Fact is *more* real than you or I. And it's kind. Completely benign. It's like—like a father of infinite patience and strength."

She slapped him. With her hand bent back, its heel stretched tight, Thorn rocked Rado back in the seat. He flushed, glared, and grabbed her by the front of her cloak.

"Who do you think you are?" he snarled.

"I know who I am. Who are you?"

He relaxed his grip. "You can't understand what it was like. We can't hurt it, Thorn. *It is a god.*" Rado turned his face to the sky. "How long was the band on me?"

"Oh, to a count of ten, twelve."

"It seemed like days to me. I knew I was in the worship hall, I could still see everything, but I was also somewhere else. It knew who I was, Thorn. It called me by name."

"How could that be? You must have imagined it," she said.

"The Fact knows me," Rado said gravely. "And if it does, it may also know why we came here."

"Then we have no time to waste. When the sun sets, we'll make for Yestigol. If your assumption is right, the Brethren have a secret boat dock under the citadel. With luck and the Goddess's blessing, we'll be able to hide on board one of their ships."

"You won't consider doubting what we're supposed to do, will you," said Rado. "You can't imagine that our purpose might be wrong."

"My lord, after what I've seen today, I'm convinced more than ever that our task is not only just but desperately necessary."

The glowing red frog above the inn's door greeted them. The count put the driver's fee in his hand. He gave him the exact fare. For some reason, it was no fun throwing gold at Miyestans anymore.

X

A coil of soft black rope hit the ground. Count Rado peered out the open window of the Dolphin Suite. The walls of the inn blended into inky darkness just two floors below, and the slender silk cord vanished with them.

"You can't expect me to climb down that," he said.

Thorn pulled the laces of her gloves tighter with her teeth. "You can always jump," she retorted.

"Lot of Sentinel foolery, this swinging on ropes." His sword clinked on the window frame. Rado adjusted his cape around the scabbard. For the sake of silence and mobility, Rado wore his sword over his back.

"That's a striking outfit," he said. Thorn had donned a close-fitting suit of black suede that covered her from head to toe.

"I've had it for years," she said breathlessly. The waist was a bit too tight. That bothered her vaguely. Ten months ago, the last time she'd worn the stalking suit, the fit had been perfect.

She slipped the black linen hood over her head and

tied it loosely under her chin. The eyeholes were
screened with gauze. Thorn could see out, but no one
could see her eyes.

"Are you ready?" she asked.

"Does it matter?" Rado let the silk mask fall out of
his floppy hat. It hung down, concealing his features
from the mustache up. "You may precede me, my
boy," he said with affected grace.

Thorn hopped onto the low sill. She twisted the
rope around her hands and stepped out into space.
Turning slowly from the torsion in the strands, she
whispered, "When I get to the bottom, I'll twitch the
rope twice, like this." Flip, flip. "You come down
then."

"Of course."

She eased down half her body's length. "Don't
think you can bow out on me at this late date. Wait
for the signal, then hurry down."

"I don't see why we can't go out the front door like
civilized persons."

Thorn didn't answer. She wriggled down the rope
and was lost in the shadows.

Rado watched the black cord twist and strain. An
amusing thought formed in his mind. If I were to cut
the rope, she'd fall three or four stories onto hard
paving. That would be one way to remove the thorn
in my side. . . . He actually saw himself put the edge
of his dirk to the writhing rope. It would be easy.

Why not? He still had a box full of Temple gold,
and it might be years before the Sentinels tracked him

down.

One year. Two at most.

A hump snapped in the rope, then another. "Another dream lost," Rado mused aloud. He climbed onto the sill. For a moment everything seemed sharp and clear. The touch of steel on his back. The smell of his deerskin gloves. The creak of his boots as he bent his knees and ankles to make the step into thin air.

He didn't climb down so much as control his fall. Rope hissed through his hands until the scorch of leather and the heat on his palms forced him to tighten his grip. Rado jerked to a stop somewhere between heaven and hell. His impetus sent him banging into the inn. He spun around twice before halting his dizzy course by planting both feet on the wall. Thus braced, he descended the final stories to Thorn.

"What were you doing up there, a jig?" she asked.

"I was trying to hang myself," Rado retorted.

"So what stopped you?"

"I decided I was making a noose for the wrong person!"

They tiptoed to the mouth of the alley. The street seemed deserted, as it should be; it was well past the tenth hour. Rado started out, but Thorn blocked him. With expressive hand gestures, she indicated he should look again.

Across the road was an imposing yet anonymous building, half the height of the Red Frog. The regular lines of the walls, corners, doorways, and windows were interrupted by a different contour. Rado studied it, let his vision lose focus from the usual modes of recognition. And then he saw the shadow was a man.

The stiletto was in Thorn's hand. Rado shook his head. Pass him by, he signed; it will be quieter that way. Thorn shrugged and replaced her weapon.

She dropped on her belly and crawled. Following the line of the next house, she zigzagged over the ground with a serpentine motion Rado admired but could never hope to copy. The soles of her soft shoes disappeared around the corner.

Rado steeled himself and gathered his cape around him. The brim of his hat bent down as he hugged the wall, and he stepped lightly from the alley to the inset door of the neighboring house. He thought he was alone in the black recess and nearly cried out when Thorn's gloved hand touched the back of his neck.

"Don't do that!" he said through clenched teeth.

"They're watching the inn," she whispered. "Now do you see why we didn't leave by the front door?"

They eased from hiding and continued down the street, leapfrogging from doorway to pillar to alley, a black phantom and a caped ghost dancing a secret, silent minuet. At the lower end of Cormoring Way, Thorn walked out of the shadows and surveyed the upper windows and rooflines around them.

The count hung back. "What are you doing?" he called.

"Looking for clouds."

"At night? Are you mad? Come back before you're seen!"

She returned with maddening leisure. "There's more than one reason for the curfew, my lord. It keeps the common folk away from halls of vice, true, but it also prevents them from seeing the Brethren's flying clouds."

"What are you raving about?"

"Lights in the sky, my lord, and a curfew. What does that add up to? The Brethren have some sort of flying ship by which they go to Prios quick as a crow." She craned her head to see the strip of night sky between the high houses. "They keep watch over the city, but they won't see us. The clouds are too noisy. I shall hear them before they see me."

"You're mad as a stoat. Flying ships indeed!"

Her hooded face turned to his. "Do you think such things are beyond the power of the Fact?"

Heat flowed into his face. He remembered the omniscient presence he'd felt that afternoon. The hair on his neck bristled. Rado ached for his pipe.

"We're wasting time. Let's move on."

Cormoring Way ran from the Princes' Plaza south until it ended on Barinade Way, the central avenue for the east-west section of the city. Thorn started to run. She had a peculiar slow lope that covered ground as fast as most men's sprinting but didn't tire her as soon. The count labored to stay with her but failed. He was too big, too used to ale and smoking resin to run very far. He settled for keeping her back in sight.

An abrupt right turn at the end of Cormoring Way announced its transformation into Barinade. The count sagged to a halt. He leaned on a lamppost to regain his wind.

Thorn came dashing around the corner, running hard. "Hide, hide!" she sputtered as she breezed past the stationary Rado.

The sound of many wheels washed up the street. Rado looked for an alley or dark doorway. None! The Cormoring-Barinade junction was walled in by a featureless brick fence as tall as a man. He cast about wildly for Thorn, but she was nowhere to be seen. The noises grew louder. Lights bobbed on the wall to his left, lamps from the oncoming go-abouts.

Rado crossed the street on the run. He leaped and slammed into a lamppost a few steps off the ground. Climbing with an agility he thought he'd never possess, he was at the top of the pole, six steps high, just as the first go-about entered Cormoring Way.

A three-wheeler rolled right under him. Six guardsmen were in it. Behind them came a horseless landau much like the one they'd hired to see the sights on Banner Street. Two men sat facing each other in the landau. The last vehicle in the caravan was a heavy wagon. A canvas screen surrounded the wagon bed on three sides, but from his high perch, Rado could see what was in it.

It was a flower.

At least, that's what it resembled—a great bronze flower with four petals, each as wide as a man's arms could reach, and a pointed stem in the center. There was a hole bored through it. From the way the wagon frame protested, the flowerlike thing was solid metal and very heavy.

The go-abouts proceeded around the corner and were gone. Rado closed his eyes and sighed. If just one Miyestan had looked up . . .

"My lord has certainly risen in the world," Thorn said. She was at the foot of the post, leaning on it with one hand.

"Blood, I thought I was for it then." He wrapped his arms around the post and slid down. "And where in deepest Chaos did you go? I couldn't find you anywhere."

"I was in plain sight all along," said Thorn. "I watched you throw yourself up the pole. You haven't moved so fast since that alehouse caught fire on Oparos."

"Ha. Most amusing." Rado slapped the dust from his sleeves and trousers. "You would do better to think of me next time danger threatens. If I'm caught, you'll have no chance at all."

They jogged along vacant Barinade Way. The street rose on a steady grade for five or six bowshot. The count panted in time with each strike of his bootheels on the bricks. The smell of the sea was stronger here, especially when they came to a dogleg in the street. The road crooked right, and the grade steepened suddenly. Rado stumbled when the street abruptly changed into a set of wide steps.

The ancient citadel of Yestigol frowned from the hillside on which it stood. City houses ceased half a bowshot from the lower gates of the stronghold. Two concentric walls, sloping backward and faced with rusted iron harrows, ringed the citadel and separated it from the street.

"There's a grim sight if ever I saw one," Thorn said.

"It wasn't made to be pretty," Rado replied. He'd served a stint in the city guard of Pazoa, so he knew something about fortifications. The Kurukish design of Yestigol was still evident; all the later colonists from the Homelands had done was heighten and thicken the existing defenses. The lowest section of the citadel, the part melded with the city wall, was roughly triangular, with the apex pointing over the cliff and out to sea. Standing on the triangular base was a squared casement three stories high, equipped with loopholes and sally ports. Atop the casement was a tall hexagonal tower. A dazzle lamp burned on the highest platform of the tower, and against its glare, they could see guards patrolling.

The outermost wall had a double-width gate. It was standing open. Thorn ghosted through, stiletto in hand. The count followed, with his dirk drawn. The parade ground between the walls was empty. The second wall seemed to have no gate at all. They split and went to the far ends of the counterscarp. When they met again in the center, they'd still not found a gate.

"There has to be an entry," said Thorn. "A postern, something!"

Rado swore softly. He looked back at the gap in the

first wall. "The cunning bastards," he said. "This whole place is a trap—a bloody massacre pit." He pointed to the gate. "See it? See how ridiculously wide it is? The enemy is supposed to break into this confined lane and find a blank wall before them. And then—"

"Total butchery." Thorn shook her head. She hadn't flinched from killing in years, but wholesale slaughter still disgusted her. "So where is the true entrance?"

"We're probably standing under it. A scaffold or gangplank perhaps, lowered from the top of the inner wall."

"There's no other way in?"

Rado swept the rim of the wall with his eyes. "Not from here, I'll swear on it."

Thorn turned to the inner wall. She reached up and carefully hooked her fingers over one of the harrows. The blades curved upward like scythes and stuck out almost three handwidths. Thorn put a foot on a lower harrow and pulled herself off the ground.

"You'll be cut to dogmeat!" Rado said hoarsely.

Thorn dropped down and came back. "No invader's attacked Miyesti in the last century, my lord, and no one's seen to the sharpening of these blades in half that long. They're jagged, but with care we can climb right up."

Thorn swung up on the same two blades. Rado remained where he was, watching her pick her hand- and footholds gingerly. Thorn looked down and

waved for him to follow. His barely contained sense of
mutiny was about to break out in earnest when a
marvel changed his mind.

A cone of white light hit Yestigol, and a monstrous
thrum filled the air like the song of all the locusts in
creation. A dark mass, larger than the citadel tower,
ascended rapidly over the cliffside. The white light
shone down from the thing, and a dazzle inside Yestigol stabbed back at it.

Rado dropped his dirk and stared.

The tower's lamp traced along the hull of the biggest ship Rado had ever seen. The keel was clearly visible, and the upward curve of the hull was lost in the
night. Small boats hung below the monster, and the
thrumming came from them. The ship was flying,
flying through the air with the ponderous grace of a
sounding whale. It even had flippers like a whale.
The flying ship passed completely over the citadel
and turned toward the heart of the city. It rose higher,
and the dazzle lamp shining from its belly flickered
out.

The count scrambled up the wall, grabbing harrows indiscriminately. His tough boots protected his
feet, but in his panic, he gashed his hands badly.
Thorn was nearly to the battlement. Rado struggled
on, snagging his clothes and ripping his cape on the
hooked blades.

"Did you see it? Did you see it?"

"Shh!" Thorn hissed fiercely. "Guardsmen!"

She peered through the crenellations. A soldier was

walking the wall, halberd on his shoulder. He wore a
quilted brigandine, more for warmth than as armor.
Rado's fly-in-amber progress up the wall halted the
guard in his tracks. He stood to the battlement to see
what the disturbance was.

Thorn was on him in the wink of an eye. She held
the back of his collar and thrust with the stiletto, but
her aim was off. She felt the point scrape bone and
knew she'd missed the heart. The guard dropped his
halberd and threw himself back, trying to smash his
assailant into the wall. Her chance for a quick kill
gone, Thorn was in trouble. The man was too big for
her to take down. While he clawed for the baton
hanging from his waist, she dropped her stiletto and
clamped that hand over the Miyestan's mouth. The
struggling pair scraped to an open crenellation.
Thorn rolled backward, still holding the guard by the
collar. He flipped through the gap and plunged over.
Halfway down the wall, the harrows did their hideous
work.

Rado finally reached the battlement. Just as he did,
a second Miyestan arrived, summoned by the sounds
of combat. He lowered his halberd and charged. Rado was between him and Thorn, and his back was
turned.

"Rado, behind you!"

Rado sidestepped the halberdier's rush like a bull-
fighter. The Miyestan recovered and cut at him with
the axe edge. Rado backed away, whipping the cape
off his shoulder and drawing his sword. Thorn would

have rushed the guard's back, but he was standing on top of her stiletto.

The halberd's reach was long, but it was a clumsy weapon to duel with. Rado parried, parried, and thrust when the guard exposed his chest. The Miyestan was good. He didn't waste effort trying to chop down his foe; instead, he forced Rado farther and farther back. Soon the casement wall would prevent any more retreat. The sword-bearing intruder would be at his mercy.

Thorn picked up her stiletto once the guard advanced off it. She saw Rado's approaching predicament. She shifted the stiletto to throwing position.

Rado's heel bumped stone. This was the end. The halberdier permitted himself a grin of triumph, then lunged.

Rado stepped forward to meet him.

The thick halberd met only air. The spear point chinked against the casement. Count Rado pirouetted on his heel and ran his sword into the man's chest. He caught the halberd shaft under his arm to prevent its clattering on the battlement. Rado recovered his blade, and the Miyestan fell on his face.

Thorn came up. "Thank you for the warning," said Rado.

"I serve and protect," she replied. "That was well fought, my lord."

"Surprised?"

"In truth, yes. After your duel with Geffrin, I marked you for a mannered sportsman, with no grit for a close-in kill."

Rado wiped his blade. "Learn a lesson, then. Geffrin was a duelist of the Emerald School and a gentleman. This poor lackey was neither."

The city bells tolled midnight. A ponderous chime rang from the tower above Yestigol, and under the cover of its clangor, Rado and Thorn hurried down the steps to the tiny bailey between the inner wall and the casement. Arrow slits glowed from within, indicating which rooms were occupied by still-awake guardsmen.

"Which way now, clever lad?"

"Inside and down. There are bound to be galleries and dungeons under the foundations."

"And a regular army of guards to fill them. Do you propose we cut our way through the entire corps?"

"What do you suggest?"

"Practically anything else!"

Thorn cat-footed back up the steps. With fingertips and flexing toes, she climbed the face of the casement and vanished over the roof. Rado sweated long minutes in the corner shadows. The tower bell fell silent. He heard the stirrings of the garrison inside the casement, muffled by layers of stone and mortar.

A knot the size of his fist banged into his nose. He flinched and grabbed the thick, musty rope attached above it. The round outline of Thorn's hooded head appeared over the edge of the roof.

"Climb," she whispered.

It wasn't pleasant with his lacerated hands, but Rado made it. Thorn had a vast quantity of heavy rope in coils atop the citadel. "Where did you get all this?" he queried.

"The bell tower."

"You mean you cut down the rope from a city bell tower?"

"I waited until they were done chiming the hour. Now hurry. We've only an hour before they need to ring again and discover the rope's missing."

They dragged the loops of hemp across the roof, past the base of the tower to the cliffside. The strait spread around them on three sides. A warm, salty updraft assaulted their eyes as they gazed over the edge at the sea so far below. Waves broke in white angles against the base of the cliff.

"You don't imagine— Surely you're not thinking—"

"Of climbing down? You wouldn't go through the citadel. This is the only other way," said Thorn. "Now let me tie this off. . . ." She wound the rope around one of the conical Kurukish tile anchors, which were set like teeth along the roof to hold the clay shingles in place. Knotting and reknotting the rope, Thorn recited the temple catechism "To Banish Fear."

"Thorn?"

"Yes, Rado?"

"I'm not sure I can do this."

"Must we have a tussle every time an obstacle appears? You—"

"My hands are cut. I just barely managed to climb

a short way up a moment ago. I don't think I can hold a rope for a long descent."

She dropped the rope and came to him. Turning his hands over, she examined his lacerated palms. "Your pardon," she said. "I didn't realize it was this bad." They went to the edge and checked the drop again. From where they stood to the bottom of the cliff was a fall equal to the height of the citadel from casement to tower top: three quarters of a bowshot.

"Lend me your knife," she said.

"Ah . . . I lost it. Climbing the wall."

"Then draw your sword." Warily he pulled the blade from its scabbard. Thorn picked up the hem of his cape and speared through the leather with the sword tip. Rado protested the mutilation of an expensive garment. She ignored him and cut off a wide leather strip from the hem of the cape. This she split into two equal segments.

"Wrap these around your hands. That should protect them," she said.

"This is a Gwello cape," he said peevishly. "Do you know how much I paid for it?"

"With whose money?"

The count would descend first. This pleased his vanity, until Thorn remarked that if he slipped and fell, she didn't want to be below him. He snorted and took his place on the roof's rim. Rado wrapped the line behind his back. His boots hung over the precipice. " 'O noble, courageous vanguard, ever in the fore!' " he quoted, and went over the edge.

He swung around and braced his feet against the citadel. His hands burned under their expensive leather wrapping, but it was endurable. Before lowering himself out of sight, Rado asked, "What if there is no boat dock at the bottom?"

"Then we'll climb back up and try something else," said Thorn.

"You're a mad boy, Thorn-in-my-side. Ho, away!"

"Quietly!" His hat sank below the roofline. Thorn tarried for a count of thirty, then started down the rope herself.

Wind took Rado's hat, and his mask went with it. The heavy cape billowed and snapped, pulling him away from the citadel wall and dashing him back. Desperately Rado unhooked the frog at his neck and let the Gwello garment fall. It fluttered out, a headless bat with satin lining, and eventually landed in the churning surf.

A loophole appeared beside his feet. Rado paused to peek inside. It was an arsenal room full of weapons. A single Miyestan sat by a lamp, his back to the loophole. The count restrained an impulse to shout vulgar things about the guardsman's deaf-and-dumb ancestry. The man scratched an ear, an armpit, and his backside in that order. Rado smothered a chuckle and moved on.

The cliff face was remarkably smooth and vertical, and after descending a way, Rado realized why. Long ago the Kuruks had quarried stone from the face of the cliff, thus providing themselves with a ready source of building blocks and also making the cliff harder to scale. He marveled at the daring of the Kurukish stonecutters, chiseling out slabs of limestone while dangling from rope platforms or raised on rickety scaffolds. Here and there were other signs of men long dead. Names and slogans carved in the soft rock, forgotten craftsmen's small bids for immortality. Rado couldn't read Kurukish. Thinking of the risks those men took, it saddened him that now he couldn't even read their names.

His hands ached. He tried coiling the rope around his arms to lessen the drag on his palms. It helped a little. By the time he could see the rocks at the cliff base clearly, blood was oozing out from under the edges of the overlapping layers of leather. He wanted his pipe so badly he could curse.

Above, he saw Thorn's slight figure descending, legs twined around the rope. She really is much too skinny, he thought between his pain and pipe need. A real woman ought to have more meat on her bones.

All these musings came to a shattering end when the rope ran out. Rado suddenly found his feet swinging without anything to wrap around. Panicking, he climbed until his legs were securely on the rope again.

Thorn was soon over his head. "Why have you stopped?" she called.

"There's no more rope! You idiot, you didn't allow enough when you cut it!"

"We can't lack for much," she said. Thorn let go with one hand and leaned far out. "It's scarcely twice your height to the ground."

"Yes . . . onto enormous, jagged rocks!"

He was right. Heaps of saw-toothed boulders covered the narrow beach below them.

The rope swung away from the rock face and fell back. Rado's hip jarred painfully against the cliff. He saw that Thorn was kicking off, causing the wild oscillation.

"What are you doing?" he asked.

"Swing," she said. "If we can swing out far enough, we can jump into the surf."

"Oh, no! Not for all the gold your temple owns!"

Thorn pushed off in ever more violent thrusts. Rado had little choice but to mimic her posture or else be dashed senseless against the cliff. His feet hit the rock and his knees bent, absorbing the impact. Then he sprang out, farther, higher.

"Next time let go!" cried Thorn.

"Never!"

They fell back with such impact that Rado's legs buckled completely and his heels struck him smartly in the rear. His baldric slipped under his arm and clanked loudly. There was a second sound, the kiss of steel on steel.

They pushed off once more, hard. Rado shut his eyes, expecting to swing in and splatter his brains on the limestone. The impact never came. Instead he felt wind rushing up his trousers while the pounding of the sea grew louder. And closer.

"*Thoooorn!*"

Rado smacked into the sea on his back. He came up spitting, still clutching a length of rope in his hand. Thorn was treading water nearby.

"You tricked me!" he sputtered. "You cut the bloody rope!"

She handed him back his sword. "Why do you think I had you go first?" Seawater shone on her suede outfit, making her look like a seal. "Come, my lord. I see a light on shore."

Ompy, the god of chance, played them fair. They reached the rocks during an outflow and hurriedly scrambled onto the higher boulders before the next wave crashed ashore. As the count sat with water dripping from his eyes and nose, Thorn hopped from rock to rock toward the shielded light.

She waved to Rado from a distant perch. Wearily he stood and stepped wide over the rugged stones.

"Do you see something?" he said too loudly. She hissed for silence and pulled him to his knees. Thorn pointed through a cleft in the rocks.

Inside the outermost point of the headland was a wide niche cut in the rock and screened by piled up boulders. A high-walled dock of black stone merged into the sea-stained cliff. From the strait, one could sail right by the place and never see it. But Thorn and Rado's point of view was different. Rado's deduction had been correct. The Brethren did have a secret boat dock.

A vessel was there, tied to the black dock. The low, razor-bowed felucca was chained at the stern. Leather fenders held the bulwark away from the dock. The felucca's twenty oars, ten per side, stood vertically in their locks.

Three Miyestans were in sight—one on the dock by the stern, and two others on the bow of the boat. Rado looked into the niche. It was more a cave, really, going back into the cliff some distance. A wooden barracks were built near the rear of the cave. The windows were light, and smoke trickled from the chimney. Dark shapes moved across the windows.

"More guards," Thorn whispered.

"More likely the ship's crew," Rado said. "How are we getting aboard?"

"We could swim to the bow and go up the hawse-hole."

"You might be thin enough to mouse through that hole, but I'd never fit," Rado said. She decided he was right.

"You know boats better than I. How would you get on without being seen?" asked Thorn.

"I always go up the main gangplank." He was about to add a pungent epilogue when the door of the barracks banged open and a dozen Miyestans filed out. Thorn and the count crouched lower, even though they were invisible beyond the ring of dazzle lamps.

A group of men appeared from the recesses of the cave. In their white cassocks and gold emblems, they were obviously high-ranking Brethren. They walked in pairs to where the men from the barracks had assembled. When they were close enough, Rado recognized the mysterious Goss, the man who had questioned them in the common room of the Red Frog. The older man on his left was the prelate who had led the ceremony they'd seen in the worship hall.

"As I suspected," muttered Rado. "That Goss is no subprelate. He's the prelator's right hand man."

Goss and the prelates stopped to greet the waiting Miyestans and inspect the crew. Thorn dug an elbow into Rado's ribs. He looked where she pointed. The three men by the felucca had departed to join their comrades in line.

They lowered themselves through the piled-up boulders to the water's edge. There was a second boat slip on the other side of the dock. Thorn slid into the water and swam in gentle, silent strokes to the dock. Rado disdained getting wet a second time. Shielded by pilings and planks, he walked around the slip and climbed onto the dock. Recklessly he stood upright and strolled down the felucca's gangplank with the brazen gall of the vessel's master. By the time Thorn had scaled the hull and crawled into the starboard apostis, Rado was sitting on the steps leading to the poop. Dripping, Thorn walked heel to toe along the outrigger rail. She didn't want to leave wet footprints on the deck to advertise her presence.

"Comfortable?" she asked the smug count.

"I am dryer than you, at any rate. Shall we go below before the noble Goss spots us?"

Down a vertical ladder they went into the hold. It

was as black as an eel's belly there. By the weak rays
that filtered in through the oar ports and deck grates,
they saw that a forest of rods and bars filled the felucca's hold.

"Where are the rowers' benches?" Rado wondered
aloud. "A ship this wide should seat three men to an
oar."

There were no benches at all, just a catwalk above
the keel. Rado and Thorn moved among the ordered
rows of beams, frozen in locked lines between the
oars. Thorn touched one of the vertical rods. It was
cold iron.

"What is all this?" she asked.

"Never mind that," said Rado. "What is *this?*"

In the center of the hold, where the mainmast an-
chor ought to have been, was a massive block of metal
with odd protuberances and wheels attached to it.
Thorn ran her fingers lightly over the casing, but
quickly drew her hand away.

"It's alive!" she murmured. Rado touched it. A
light vibration passed through the chill iron skin into
his hand. There was some potent spirit trapped inside
that block, buzzing with frustration to get out.

Boots rattled on the deck overhead. A forward
hatch flew open. Without a word, Thorn and Rado
jumped from the catwalk. They fell among the hull
ribs and rolled toward the keel. There they lay mo-
tionless in the rancid, oily bilge while the felucca's
crew readied the vessel for sea.

"Look alive there, Marpo! Get some grease on

number four linkage. It rattled like an old maid's teeth on the trip out. I don't want His Excellence to hear nothing like that going home!"

"Ho, Vam! Are the jars refreshed as I ordered?"

"I saw them filled myself. What do the measures say?"

"I haven't been to the wheel to see, have I?"

Crewmen bustled back and forth over the hidden pair, making adjustments to the queer machinery in the hold. One man bawled for light, and a dazzle came on. Rado shrank back under the catwalk planking.

"Is everything prepared?" asked a familiar voice.

"All is as it should be, Prelate Goss."

"Thank you, Jatt. Tell Captain Pestarc to get under way."

Thorn pushed up to the underside of the catwalk. The planks were gapped for drainage, and she peered between the boards.

"I wanted to take a moment to tell you the *Oribos* is almost finished," Goss said. "The bronze casting was a success, just as the Fact said it would be."

"The Fact is never wrong," said the man with Goss. "When will the new ship be ready to put to sea?"

"A crew has to be trained to operate the new machinery, supplies have to be gathered, the Speakers picked . . . Three months. Two if we press."

"Haste isn't necessary," Goss's companion said. "The mission of the *Oribos* is the greatest of our generation. It will be the first formal Speaker mission to the Homelands. We want everyone who sees the new ship to know the wisdom and strength of the Fact."

"They will know, Rhom. Not even the jaded citizens of Pazoa will be able to shrug off the *Oribos!*"

Bells jangled from the deck. "We'd better go up," said Goss. "The hold is too noisy for comfort when the machinery is working."

"Did you hear that?" whispered Rado. "They're sending Speakers to Pazoa!"

"Yes, on a new ship. It must be stopped."

From above, a voice bawled, "Release mooring chain! Push off those fenders! Oarmaster, drop oars!"

A ghastly squeal filled the hold. The rigid rods and beams began to move. When the felucca was clear of the dock, the oars fell until they were straight out from the boat's sides. A steady throbbing shook the hull. Rado dared to raise his head over the catwalk. The stout iron wheels on each side of the metal block were rotating. Bars connected to the oars quivered with the transferred motion.

"Oarmaster, give me thirty beats per measure!" the captain shouted. The beams alongside the block rose, swung forward, and fell. Twenty oars bit the water, and the felucca surged forward.

Rado ducked down. "You must see this!" Thorn stuck her head out. A swinging beam barely missed her at the bottom of its downward circle. Thumping and creaking, the block turned the wheels, raised the beams, and rowed the ship.

Under the catwalk, Rado said, "An oared ship

without oarsmen! Isn't it fantastic?"

"Whatever it is, it's contrary to nature," Thorn replied. The noise of the mechanism was deafening. "You can't get something from nothing," she said close to the count's ear. "The Brethren must have a powerful spirit enslaved to turn these machines. Did you hear that sailor's remark about jars? They must have to feed the monster prodigious amounts."

Conversation ended there. It was too much to talk over the rowing racket. Thorn and Rado braced themselves between the felucca's ribs and settled in for the short voyage. They shared a common unspoken thought: What miracle could there be in the new ship Goss mentioned, if it was more powerful than the wonderful mechanism of the felucca?

The *Promicon* sliced the sea at an untiring thirty beats per minute. At that rate, the crossing to Prios Island would take little more than an hour.

* * * * *

The rhythm of the oars changed. Instead of a regular dip-pull-lift, the oars were now being held up longer: dip-pull-lift-*hold*. The felucca slowed. The starboard rank of oars was held out of the water, and the port row dug in. The felucca turned hard in that direction. The command to backwater was given, and the vessel frothed to a halt. Chain was run out on deck, and the oars were locked in their highest position. Something heavy and solid bumped the hull forward, and the *Promicon* was docked.

Sailors entered the hold to inspect the machinery. They swabbed the moving joints from pots of goat grease. That accounted for the disgusting smell in the bilge. When their task was done, the men left. The dazzle went out, and the hatch covers were slammed in place.

"Wait," said Thorn.

Time passed, hobbled by the lack of sound on board. The felucca rocked on its mooring chains. Water slapped against the hull. Thorn chinned herself on the catwalk and rolled onto the planks. "Rado, come."

They went to the forward hatch. It was closed and pinned. Thorn worked her hand through the grate, but she couldn't reach the lock. A fine thing it would be to get this far, only to be trapped by the handiwork of a conscientious sailor!

The stern was a different proposition. The hatch there was locked as well, but a scuttle into the stern-castle was not. They crawled through into the captain's quarters. It was a modest cabin, with a bunk, table, and chair. Rado found a provisions locker.

"Bread?" he mumbled through a mouthful. Thorn had gone aft to the sternlights.

"By the Mother," she said breathlessly.

Rado wandered over, guzzling sour milk from a gourd bottle. When he got to the glazed ports, he dropped the bottle. A wad of damp bread fell from his mouth.

Prios. The Sanctuary of the Fact.

The felucca was moored sternfirst to the island. Through the leaded glass panes, they beheld a fortress of gold and alabaster, bathed in unnatural light. The fortress rose in tiers, each one smaller and set farther back. Ringing the fortress were the black hills that were Prios Island.

The lower course of the fortress was a smoothly curving wall of translucent white that seemed to glow from within. Starting at the third tier, the sanctuary was pierced with a thousand diamond-shaped windows and hexagonal doors. Lamps buried in the causeway threw beams on the gleaming walls. Tiny men moved across the face of this porcelain fortress, the white of their cassocks looking faded and yellow against the walls of the sanctuary.

And emblems! From the fifth tier on up to the top, the flat roofs were thick with row upon row of Fact emblems, wrought in golden rods. Behind each were slanting black panels that set the emblems off in high relief. These were put in proper scale when a four-wheeled go-about rolled under them; the wagon could have easily been driven through the center of the open diamonds.

"Do you have it?" asked Thorn, not taking her eyes off the awesome edifice.

"Have what?" asked Rado numbly.

"The Goddess's weapon. Do you have it?"

He reached around to the small of his back. In all the climbing and hiding, he'd forgotten about it. Rado pulled the canister strap off and set it on the sill. For months, they'd carried this thing in the bottom of the coin box, padded by sacks of gold. Thorn had put it there deliberately, for she knew Rado would fight hard indeed to keep the temple's money for his own use.

The cylinder was covered with lambskin, sewn with the fleece turned in. Rado picked at the lacing.

"No," said Thorn. "Don't open it till you must."

They left the sterncastle by the ladder to the poop. From behind the stern rail, they could see the whole harbor. A long mole, built of the same glassy white stone, jutted out from shore. It bent halfway along its length, forming a sheltered anchorage for the Brethren's ships. Besides the felucca, there were two galleots free-anchored in the harbor. Across the bay, still standing in builders' stocks, was the new ship, the *Oribos*. It was a blocky, black vessel, with high sides and no oar apostes.

"No masts," said Rado. "Hardly looks as finished as Goss said."

"Maybe it doesn't need masts," Thorn remarked.

The well-lit mole was deserted. A few men were busy at the far end with a winch and boom. They were trying to hook a cask floating in the water.

Thorn and Rado went down to the main deck and leaped from the starboard apostis to the mole. The pier was paved with ordinary slate. Thorn ran a hand over the seamless white rock of the seawall.

"There's not a crack in it," she said. "It's one long,

continuous piece!"

"Who cares? Let's find a less exposed place, shall
we?"

The mole was twenty steps wide. The outer wall
was in shadow, as the lamps were arranged to shine
into the harbor. Thorn skulked ahead, running in a
low crouch. When she saw the way was clear, she sig-
naled for Rado to join her.

Rado stood. His shoulders topped the mole wall,
and many pairs of hands reached over the wall and
seized him by the arms.

"Thorn!" he cried, but she was already running at
him, stiletto held point down as she came. More guardsmen emerged from the dark side of the mole. They
were armed with batons only, and Thorn weighed into
them without hesitation. Rado saw a flurry of batons
and white tunics, and Thorn disappeared. Then guards
began to fall from the melee, falling to the slate with
bright streams of red splashed on their chests and backs.
Rado struggled. At least six men had him. A seventh
Fact guardsman took his sword.

The staccato rumble of running men ascended the
causeway. Rank upon rank of guardsmen and Brethren bearing sticks flowed into sight. The men who
were fighting Thorn drew off, surrounding her, con-
taining her, but keeping out of reach of her deadly
hands.

"If you have any ideas about what to do, now is the
time to vent them," Thorn shouted.

"How about back to Harbor Town? Or better yet,

Pazoa?" answered Rado helplessly.

The battalion of Fact men closed in around Rado and Thorn. It was obvious they wished to take them alive, with batons, but no one could get close enough to Thorn without paying the price in blood.

Goss parted the massed guardsmen and stood before Rado. "Tell your man to put down his weapon," he said.

"Oh, he never listens to me," said Rado. "I ought to discharge him, really. But where would an incorrigible lad like him find another master like me?"

Goss nodded sadly. He raised his hand, and a squad of crossbowmen shouldered to the fore. They leveled their bows at Thorn. The bursting of the guards' go-about in the street flashed through Thorn's mind. Thunderbolts. Wordlessly she folded the tines of the stiletto shut and laid it on the ground. Goss picked it up. He handled it curiously, unafraid of the blood that coated the shaft and tip. The prelate looked at Thorn. "Quell him," he said. A guardsman stepped forward and felled her with one blow on the back of her head. Rado, who to this moment had been expecting Thorn to break loose and slay all and sundry, gave up and relaxed in his captors' hands.

Goss faced him. "Count Rado, are you all right?"

"I'll live," sighed Rado.

"So you shall," Goss replied. Men hoisted Thorn's slack body on their shoulders. They paused as the prelate peeled the hood from Thorn's head. "I'm not sure I can promise as much for your valet."

XI

Thorn and Rado were separated once they were inside the sanctuary. A cloth was thrown over Rado's head so he couldn't see where he was being taken. Guided by two Brethren and escorted by four more, he was led along a long, straight passage, up a flight of steps, around some turns, up another floor, and down a narrow hall. He heard a key turn in a lock. His arms brushed the sides of a doorway. The cloth was whisked off. Before he could utter a word, the door swung shut. The key rattled again, and he was locked inside.

As cells went, this one wasn't terrible. There was a bed with a blanket, a table and chair, a pitcher and basin filled with cold, fresh water. The copper chamberpot was empty.

A window cut through the wall, but it was higher than Rado could reach. He pulled the chair over and stood on it. The window was stoutly framed with iron and was too small besides. All in all, he was very neatly bottled up in what was probably most often used as a guest room for Brethren visiting Prios to commune with the Fact.

They had taken away all the metal he had—sword, coins, even his bootstrap buckles. Rado lay down on the bed, tucked his hands under his head, and waited. Someone would come.

The window lightened from gray to white. Elsewhere in the complex, bells sounded, and the scraping of chairs and scuffling of feet filtered into the count's humble room. Men passed in the corridor outside. A new day in the sanctuary of the Fact had begun. Rado wondered, Do they know who they have in this damned stone box? Infidel! Libertine! Assassin! If there was one thing he was baffled and terrified by, it was religious fanatics. His unfettered mind conjured up ghastly scenarios of the justice meted out by the Brethren.

Fear did not prevent him from falling asleep. He dozed fitfully on the hard mattress until the grating sound of a key in the lock snapped him awake. Rado leapt off the bed. He combed the loose hair out of his face with his fingers.

The door swung into the hall. Prelate Goss stood there, with one guardsman. Goss saw Rado was well back from the door, so he handed the key to the guard. He stepped inside, and the door was closed and locked behind him.

"Good morning, my lord. I hope you are feeling refreshed?" asked Goss. He set a cloth bag on the bed. "We are returning most of your possessions." Rado thumbed through the items. "You'll under-

stand that your weapons have been retained. They are
being kept in a safe place."

The lambskin cylinder was in the bag. Rado bit his
lip to avoid smiling. Facing Goss, he said, "What is
to happen to me?"

"That is entirely up to you, my lord. You have deliberately violated a sacred place. This sanctuary is
forbidden to all those not wearing the headband of
the Fact. It is within our right to punish you for this
infringement."

Rado felt an upswell of confidence. He dragged the
chair under himself and sat. "It would be a serious
breach of etiquette for you to harm a noble of the
Homelands," he said.

"No one here will harm you."

"What, no axe? No fiery stake?"

"No, my lord. The Fact teaches us mercy toward
those who injure us. Should the prelator decide, you
may be held here for a course of instruction in the
tenets of the Fact. Then you will be released."

Rado laughed. "Going to make a brother out of
me? That would be a better trick than all your magic
lamps and horseless carts combined."

The prelate was unperturbed. "The length of your
stay depends on how willing you are to tell us why you
came to Prios."

He shrugged. "It was a lark."

"A lark? To penetrate our citadel in Miyesti, killing
two men, and stow away on the *Promicon?*"

Rado uncrossed his legs. Goss knew more than the

count had imagined. The prelate clasped his hands behind his back and continued. "Why did your valet resist so violently when caught? Several of our men are quite badly hurt."

"Thorn is very excitable."

"Why does she pretend to be a man?"

The spring uncoiled from Rado's spine. "What makes you say that?" he asked slowly.

"She awoke in confinement and fought like a mad wolf. It took six men to subdue her, and when she was stripped in a search for weapons, the truth was evident. This is no lark, my lord. The woman you call Thorn is neither crazed nor is she a pervert. Someone taught her to fight and to wear men's clothes."

"What of it? There are many strange cults in the world."

"One of the strictest rules of the sanctuary is that no woman is to ever set foot on Prios. Your companion has defiled the fortress of the Fact. I am afraid the consequences in her case may be grave—unless, of course, you can explain your extraordinary persistence in coming here."

Rado rubbed his hands together and looked away.

"Who is that woman? Why did you bring her here?" Goss demanded.

The count crossed his arms and said nothing.

"You're being very foolish, my lord. The truth will come out in time."

"Ah, yes, the thumbscrews, the boots, the rack, eh?"

Goss looked genuinely shocked. "Brethren do not torture!" he said with verve. "Such methods are an abomination to us!" His features relaxed. "I can see that you will have to be introduced to the Fact. Once you have been tapped by the goodness and glory of the Fact, you will genuinely desire to cooperate."

"My mind is not easily changed," said Rado.

The prelate essayed the slightest smile. "It is not your mind we will convert," he replied smugly. "It is your soul."

* * * * *

Goss left Rado alone with his fears. The prelate's promise was more chilling to him than any threat of torture. It was one thing to break under horrible pain, but quite another to be treated politely, respectfully—and be served up to a higher power unwillingly.

A feeling of naked helplessness gripped Rado. He tried to summon back the euphoria he'd felt in the worship hall, when the presence of the Fact had first come to him. He couldn't. Like the words of a song he'd sung for years and then forgotten, the experience of the Fact eluded his memory. He remembered the event, but for some reason could not draw the sensation of the Fact's touch out of the past. It was no longer real. It was a waking dream with no connection to reality.

He wondered what had happened to Thorn. Goss's

description suggested a brawl she'd ultimately lost. Rado believed the prelate's disgust when torture was mentioned, but knowing Thorn to be dangerous, and as a woman unqualified for conversion, there seemed nothing between her and the headsman's axe.

A hollow, lost sensation followed this realization. It didn't make sense. Thorn was the knife at his throat. Let the Brethren remove it, he didn't care. She'd be gone, and he'd be free of the temple forever.

Forever free and converted.

Brethren came to his room at irregular intervals. They always came in pairs, one to hold the key and block the door, while the second brought in food, water, or an empty chamberpot. Rado tried to time the day by their visits, but his estimations never meshed. The Brethren had no schedule that he could determine.

Night and day betrayed him, too. His first day in captivity was extremely long; the window stayed light for at least eighteen hours. An amazingly brief night followed, and then it was day again for another eighteen hours. How could this be? Did the Fact command the cycle of the sun?

Part of the mystery was dispelled on the third day. In the middle of what Rado thought was a sunny afternoon, the room suddenly was plunged into darkness. He pushed the chair to the window and peered out. No sooner was his face in front of the glass than the "daylight" blossomed blindingly in his eyes. So that was it! The Brethren had a dazzle lamp set below his window. They were manipulating his sense of time to confuse him and weaken his resolve.

Anger made Rado resolute. I will resist, he vowed silently. All the same, he had hopelessly lost track of the time he'd been on Prios.

They came for him while he slept. He had no warning. Usually Rado could hear footsteps in the passage, hear the click of the key in the lock. When they came for him, he heard nothing until a voice summoned him to wake. He opened his eyes and saw his bed was ringed with Brethren.

"Arise, Rado of Hapmark. Your hour of communion is at hand," said the subprelate leading the group.

"No," he said.

"We have specific instructions from the prelator himself to compel you." The half-dozen Brethren standing around his bed carried leather-wrapped batons. "Whatever you choose to do, the outcome will be the same. Would it not be better for Count Rado to go to the Fact on his feet, rather than being dragged like a cringing felon?"

The man had a point. Rado got up and reached for his trousers. His clothes were filthy from climbing and lying in the felucca's bilge. He wished Thorn was on hand to clean them. He stood and stamped his feet into his boots good and tight. With all the aristocratic hauteur he could muster, Rado put on his jacket and reached for his bag of possessions.

"You won't need that," said the subprelate.

"These are important," Rado insisted.

"You'll be returning here later. All your trinkets will be where you left them."

His hand retreated from the bag. Through the open top, he could see the cylinder with the Goddess's weapon in it. It was too bulky to smuggle out. The Brethren watched every move he made closely.

"Shall we go?" Rado asked airily.

They marched out of the room. Two Brethren preceded Rado and the subprelate. The rest fell in step behind. As they went, Rado was reminded of a play he had seen in Pazoa once. *The Usurper*, it was called, by some fellow named Britheme. In the climactic scene, the rebellious prince Casmar is marched to the scaffold. He turns to his lover trailing behind him and says, "Do not weep, my darling. The headsman takes pride in his art. I am sure the axe is sharp." Rado wondered how sharp the Fact would be.

Rado and his escorts ascended no less than eight sets of steps. The higher they went, the richer the furnishings became. From the ascetic stone walls and floors of his room's level, the sanctuary gained thick carpets, tapestries, ornate lamps and statuary. The sanctuary took on the air of a palace instead of a prison.

Upon leaving the eighth stairwell landing, they were met by Prelate Goss and three men identically dressed in emblem-free clothing. The subprelate turned Rado over to Goss and departed with the rest of his men. Rado watched them go.

"Come," said Goss, extending his hand. "It won't be necessary for me to call them back, will it?" Rado said no. "That's good. You're about to have a sublime experience, my lord. I wouldn't want it spoiled by batons and fisticuffs." The prelate linked his arm in the count's. "Come," he said.

"Before you commune, there are some preparations we have to make. The Brethren with us are very skilled in such matters."

"What will they do?"

"Nothing hurtful, I assure you."

They entered a small room. It was lined on three walls by tables laden with metal tools and jars. A single high chair stood in the center of the room.

"Take off your jacket and be seated," said Goss.

One of the simply clothed Brethren took Rado's coat and hung it on a peg. Rado sat, and another man whipped a cloth around his neck, draping the ends evenly over his shoulders. He busied himself behind Rado's back with tinkling metal and glass.

Something cold touched the back of his neck. "What are you doing?" Rado asked sharply.

"Cutting your hair," said Goss. "The communing process requires it." Rado fidgeted in the chair while the man snipped off his smooth hair well above each ear. Cascades of brown hair spilled down his chest. The third brother promptly swept the locks away with a soft brush.

The barber brother dampened a towel with a sharp-smelling liquid. He wiped the loose hair from Rado's head and swabbed across his temples. The acrid lotion chilled his skin. The barber dropped the towel and picked up a razor. He stropped it expertly on a strap hanging from the back of the chair.

"Leave the mustache, please," said Rado. Goss was unmoved.

The brother shaved patches on either side of Rado's head, from his ears forward. More of the cold liquid was applied, stinging where the razor had scraped his skin. When the barber was done, he gave way to the man who until this time had been busy mixing something in a bowl. The apothecary brother stirred the white paste in the bowl vigorously. He dipped a flat spatula into the paste and proceeded to smear dollops on Rado's newly shaved skin.

The third brother removed Rado's boots and washed his feet in a pan of warm water and vinegar. He blotted them dry and slipped woven rag sandals on the count's feet in place of his boots.

"Stand up," said Goss. The Brethren dusted Rado off from collar to cuffs. "Very good. Lennic will remain with us. The other two may go." The paste mixer, Lennic, washed his hands. He, Goss, and Rado went out.

At the end of the corridor was a moving room, much larger than the closet in the Red Frog Inn. How high it lifted them Rado couldn't guess—somewhere near the peak of the sanctuary, if not the topmost

level. Here again the decor was different. The walls
were sheathed in sheets of pale gray metal. The floor
from wall to wall was a spongy yellow stuff that Rado
first took for hide, but it was plainly not hide, since
the floor ran in all directions in an unbroken sheet.
No animal in the world had such a large and perfect
skin.

"Wait," Goss pronounced. He went ahead to a pair
of doors made of the same gray metal. He reached
under his cassock and brought out a Fact emblem, a
three-dimensional mated pyramid. It was a tiny rep-
lica of the image standing in the worship hall. Goss
touched the point of the object to the seam between
the doors. With a soft click, the doors parted inward.
Goss waved Rado inside.

The room beyond was perfectly circular. The metal
walls extended inward, forming the floor as well. In
the center was a deeply cushioned chair. A metal
stand jutted up behind the head of the chair.

"My lord, if you would sit—"

No! Run! Rado's mind screamed. *Put your fist in
the helper's face and run like all the damned spirits of
the dead were after you!*

"Please, Count Rado. You are so near. Please sit
down," said Goss.

Rado fell heavily into the seat. Lennic crossed behind him and disturbed some apparatus on the back
of the chair. A horizontal frame unfolded forward,
touching the crown of Rado's head. Lennic handed a
thick copper band to Goss.

"Tell me the truth," Rado said. "Am I going to die?"

"No, indeed. You are most definitely going to live," said Goss. He seated the band on the count's head. The prelate adjusted some screws on the outside rim of the band, tightening them until Rado felt contact all around the shaved patches on his skull. Lennic passed a black cord to Goss. The prelate attached the cord to the largest screw on the right half of the band. Rado saw the cord was actually a strand of copper wire covered with black wax. A second wire just like the first was attached to the screw on the left side. Lennic came around and positioned Rado's feet precisely on a metal plate at the bottom of the chair.

Goss smiled. "I envy you," he said with real emotion. "The first time I spoke with the Fact was eleven years and nine months ago. There is nothing like the first time you hear the voice of god."

"You could speak to the Fact?" asked Rado. His mouth was so dry his lower lip split as he talked.

"Oh, yes. It will hear you, too." Lennic remarked that everything was ready. Goss nodded and went to the doors with him. "Commune well, my lord." He turned his back. The twin doors closed of their own accord.

Sweat trickled through the stubbly hair behind Rado's ears. He reached up to pull the band off. It was stuck. Between the tight screws and the sticky white paste, the band was not going to come off easily. Feverishly he felt for the screws that would loosen the damned thing.

The light faded. Rado froze. "Here I am," he said loudly. "What are you waiting for? You're a god, aren't you? Show me your divinity!"

He shuddered. His head slammed back against the cushions. Rado's arms slowly bent across his chest in deathlike rigor. His eyes rolled back until only white showed. Ripples of preternatural motion ran through him from head to toe, then ceased. Gradually every part of Rado's body relaxed. Only the cables on the headband kept him upright in the chair.

He was gone. The body remained, a living suit of flesh, but the mind and soul of Rado of Hapmark had departed from this world.

Fourth: The Unbeliever

Belief consists in accepting the affirmations of the soul; Unbelief, in denying them.

Ralph Waldo Emerson,
Representative Men

XII

The field of rye stretched to every horizon. It was early rye, still yellow with new growth and lacking the heavy head of the grain when ripe. The smell of fresh life was in the wind, and the rye stalks sighed with it.

Rado couldn't believe it. The last thing he remembered was the weird room in the sanctuary of the Fact—and the pain. He plucked a rye stalk and stuck the broken end in his mouth. Sweet. He dug his hands into the black earth. Mealy worms and pillbugs scurried away from his probing fingers. A single blind earthworm waved its blunt nose to the sky, then oozed back into its fertile hiding place.

"Do you like it?"

Rado started. "Who said that?"

"Does this scene please you?"

He whirled in a circle. He was completely alone. "Who's that talking?"

"I am the Fact."

"Where are you? Why can't I see you? Where am I?" Rado shouted.

"So many questions! Didn't my Brethren prepare

you for this moment?"

His knees lost their bones. He sat down hard in the tender grain. "No," Rado said faintly. "No one prepared me for this."

"I am sorry. Still, do these images please you?"

"Yes. Yes. Where am I?"

"Nowhere . . . and here. You are inside me."

"How can that be? I was in the room with a band on my head—"

"Yes, a crude thing, the headband, but it is so hard for me to make myself known without them. Since my Brethren did not prepare you fully, I will grant you an explanation. This place, this field of winter rye you see, I made from thoughts in your mind. Did you live near a field like this once?"

"In Teraza, almost thirty years ago . . . I was four years old. I used to hide from Nanna in the rye." A tear formed, grew heavy, and rolled down his cheek. "How could you know these things? Even I had forgotten them."

"I can read every memory you have as easily as you can speak." The wind changed direction. It blew on Rado's face, cooling the hot flush of memory burning there. "Why are you here, Rado? Why have you sought me by clandestine means?"

"If you have to ask you can't be much of a god," Rado replied.

"How skeptical you are. I can take answers any time I choose. It is painful to take without permission, however, and I already find a great reservoir of anguish within you, my child."

"I'm not your child," the count retorted. "I'm a prisoner of the Brethren. I don't want to be here, and I truly don't want to talk with you!"

"I see. Who brought you to the place of communion?"

"Goss."

"The first of my guardians. I understand now; he wishes me to empty your mind, to know what you know. Very well, it will be done. . . ."

Rado jumped up. "No, don't! Please!"

"It will be done."

"Then—then grant me a favor. You can afford to be generous to poor Rado."

"What do you want?"

"Let me see you. I want to see the Fact." A finger tapped him on the elbow. Rado flinched and almost screamed. There was a young boy beside him. He looked about twelve. "Are you the Fact?"

"I chose this form for your sake. Do you know it?"

A trail of ice grew along Rado's spine. The boy Fact was himself. "Choose someone else," he whispered.

"No, this is best." The boy Rado held out a dirty hand to the grown Rado. "Touch my hand and your torment will be brief. I promise it." The true Rado hesitated. The boy added, "You cannot trick me, Elder Self. Any deception you make will increase the depth and clarity of your memories. I shall know instantly when you lie." The boy's face lost its harsh cloudiness. "Hurry, take my hand! Reliving is less a shock than living."

Rado took the Fact's hand in his. Spasms passed
through him to the boy and back again. The rye field
disappeared in a flash. In its place was a squalid farm-
yard in the south country of the Homelands. Rado the
man and Rado the boy stood apart, watching a haggard and dirty young woman huddle under the blows
of a whip. A tall bearded man in the flower of youth
and strength was shredding the clothes off the woman's back with his lash.

"Mother," said the Rados together.

"Slut!" shouted the man. "How dare you bring
that squalling bag of pus to me. I did not make him!
It was the cross-eyed idiot swineherd, yes? He's the
father, isn't he?" He punctuated the question with
an especially vicious cut. The woman, doubled over
on her knees, wept an affirmative. The bearded man
stayed his hand.

"That's better," he said, panting. "Now get out of
my sight and off my land. And take the little bastard
with you." He stalked off, coiling the whip under his
elbow.

The woman raised her head. In her lap, protected
from the whip by her own back, was a red-faced baby
boy.

"Poor woman," said the Fact. "In love with the
youngest son of the estate's lord, she bore him a son
he didn't want and couldn't acknowledge. That is us,
Rado. Not a count or lord at all, but a poor, rejected
bastard."

Rado held out his arms to the battered woman, his mother. His hands passed through her like smoke. He couldn't embrace a memory, even the first memory of his life.

Then his heart hardened and he glared at the Fact. "Some great god you are, showing me this little fable. No suckling babe can remember so early a time! You made up this ugly scene to break me!"

The boy brushed tears from his face. "Deny it, Rado. Deny it as often as you can. If I dredged your mind a hundred times a day, it would still yield this 'ugly scene.'"

He grabbed the boy Fact by the throat and shook him. "Hunter's blood, I ought to wring your neck like I'm supposed to—"

"I see," said the Fact. "You want to kill me? Is that why you came to Prios? To kill *me?* Not many men have the ambition to commit deicide. Not even you, Rado. I would know more of this."

He shoved the red-faced boy away. "I have nothing to say."

"As you wish. Nothing need be said, after all." Before his eyes, the boy Rado grew into a young adult and then a man. The fully grown Fact Rado came toward him.

"Keep back! I don't want you—I don't need you! This is all jiggery-pokery. It isn't true! It isn't *real.* . . ." His protestations were choked off when he and the Fact Rado touched. Flesh flowed into flesh, bone and bone melded as one body. Rado and the Fact were joined, and their minds became a unity.

*   *   *   *   *

It was raining that night we ducked into the Knuckle Bones gaming house. Pazoa had been soaked every night for a week, and that as much as anything made us itchy and reckless. It's not hard to want diversion, any diversion, when the most exciting thing you've done in seven days is watch the leaks in our ceiling fill every pot the landlord would lend us.

So we dashed into the Knuckle Bones, even though we knew we'd find Captain Sasrel there. We owed the captain money. A lot of money . . . twenty-two ducats. We hadn't won a pool of tiles or a roll of dice from Sasrel since the last full moon.

Lusha, the barmaid, gave us a hearty greeting as we swept aside the beaded curtain that served the Bones as a door. We gave her a hearty one back, hefting a tit on our way to the ale tap. She squealed and said a filthy word in our ear. She was a game lass, that Lusha, but she had no teeth and a hairy mole where no woman should have one, so we'd only given her a toss on the sheets once.

"Ho there, Cracks! Draw me a brimmer," we said. "Cracks" Duormo, the barkeep, spat red chewing resin on the floor.

"Money, Rado. It takes money to buy drinks in this establishment," he rumbled. Cracks was as broad as he was tall, and not fat at all. He got his name from the glass eye he wore, having lost the real one in King Talton's day to a warden's branding iron. Not long after that, somebody now a corpse had whacked him on the head with a hammer. Duormo lived, but his glass eye was cracked. Cracks.

"I paid you off, didn't I?" we said in our most winning way.

"Aye, and from now on it's coin on the counter for you, lad. I should have my ass strapped for giving you credit in th' first place."

We were about to argue more—we argue with Cracks all night sometimes, just so we can cadge one drink—when a gold duc with Talton's hook-nosed profile hit the bar top.

"You owe me twenty-two of them, Rado," Captain Sasrel said. He'd been cashiered from the army years ago, but he still wore the blue and sable of Pazoa as if it were the day he'd been commissioned.

"I'll pay you, Saz, as soon as I get some coin in my pocket," we said.

"Not good enough. At the rate you gamble and lose, I could be dead before you pay me."

"With any luck." His etched sneer deepened.

"That tongue of yours will be the death of you, Rado." A steel shank as long as our palm appeared in his fist. "Maybe I'll do you a favor and save you by cutting it out."

Cracks's leaded club thumped on the bar between Sasrel and us. "No blood in the bar," he said. "You want to fight, go out in the street like everybody else."

"No need to fight," we said, motioning for Cracks to fill a mug for us. "If the captain wants to be paid right away, maybe there's some other arrangement we can come to."

Now, at this point in the tale, we should explain that our chief source of turning coin was as a duelist for hire. This works two ways. Say some careless gent gets himself challenged to tickle-play with swords, and he doesn't know a rapier from a roasting spit. He can, according to the code of the Schools of Sword, hire a blade to stand in for him. That's us. Or, not as honorable but usually more lucrative, we could be hired to pick a fight with some cluck another man— or woman; we've been hired by women—wants skewered. We were one of the best graduates of the Moonstone School of Fencing, and we did well for ourself. So well, in fact, we had to spend a year in Vendrollo after killing three opponents in as many days. At the time we faced Sasrel in the Knuckle Bones, we'd been back in Pazoa only five weeks.

Yellow greed showed in the captain's jaundiced eyes. "Maybe there is," he said. "You've got more balls than sense, and a little enterprise of mine could use a man of your brash talent. Let's talk it out in private."

"I'll need ale to think," we said.

Sasrel slid the duc to Cracks. "Send a pitcher," he said.

We should have run when he did that. Sasrel buy-
ing us drinks? Sasrel made love to every coin he pried
from a beggar's cup. He loved gold more than food,
and a lot more than he loved women. Yes, we should
have hurled ourself through the Bones' window right
then, but we didn't.

The captain and us went to one of Cracks's private
booths. Booth was a kindly word to cover such a cub-
byhole. It was really just a bench faced with a plank
for mugs and elbows to rest on, screened by an espalier of smoke-stained wood. We squeezed in. Cracks
brought a pitcher of pale Bothland, the best ale in
Pazoa. While we poured and drank the first of many
that night, Sasrel began his tale.

"What do you know of the Temple of the Mother
Goddess?" he asked.

"Here in the city?"

"Umm."

"It's a very big cult, and very rich. They say the Pazoa temple is the founder of all the others around the
world."

"Bright lad. Right all around." He leaned closer
and gifted us with his rank breath. "I want to take
someone out of the temple."

We almost spit out the delicious Bothland. "Who
by the blood could you want from a closed commu-
nity like the temple?" we said.

"A woman." Something like rage flared from his
scarred neck. "Her name is Vitia Parviel, or it used to
be. The bitches inside call her 'Ariaph.' She's a supe-

rior acolyte of the Inner Temple."

That time we did choke. Priestesses of the Inner Temple were the holiest of all the orders. Unlike most other grades, Inner Temple acolytes took vows of silence (when not inside the temple), chastity (always), and wore masks of woven rattan when out in public. The temple taught that a woman's eyes were her most revealing and vulnerable place. It is through the eyes that evil is most clearly perceived.

Sasrel brushed golden droplets of ale from his sleeve. "Yes, I know. It makes me want to puke, too. Bloody priestesses take good women and shut them away from life, from men. Not natural, I say. Well, I mean to have Vitia back, if only for a few hours."

"Uh, Saz, if you don't mind my asking, how did you ever get to meet a superior acolyte, anyway?" we asked.

"She wasn't born a bloody acolyte, was she?" he barked. Heads beyond the espalier turned toward us. Sasrel hunched lower in the booth. "We grew up on the same street. Street of the Yarn-Spinners, here in Pazoa." He belched and took a deep swig from the pitcher. "I was only fourteen when I asked her, and she said yes."

"Asked her what?"

"To marry me, you clucking dandy! When I turned sixteen, I ran away to the wars, and she promised to wait for me. In two years, I was commissioned, and then she wouldn't have me! Said I swore too much and drank and talked war and slaughter and—"

Sasrel gripped the plank hard. This was more real feeling from him than we had ever seen before. It made him seem almost human. Made us kind of queasy, we tell you.

"I got mad. I—I hit her . . . just a cuff on the ears, but she screamed and her whelp brother charged in and, well, I gave him the working end of my poniard. The city watch caught me, but the siege of Vendrollo was on then, so I didn't get punished any worse than loss of pay and fifty lashes. Vitia's brother lived. He's a cripple and has a silversmithy on Furnace Lane.

"Vitia ran away. By the time I got back from the war, she was gone and no one knew where she was. I asked hard, broke a few heads just to make the truth come out, but nobody knew, not even her brother. I figured she was gone forever. Then, a week ago Marksday, I seen her. In a line of acolytes, wearing a basket on her head, but I knew her! She never left the bloody city, damn her!"

"Saz, I can't get into the temple. Even if I could, it's ten bowshot across. How would I find her? If I did, how would I get her out? It's impossible."

"Ho there, lad. That's the wonder of the thing. You heard of tactics?"

We hid a smile under the rim of the mug. "Some idea, yes."

"I got a tactic. This is what I want you to do." He related a three-step procedure and told us how, when, and where to do it. "Once you have her, all you do is deliver her to my digs at Chimney-Under-the-Bridge."

"What are you going to do with her?"

"Talk. Talk her into coming back to me, that's all."

Then is when we should have gotten up and run for the door. Right *then*. But, no, all we did was say, "What payment are we talking about, Captain?"

He astonished us. "How much do you want?"

We were truly getting tired of snorting fine ale from our nose. We blew out the Bothland brew and said, "Cancel my debt and pay me ten ducats."

"Done. Give me your hand on it."

"Aren't you going to haggle? Aren't you going to swear and call me a scum and a whoreson and a thief?" He was not. He held out that hard, ugly hand, the one with the finger missing. And we, like the newest babes in the rye, shook it.

* * * * *

Far down the coast, the river Grydon empties into the sea on a wide estuary. Ships of noteworthy size ply the lower Grydon, fishing and moving cargo. Yet the tractable and profitable river begins in the heart of Pazoa at the Sheltered Spring, a natural well enclosed by a circular wall since ancient times. More recently, King Talton's conqueror, Edram the Swift, erected a roof over the spring as a token of gratitude to the Mother Goddess for her divine assistance in his cause. So *he* said. At any rate, the Sheltered Spring became a secular shrine for devotees of the Goddess, and groups of priestesses go there daily to fetch water for the temple gardens.

Act the First: We were to secret ourself inside the walled spring with a sack, a rope, and our sword.

Act the Second: Sasrel would make himself known around the temple. He reasoned that this would induce Vitia-Ariaph not to leave the temple except in a crowd of her sisters. The only likely crowd would be the daily visit to the spring.

Act the Third: We wait until Vitia appears, seize her, and carry her off to Sasrel's tender embrace.

If we'd thought for ten heartbeats continuously, we'd have given back the ten ducats and run the scarred pustule through. But we had wrongheaded notions of loyalty to our paymaster in those days, and we took to skulking around the spring watching for the beloved Vitia.

Sasrel had given us a numbingly detailed description of her. We'd never heard so minute a description of a woman he'd never seen stripped. Love is a strange affliction. That's why we kept dodging it in favor of good old belly-bumping.

Luck, that elusive spirit that we seldom found at the gaming table, sent the woman Vitia into our hands after only two days. Despite the shawl and rattan mask, we knew her right away. She wasn't especially beautiful. A pleasant, bovine face with a receding chin and auburn hair. Nicely but not extravagantly padded out. We would have passed her a hundred times on the street without a second look.

We reached up with our sword and knocked the torch off the bracket. It hit the floor and went out. It was early twilight and getting dim outside. It was already dark inside the shelter. We circled through the hall, sending the torches one by one to the mossy stones. A few patrons complained, but not loudly; a drawn sword does wonders to people's manners. We came up behind the temple priestesses. There were five of them. Two were Inner Temple acolytes. We could ignore the others. At close range in bad light, we could easily identify Vitia. We sheathed our sword and plunged into the small band of women.

We weren't gentle, we admit. We were too excited, too churned up inside. We pushed the three non-acolytes into the spring. The first masked woman wasn't Vitia, so we pitched her in the water, too. After a quick peek to confirm that we had our quarry, we covered her head and shoulders with the bag and slung her over our shoulder. She and her sisters were screaming, but no one tried to interfere.

We ran with the woman over our shoulder along the route we'd planned beforehand. Chimney-Under-the-Bridge was a run of filthy brick houses built under the pilings of the Hockdan Bridge. Parts of the houses were truly built of old chimney brick discarded from the smelters on Furnace Lane, hence Chimney-Under-the-Bridge.

There we were, kicking the door to Sasrel's digs, yelling to cover the woman's screams. It wasn't what you'd call a smooth situation. Suddenly Sasrel was at the door. "Get in!" he bellowed.

"Over there," he said. We lowered Vitia to the floor against the dingy wall. While the sack was still on her head, Sasrel grabbed her wrists and tied them with thongs to two rings mounted in the sooty bricks. Her hands secure, he yanked the sack off. The shawl and mask went with it, exposing Vitia's weak blue eyes. She gazed at Sasrel in unconcealed horror, her lower lip trembling with as much fear as we've ever seen a mortal muster.

He hurled a torrent of obscenity and violent language at this inoffensive priestess such as we had never heard. Sasrel was raving, spit flying from his lips. He punctuated his vicious tirade with a kick delivered with his hobnailed infantry boots.

That was too much for us. It was clear that talk had never been his aim. We hadn't reckoned on his consuming desire for revenge when we entered into this hideous plot. We took hold of the hilt of our sword and stepped forward. Sasrel's back was to us.

"Captain," we said, and that was all. He lashed back, his studded leather wristband striking us across the eyes. The blow laid us out as stiff as yesterday's fish. The ugly swine stooped over us, laughing, and took back the ten ducats he had paid us. Then his boot met our head, and we missed the rest of Sasrel's reunion with his precious Vitia.

XIII

We awoke blind, or so we thought. We thought we were still in Sasrel's place; we could smell the smoky walls. Our head was splitting, and we raised one hand to our face. Cloth. There was a hood over our face. We tore it off and sat up. A hammer of pain thudded between our eyes.

We were surrounded on three sides by women—a hundred women at least, sitting in neat tiers three deep. They were gowned from the neck down in bone gray drapes, giving the ghostly impression of a hundred heads lying on a triple row of pillows. Only these heads blinked and gazed with unpleasant focus right at us.

The room was a vast chamber, mostly black with darkness. Columns rose behind the women's ranks. Tawny light played over the stone pillars and stony faces. At our back burned a fire on a great open hearth. We knew then where we were: the Temple of the Mother Goddess.

A woman in the center of the first row facing me stood. She was elderly and gaunt, with the sort of whittled look old women often get. The drape fell straight from her shoulders, concealing arms, figure, and feet.

"Are you the swordsman Rado?" she asked. We didn't answer quickly enough, so she repeated the question. We admitted we were.

"You have been brought before the assembled acolytes of the Inner Temple in order to bear witness to the judgment of their will. You have been found guilty of sacrilegious rape and murder in concert with one Sasrel, a former captain in the army of the city."

Everything became clear in one thunderous instant. "I didn't do it! I didn't! He—Sasrel—paid me to bring the woman to him! I didn't—"

"The captain told us the entire truth," said the woman, evidently the judge or high priestess. "Your complicity is the same as if you had been a willing partner. You are guilty."

"No! No! I didn't know what he was planning to do to her! He said he wanted to talk to her, to persuade her to come back to him."

The high priestess hung her head. Slowly she raised it until our eyes met. We remembered their injunction about an acolyte's eyes and looked away.

"Talk? Persuade? Let me show you man's persuasion!" She nodded to the assembly on her left. The tiers dissolved. Four workers from the outer temple were there, holding the corners of a canvas stretcher. They came to us. A body filled the stretcher, a body covered by a sheet.

"Look," said the priestess. "Lift the shroud and look!"

We didn't dare refuse. We picked up a corner and quickly dropped it. The elderly priestess stormed over and flung back the sheet.

"This is the work of an insane beast," she said. "Look on it, hired man, and know the guilt you bear!"

We're not squeamish. We've seen any number of dead men and women in our day, but we never saw anything like what Sasrel did to that poor creature. He used his fists and boots on her until she was nothing but pulp held in by blackened skin.

Sick bile grasped us by the throat. We couldn't dishonor ourself and insult the temple by being sick. We clenched our teeth and breathed fast through our nose. "What," we panted, "happened to Sasrel?"

She crossed the worn stone floor to the other wall of priestesses. There she paused and jerked her head for us to join her. Cautiously, sweating, we did so.

The second tier of women broke silently apart. They stepped down from their high stools and moved aside. Behind them were two large columns. In the billowing firelight, we could see a scarecrow standing in chains between the columns. We almost laughed! They hadn't finished dressing him, as a heap of rags lay at the straw man's feet.

No. Oh, no. Our hands flew to our face. We backed away, only to bump into a wall of silent priestesses. It wasn't a scarecrow. They weren't rags. They had flayed Sasrel alive.

We dropped on our belly at the high priestess's feet. "Spare me, Mother! I took the captain's money because I owed him gold, but I would never have done it had I known what he planned! Why—why, when he started to hit the woman Vitia, I tried to stop him, and that's how I got this mark on my face!"

She said, very quietly: "I know."

We stopped groveling. "You know?"

"Temple Sentinels found Sasrel drunk in a tavern not four streets from his rooms. They forced him to return there, and they found you lying on the floor unconscious next to our ravaged sister. Later we put the beast to the question, and he told of your true part in the crime." She studied the ragged red thing hanging above the floor. "He howled his damned soul out of his body, but he never begged for mercy." She ordered Sasrel's remains taken down and displayed on the outer wall of the temple. It hung there for weeks with a sign around its neck proclaiming *Rapist-Murderer.*

When the bodies were gone, the priestesses took off their long drapes. Young female lackeys carried them away in huge armfuls. For a moment, all was bustle and talk, and we thought we were free. We started looking for a door. We found one, but as we reached for the handle, it turned and opened. A group of hard-looking women entered, clad in kilts and polished cuirasses. The maces they carried on their shoulders didn't look ceremonial.

"Come here, man," said the high priestess. She was perched on one of those tall stools, her back to the flaming hearth. The kilted mace-wielders surrounded us. One of them poked our knees from behind, sending us to the floor.

"You are nonetheless guilty as described, hired man, and for that reason, you are indentured to the temple until we see fit to release you."

"You mean I'm to be your *slave?*" we asked.

"Would you rather have the captain's freedom?" Not by the Hunter's blood! She went on to say that the acolytes of the Inner Temple had discussed the matter, and they'd decided we were perfect for an undertaking they'd been plotting for some time.

"We want you to make a tour of the eastern colonial cities," the high priestess said, "posing as a wealthy titled man from the Homelands. The temple will provide coin and clothing."

We had to smile. "This is punishment? I'll do it. When do I depart?"

"Still your tongue! You don't know what you're agreeing to. You make take any route you choose, so long as you arrive in Miyesti by the end of the summer."

"What's in Miyesti?" we asked.

"A god."

"A god?"

"Yes, a very new god, whom we want you to kill."

Ah, we thought. This whole gang has been breathing butter. They're insane! But we're nothing if not diplomatic, especially after seeing what they did to Sasrel. We said, "Is this god made of solid flesh that I can stick my sword through?"

No one knew, she said. Before we could protest, the high priestess launched into a brief history of the Brethren of the Fact and of the inroads they'd made in the ranks of the true believers. In the east, all Miyesti had fallen under their influence, and Tablish and Oparos were turning to the new god as well. There had been a considerable loss of pilgrims and tithes from the colonies to the temple.

"There are more disturbing things," she said. "The teachings of this Fact would place women under men's feet. We have not endured a thousand years to make the lives of women honored, only to see it all lost to an upstart deity no one ever heard of in my mother's time."

"But, Lady," we said, "how can a man kill a god?"

"With a god's weapon," she said cryptically. One of the mace-armed women, a Sentinel of the Temple, stepped out of line and set a gray cylinder on the floor between the high priestess and us.

"Inside this case are the Tears of the Goddess, the most virulent poison known in heaven or on earth. By the ancient formula set down in the Millennium Book, the secret archive of the temple, this small portion was prepared for just this mission. You will take the Goddess's Tears to Miyesti in a roundabout fashion to allay the suspicious Brethren. Once there, you will administer the poison to this rogue god, in whatever form he takes."

A sweat of futility spread across our brow. "I don't see how I can do this," we said. "If this god lives among mortals as you say he does, he will be protected by scores of loyal followers. How am I to reach him?"

The high priestess clapped her hands. One Sentinel detached from the pack and came to her. The Sentinel knelt on one knee, head bowed.

"Eridé," said the priestess, touching the girl's hair. "You are the finest fighter of all the Sentinels. If your black temper did not force me to discipline you every week, you might now be one of us in the Inner Temple." She sighed. "Will you accept charge of this man, Rado, go with him, and hold him to the sacred task I have set for him?"

"Mother, I would die at any hour for you and the temple," said Eridé. "But please don't tie me to this vile man. I would sooner blood my hands than have to nurse this greedy weakling around the world."

We hopped to our feet. "Now, wait a minute! I don't care if this is a temple, people who say things like that to me had better have steel to back it up!"

"Be silent, both of you; I am thinking." The high priestess studied the Sentinel, then us, then the Sentinel again. The chamber was silent save for the hiss of burning wood.

"You," she said, meaning us, "could not be trusted ten steps beyond the confines of the temple. And even if we filled this room with gold, we could not buy enough resolve in you to breach the wall of guards who must encircle the Fact god, as you so rightly deduce. Therefore we will send with you our Sentinel, Eridé the sullen, to protect you from harm and to insure your fidelity to the mission." We started to protest, but she cut us off with a single glance. To the Sentinel, she said, "Eridé, when you were left at the temple gate as a baby, there was no room left in the nursery for another child. The war was very vicious; orphans and foundlings filled the halls to bursting. I was a callow acolyte then, and I pitied your swollen belly and wrinkled limbs. You never cried, Eridé, not ever. When the nursery walls seemed poised to collapse under the screams of a hundred infants, you lay silent in your crib."

We watched the Sentinel's face. There was an obvious bond between her and the high priestess, but she remained dry-eyed all through the story.

"You have always chosen your own way. The Goddess only knows how you and my predecessor managed to get along. I have borne your stubbornness and wilfulness for longer than was wise. The time has come to purge these vices. You must dedicate yourself to my will, not as your teacher, but as First Acolyte, Beloved Daughter of the Goddess.

"So I charge you thus: You *will* go with this man, guide him and guard him wherever he goes, until his debt for the crime against our sister Ariaph is paid. You *will* submit to his commands and obey him as you would me, except when such commands conflict with the higher purpose of your charge. Is that clear, Sentinel?"

"Have I no choice, Mother?"

"None." The old woman's tone softened. "When the deed is done, I pray you will understand better the cost of command." She motioned, and Eridé rose to kiss her hand. We were escorted out of the hearth room, and the preparations for our coming journey began.

* * * * *

We didn't leave the temple grounds until it was time to take ship for the east. Eridé, our watchdog, stayed on our heels at all times, a sullen presence so unnerving we decided to chance death by provoking her.

"You know, if I'm to be in disguise as a harmless wastrel, you ought to be disguised, too," we said.

"Why?" said Eridé.

"Well, it's very odd seeing a woman in armor away from the temple. And the farther away we go, the stranger and more noteworthy it will be."

She accepted that. She said, "How could I be disguised?"

"The obvious thing is for you to be my wife," we suggested.

"I would rather have nails driven through my ears." Looking over her lean, angular body, I agreed. Eridé said, "Sister would be more suitable, I think."

"Ha! Use your head, woman! We don't look anything alike, you and I, praise the gods. Besides, why would a lord from the Homelands drag his unmarried sister around the Adamantine Sea with him?"

She bristled, tendons standing out in her neck. "Who would a lord take with him on a long sea voyage?" she demanded.

Inspiration struck. "His manservant. His valet," we said. Eridé, surprised by the soundness of this notion, finally agreed. She was used to wearing mannish dress and fancied herself more of a fighter than us, so we bought a few sets of servants' togs, all in dull brown or gray. A barber cut her yellow hair off shorter than mine, and a cobbler fitted her with boy's ankle-high boots. She complained about the fit, the cut, and the color of her garments incessantly. Finally we burst out, "You're supposed to obey me, not be a constant thorn in my side!"

Wit is one of our gifts, if we say so ourself. Since we couldn't call her Eridé, a girl's name, we fell to calling her Thorn.

It was at the cobbler's that we first tried to escape. While her feet were locked in the shoemaker's forms, we stole out the back door of the shop and ran to the waterfront. The gold and our new wardrobe were already on the ship. If we could get even half the hoard away, we could go anywhere and live well for many a day.

Thorn caught us as we were waddling down the gangplank with the coin box in our arms.

"Ah! Hello! I came to fetch the money to pay the cobbler," we said lamely.

"I already paid him," said Thorn.

We tried twice more while still in Pazoa. We bought some powdered essence of Hudmum, the white kind that puts you to sleep. The problem was Thorn didn't drink anything but water, and snowy Hudmum floated conspicuously on the surface of water. We staged a fire in the inn where we stayed and jumped out a second story window. She chased us down in her bare feet. This time we tried to fight. We threw punches that hit only air. She took us down with three blows—one in the throat, a kick to the knee, and a foot in the balls. As we lay on the wet street gasping, she showed us the stiletto for the first time.

"Now hear me, my lord," she said coolly, "I tire of your games. If you try once more to flee, drug me, or attack me, I will drag you back to the temple and have them skin you with the dullest flensers I can find. If you believe me, nod your head." We believed her.

We sailed that night. We brooded over the injustice of our fate for a while, then had a revelation. As long as we were with folk who didn't know we were Rado the swordsman, then we *were* Count Rado of Hapmark, and we'd better get used to it! We began to spend temple gold freely, tipping lackeys and barkeeps and fancy girls extravagantly. Every ducat spent caused Thorn discomfort. We enjoyed that. That was our second revelation.

We couldn't escape our watchdog. We couldn't beat her, either. So what was left? Cowering acceptance? We'd done a lifetime's worth of cowering in the temple; we had no intention of doing any more. If we couldn't get away from the Sentinel, we'd be so demanding and demeaning she would want to leave us.

The first part was easy. It may be that we do have aristocratic blood. At any rate, we learned to love being served. No task was too small to make Thorn redo as many times as we thought we could push her. Oh, she struck back in subtle ways. She became a master of sarcasm. Our batting back and forth became a way of life, and as the voyage lengthened into months, it became as natural as breathing to us.

Demeaning Thorn was another matter. We discovered she was a prude and couldn't bear seeing men naked. This wasn't so much due to her temple vows as to her genuine dislike of men. We forced her to wait on us in the bath, to dress us from the skin out. She foiled this tactic by learning to do many things with her eyes shut. Frustration made us cruel. We decided to test how far her obedience would go.

We ordered her to our bed. Yes, it was a roguish thing to do. We'd never compelled a woman to our company before, but we were angry enough and deprived enough (twelve days at sea from Ledrille to Oparos) to go through with it. It was like making love to a doll. We moved her about but never *moved* her.

This unhappy ploy worked, to a degree. Before we

used Thorn, she was always at my elbow. Afterward, she kept as far from us as the confines of the ship would allow. She was deeply troubled, and we didn't give a fig. Thorn in our side and stone around our neck—if she didn't like life with us, let her seek some other companion!

We were paroled off the ship in Oparos. What a time we had there! We staged the biggest bout of revelry the city waterfront had ever seen. Wine ran in the gutters, and we had a flock of fancies vying for our affection. We posted Thorn outside the door and we went at it all night, shouting through the walls for her to join in if she felt like it.

Cruelty is a terribly easy habit.

We followed the coast of Kurukland south to Miyesti. There things became radically different. We'd been hearing tales of the wonders of the city since Ledrille, and in Oparos we saw Fact Speakers for the first time. These men's sole purpose in life was to win converts for the Fact. They were simple, honest clucks who endured all manner of persecution for their faith. It was in Oparos that we first wondered if the task we had been given was right and just.

Something else happened in Miyesti. We struck Thorn.

We thought we would die in the next breath, but she didn't retaliate. That, strange to say, hurt us a great deal. Not that she didn't promise to kill us once our task was done, but to see the obedience to her fanatical mistress overcome every humiliation, every insult, shocked us deeply.

We entered Miyesti, and the Fact surrounded us with its wonders. Lamps burnt without flame. Carts moved without horses. Rooms rose and fell through houses, houses so grand no mortal could have conceived them! And other things more magnificent were hidden just below the surface. The Brethren had a ship that flies.

We feared the Fact and the Brethren. If such power could be brought to bear on a single person, how could he hope to survive? We seemed doomed, doomed to die by Thorn's hand or by the magic of the Fact. And then . . . when we touched the mind of the Fact in the worship hall, we knew such greatness! Such power and goodness! Is this the upstart god the priestesses want destroyed?

It would be an infamous crime to harm Us. The divine beneficence of the Fact belongs to the world. No, we shall not kill Us. Though we are afraid of Us, we know now that we love Us, too.

XIV

Thorn wiggled her toes. She wished she had something to kick against, just to restore some feeling in them. Suspended high above the floor, strapped arm and ankle to the heavy chair, her limbs had rapidly gone numb.

She'd fought every step of the way, even after the Brethren had taken her death-dealing stiletto. She had broken many arms and a few heads before they pinned her to the ground and sat on her. The guardians took her to a room like Rado's and locked her inside. The first time a brother came to feed her, she attacked. She made it forty steps up the corridor before an army of guardians overwhelmed her again. The batons were out, and they beat her soundly.

Thorn was put in a smaller, harsher cell. Within a day, she was out. The man serving her made the mistake of putting his arm through the wicket to reach her water cup. Thorn wrenched his arm half out of its socket before he yielded the key. She didn't get any farther than the open door before they caught her.

Goss was with them. "It grieves me to see you so

intent on escape," he said. "The Brethren do not want to take your life. The Fact has forbidden it for the time being, but we must find a way of keeping you from harming and being harmed."

They carried Thorn to a large, empty room. A heavy cubic chair, weighing at least nine stone, was the only thing in the room. The guardians put wide straps of soft leather over her forearms and calves and nailed these to the chair. Rope of disquieting thickness was looped under the arms and back of the chair, and Thorn was hoisted into the air.

"Are your bonds too tight?" asked the prelate.

"Very comfortable," said Thorn. "You should try this yourself."

"I will take my leave of you," he said. The guardians filed out. The door boomed shut, and the bolt clicked home from the outside.

The walls were shiny with dew. The courses of stone were blurred together by a coating of moss. Looking up, Thorn saw that the distant ceiling was made of heavy timbers. Cracks let in thin wedges of light.

Thorn made a fist with her right hand. Slowly she tightened the muscles in her arm. The strap did not give. She pulled from the shoulder, and the chair bobbed wildly. Then she realized the cunning of this arrangement: The seat was hanging by three points, and if she upset the balance by trying to break free, she would end up hanging in some awkward, painful position. She might even strangle herself with the rope. Thorn sat still, feeling her bruises and nourishing her hatred for the Brethren.

The straps weren't tight, but her hands and feet, lacking mobility, began to throb and tingle. The effect was maddening.

A guardian brought soup and water at long intervals. He delivered it to her lips with a cup hinged to the end of a long pole. Thorn spilled most of it on her lap.

Alone, she tried to count the hours. One of her early trials as a Sentinel consisted of sitting in a totally dark and silent room. She had to measure the passage of time and not emerge before four hours were up. If she came out too soon, she received one blow from Nandra's stick for every minute she was wrong. The same would happen if she stayed too long in the dark. Stubborn Eridé got ten strokes for tardiness.

How long is a day? The number of hours means nothing when the hours are infinitely long. Thorn counted minutes into thousands and wished for something, anything, to happen to break the flood of unbroken time.

Rado walked in.

"You!"

He tilted his face up and smiled. "How did you get up there?"

"I flew up and built the chair here! Later I plan to lay eggs. What do you think? Goss put me here."

"He is a clever fellow. I see, the suspension keeps you out of mischief. How clever."

"Save your admiration and let me down, will you?

My toes are about to burst!"

"I can't do that," said Rado.

"Why not?" she shouted. Then Thorn spotted the shaved patches on his head. "Mother preserve me," she groaned. "You're converted!"

"Not exactly." Now Thorn was confused. "Let me explain. I am not who I appear to be." He cupped his own chin in his hands. "This body is only borrowed. You see, I am the Fact."

"Ho, ho. You're a very small god, Rado," Thorn laughed.

"Only a fraction of my entirety is here. The full sum of my existence wouldn't fit into any shell of flesh."

Thorn leaned forward. The chair tipped dangerously. "I don't believe you. This is one of your stupid jests, Rado."

"How may I convince you?"

"Do something godlike."

"Very well." He circled below the chair, Thorn's feet scant inches above his head. "I cannot speak directly to your mind, alas. You are a woman, and therefore unworthy. . . . Would you like to hear the General Theory of Relativity, or of Avogadro's Law? I can tell you that your heart is beating sixty-six times a minute, and your blood pressure is one hundred ten over seventy."

Thorn yawned down at him. "Pathetic gibberish. Go away, Rado, and thank the gods I can't get my hands around your wretched throat."

"You hate Rado, don't you? You have cause, I know. As we speak, Rado's mind is communing with another part of mine. He is telling me all about you . . . how you met. Tragic, the death of the woman Vitia. Not that it justified the barbarous treatment of Captain Sasrel."

"Barbarous! Not in two centuries had such an outrage been committed against a sister of the temple. The old law is emphatic: violation of an Inner Temple acolyte is to be punished by flaying the perpetrator alive. An example had to be made. If the priestesses were not protected by the strictest code, how long do you think the Temple and its worldly treasures would remain safe?"

Rado ceased circling and sat, cross-legged, below Thorn. "It's all so unnecessary," he said calmly. "This man Sasrel died in vain. In a few short years, your temple will cease to exist. Under my worship, there will be wealth and happiness for all. Man and woman will find their place together, in the roles nature intended."

"Meaning man over woman," Thorn said. "You offer slavery to half of humankind."

Rado smiled again. "So you believe in me now?"

The truth slowly crept into her. This smooth, confident Speaker wasn't Rado. Her companion didn't have the patience to prolong a joke this far. "You are the Fact," she said. It wasn't a question.

He bowed with unconscious irony. "I am god's messenger."

"What god?" she spat.

"The one, all-seeing deity, who made and rules all worlds."

"Then you know why Rado and I came to Miyesti?"

"Yes, to kill the Fact. A vaunting aim. Did you seriously expect to succeed?"

Thorn arched her back, straining against the leather bonds. The Fact showed no fear at her display. When she finally gave up, gasping, he repeated his question: "Did you think you could succeed?"

"Succeed or die trying," Thorn answered, breathing hard.

"Hmm, yes, the credo of every fanatic. Rado is right about you. He believes you think of nothing but your mission. He thinks you never notice a sunset or hear the birds sing or laugh at silly, inconsequential things."

"The thoughts of Count Rado have less substance than gnat's piss," she replied. "Why do you task me? What do you want? Tears for mercy? Submission to your slavish faith?"

"I prefer converts to martyrs," said the Fact. "It's always better to have a city of worshipers than a pyre heaped with dead enemies."

"You have no convert here."

"So I've discovered. Pity. I detected in Rado's thoughts something that inspired my curiosity. That's my greatest compulsion, curiosity. I must always know more. I had to seek you out and experience you face to borrowed face. He admires you very much, did you know that?" Thorn laughed scornfully, rocking the chair from side to side. The Fact made Rado's face sad. "It's true. He's very much afraid of you, too. Why is that?"

"He knows what I can do. Men like him spend their lives skimming along, grasping at easy money and lax virtue. They can't fathom anyone who truly believes, who has dedication and discipline."

The Fact stroked Rado's chin. "That is true. I feel the fear he bears for me. It is the same sort of fear. Perhaps we are not so different after all. Tell me, Thorn, why do you want to die?"

"Because you threaten my Goddess, my way of life, and my world," she said.

"Your world stinks of want and barbarism. I offer something better. On my path lie unity, dignity, and strength. The Fact brings light to its worshipers. I shall ease their burdens and give them joy."

"Lies, lies! I have seen what you have to offer, and it's villainous. Do you have enough captive spirits to run machines for the entire world? What is the price of the light you bring? The streets of Miyesti show clearly what the Fact means—conformity, sterility. You would make nature man's servant, instead of keeping its mysteries. How long can your way of life be sustained? A hundred years? A thousand? What will be left of the Goddess's world once it's covered by stone and glass? Where will the rhythm of the seasons go when they have been drowned in the clatter of cogs and levers? The Fact means slow death for the world.

"The Goddess sent me bearing the gifts she values: quick death, the mercy of oblivion, and the return to the soil."

The Fact continued to smile through Rado's lips. "Thank you for defining the coming battle for me, Sentinel. The depth of ignorance I face is even greater than I imagined." Thorn formed a stinging retort, but Rado's head suddenly snapped to one side. He cocked an ear as if listening to a call Thorn could not hear.

"I must go," he said slowly. "The propeller for my new turbine ship has arrived from the city foundry. My engineers require my guidance to install it."

"The *Oribos!*" Thorn called as he rose and turned his back on her. "Built to carry your Speakers to the Homelands."

Fact-Rado looked back, frowning. "You know more than I thought. Why did I not find this knowledge in Rado's mind?"

"Because Rado is a fool, and god or not, you're a fool, too! When I don't return to the temple, the high priestess will know I failed. More Sentinels will come for you, and every Speaker you send to Pazoa will die on the dock!"

"Then I shall send more. And more. Each day my ranks swell, hastening the day when the Fact will be worshiped as the voice of the one true god throughout the world. The tide of change is with me, Eridé. If you don't swim with it, you and all your kind will be drowned."

She leaned over as far as her bonds would permit. "You've no right to call me that name. Thorn I am, and Thorn I shall be until you are destroyed!"

"A thorn is only an annoyance," observed the Fact. "You *are* a thorn. I, on the other hand, am a needle. Do you see the difference? While you were grown as a weapon to serve a decadent cult, I was forged from new metal by god. As you bleed the enemies of your temple, I penetrate their hearts and bring them light. You worship Chaos and don't realize it. I am the new order for the ages, and that is the Fact."

The Fact steered Rado to the door. "I'm glad to have had this chance to talk to you. You're a dying breed. I rejoice in your passing."

"Someday I'll bathe in your blood," Thorn replied.

The bolt slid into its slot. It sounded like a death knell.

XV

Rado opened his eyes. He was lying on a bed. His bed, in his room, in the beautiful sanctuary of the Fact. Prelate Goss was sitting in a chair beside him.

"How are you?" the prelate asked gently.

Rado touched his temples. The band was gone. The paste was gone. Stubbly hair had grown in the shaved patches. "How long have I been—been away?" he asked.

"A long time, as the Fact reckons. As men know, a mere instant. What do you want to do, Rado?"

He dropped his hands to his sides. "This may sound odd, but what I want most is sleep. I'm very tired."

Goss said, "I understand. You've been on a long journey. It's only natural for you to feel worn out. I'll return later, and you can tell me about your communion. No one else has ever spent so long with the Fact. Not even the prelator himself."

"Goss," Rado called before the prelate was through the door. "It was wonderful."

"I know. It always is."

He shut the door softly. Rado listened with his eyes closed for the click of the lock turning. He didn't hear it.

He rolled quickly off the bed, his heart hammering. Tired? He'd never felt so fired-up in his life. Sounds and pictures rose in waves in his brain, battering at the sandbar that was his true mind. While the Fact had borrowed Rado's body, the swordsman's mind had been left to roam the vast expanse of the Fact untended. Now a hundred million things jostled for his attention. For two days, Rado had wandered the cluttered halls of the Fact's mind, and he remembered what he had found. He knew the precise layout of the sanctuary, the timetable of the guardians' watch, every detail of every plan in the Fact's prodigious memory.

For a god, the Fact had made a very simple error. It accepted Rado's memories as pure facts and failed to veil its own recollections from his free, wandering mind.

Worse, Rado had lied.

As he passed through the great storehouse of knowledge inside the Fact, Rado realized this god was powerful, but not perfect; huge, but not omnipresent. His sense of awe faded. He feigned the soft smile and sleepwalker's gaze, and that was enough to convince the Fact that he adored it like all the others. After all, no one had ever been so close to the presence of the god and not been transformed into a devout believer. No one had reckoned on the will of a life-long cynic.

Rado cracked the door ever so slowly. The passage was empty. He now knew that there were magic eyes called *kamras* in the ceiling at regular intervals. These magic eyes sent images directly to the Fact. No one could escape detection within the sanctuary—unless one knew he was being watched.

The first *kamra* was five steps down the passage to the right of his door. To the left, the hall ended after two more rooms. Rado went left. A high, deep-set window was cut in the marble wall. He lifted the catch and stepped up on the sill. It was a tight fit.

From above, the sanctuary was a lozenge-shaped hexagon, the long axis parallel to the harbor. Rado knew at this hour the highest-ranking Brethren were witnessing the final touches being put to the *Oribos*. He had to act fast. He would get only one chance. The Fact might deduce its blunder at any time, and Rado would end up like Thorn, tied to a chair suspended from the ceiling.

Thorn. If he freed her, he would have a better chance of escaping from the island. On the other hand, going to Thorn was just the sort of move the Fact might anticipate. He'd have to run a gauntlet of *kamras* to get to her. No, stay with the original plan; that was best.

He raced along the alabaster portico that screened the inner wall of the sanctuary. Sunlight flickered among the square columns, creating wavering fingers of light and shadows that clutched at Rado's legs as he ran. He stumbled and crashed into a pillar. Wild, impossible things swirled through his head. Metal birds and talking windows. Voices in the air. Towers of fire that flew screaming through the sky. Dead babies in bottles. Living people under water. Rado moaned and slid down the column as his mind burned with the knowledge of the Fact.

Golden rods. Copper, copper bands. Sand melted into tiny buttons. The light of a thousand years passed through these buttons and came out as a stream of numbers, all naughts and ones.

"Ohwanohohwanwanwanohwanohwanoh." That same nattering nonsense was bubbling unbidden from Rado's mouth. "Stop it!" he hissed, slamming his fists against the stone pillar. "Stop! It! Stop! It!"

Pain drove the Fact thoughts away. Rado licked a smear of blood from his knuckles. It tasted salty, real. Good. He was Rado still.

A set of steps zigzagged up the outside of the fortress wall. He jogged up one set, then another. The lambskin case thumped against his back. The Fact had discounted the Tears of the Goddess. In its usual cryptic fashion, it made some remark about not being an insect one could spray with poison and expect to die. Rado didn't understand the analogy then, but as he pounded up the long white steps, he got a glimmer.

Poison. Not an insect? Not *alive?* If the Fact was not alive, could it be killed? If it wasn't living, what was it?

He dragged the tears around by the strap. The cold lead container cradled in his arms, a babe of death as yet unborn. Babies in glass bottles, he thought wildly. Only two more stories to go. Every breath he drew had ragged corners.

There is only one god, and that is the Fact. . . .

The roof of the penultimate story was a glade of spiky metal rods. It was through these rods that the Fact spoke to its worshipers. The voice rode on the spirits of the air until they found a headband wearer. Differently shaped rods spoke to differently shaped headbands. Thus the hierarchy of the Brethren was upheld.

Rado weaved through the tangle, dreading the touch of the golden branches. Around the far side of the roof was a circular hole cut in the wall of the highest floor. Strands of copper wire flowed from the hole. This top story was the vault of the Fact, and the tunnel was the only way in other than the official sacred portal.

The vault was capped by a tall pyramid of milky glass, and from its apex grew the tallest golden tree of all. It scraped the clouds as high as the peak of Mt. Prios, and from its lofty tip, the words of the Fact could be thrown on every wind. Rado stared at it and wondered how much gold had gone into it. From the recesses of his mind, the Fact whispered a figure. He snorted. The spire was only gold-plated.

The tunnel into the sacred vault was wider than his shoulders and half-filled with bundles of twisted wire. A flash of Fact memory told him the leftover space would be filled once new worship halls were erected in the Homelands. Rado saw the Fact's plans for more golden trees. More Fact symbols. He lay down on the cables and crawled inside.

A bitter smell emanated from within. He'd smelled such an odor before, as a boy, far away from Prios and the Fact. Lightning had struck a beech tree, bursting it into thousands of desiccated fragments. The vitriolic smell hung about the broken tree, perfume of the storm god's mighty stroke.

He was inside. Rado rolled off the wire. He was above the vault proper, on a wooden platform built to distribute the cables evenly around the Fact. He peered through the closely spaced boards.

The god looked like its symbols, only solid. Two golden pyramids, base to base, with rods protruding from all the corners. Rado climbed down the thickest bundle of wires and dropped not ten steps from the Fact.

The Brethren had carved a dais for it, four pylons leaning inward against the four golden faces of the lower pyramid. It rested there, inert, lifeless, and quite unimpressive. Heavy twists of wire ran across the floor from the underside of the Fact to other golden images. They were simple box shapes covered with tiny red jewels. The gems blinked like cat's eyes by torchlight.

These are my memory, the Fact had said, somewhere long ago. . . .

He walked around it. Had it stood on its point on the floor level with Rado, they would have been equal in height. At center, the Fact was twice Rado's width.

He touched it. The lovingly polished surface was pitted and uneven. The gold was crazed with blurred color and ridged with regular square-sided bumps. At some angles, faint lettering in some unknown script was visible. Some of the rods were broken off short, and the stump ends had melted. The Fact had fallen from a great height. Its passage through the sky had nearly burned it to ashes.

Towers of fire screaming.

Rado finished his circling. He backed off and set down the lambskin case. The hide drawstrings were dry and tight, but he worked them apart and pulled the fleecy cover down. The lead case was engraved with scenes from the parables of the Mother Goddess. Rado could tell the case was very old, because the artisans who made it had given the Goddess enormous thighs and breasts, and that style had faded centuries ago.

How did it open? The Fact's stolen knowledge didn't help him here. After much groping and tapping, he discovered that the cylinder unscrewed in the center. Wadding—ancient, pulverized cloth— oozed from the gap where the two halves separated.

Carefully, oh, so carefully, he lifted the top off. The lint fell away in gray drifts, exposing a long black tube as thick as his thumb and tapered to a point. He ran his fingers over it lightly. It was cold and smooth, just as glazed ceramic should feel. Rado lifted the tears out and blew off the last wisps of wadding.

What do I do with it? he wondered. If the Fact had a heart, he could stab the tears into it. It had no heart, no flesh, no blood to poison.

Rado circled the Fact again, the tears clasped in his fist like a dagger. Three-quarters of the way around the golden pyramid, he paused. With his free hand, Rado felt for a slight gap between the sheets of gold. He dug his fingers into the gap and pulled. A triangular panel rose, hinged at the top. Rado ducked under far enough to prop it up with his head. And there he, Rado the swordsman, Rado the false Count of Hapmark, beheld the naked Fact.

The cavity was filled with black buttons and hair-thin wires. Strands of glass so thin they bent like string. Shiny wafers of gold and silver foil. It meant nothing to him.

It was a fake, a fraud! This was not the Messenger of Unquenchable Light. This was not the source of the invisible, intangible thought that so moved men's hearts and minds with awe of its wisdom and endless knowledge. This confection of metal and glass was a stupid fetish, a cheat, like the puppet mummies carnival sorcerers used to gull the foolish with words from the "talking dead." Rado hated it, and he hated the Brethren for making such an insulting idol.

So where was the real Fact? Where did the strange messenger he had communed with reside? The priestesses of the temple in Pazoa had sent him to kill the usurping god. Here, in the most sacred sanctum of the Brethren, he found only this idiot's image.

He dashed the Tears of the Goddess against the nest of cheap glitter. The egg-shell thin black porcelain snapped, and thin liquid spattered over the bogus idol. It hissed, and threads of smoke trickled from the wires. A vile odor assailed Rado's nose and throat. Coughing furiously, he reeled away. The triangular panel banged shut.

Stinking gray vapor seeped through the seams. Rado pinched his nose and clambered with difficulty up the web of wire to the tunnel. His eyes were wet as he kicked his way over the cable. Gasping and gray with nausea, he burst from the tunnel mouth and rolled away from the sickening smoke.

There were shouts coming from the harbor. Rado crept to the edge of the roof and saw a stream of white-garbed Brethren leaving the unlaunched *Oribos* for the sanctuary. The Fact had finally realized its error. It was recalling the faithful to catch him and kill him.

Rado made a leap from that thought to another: Thorn. If there was going to be a fight, he wanted her free to even the odds against him. She was in the old Kurukish cistern, under the ground level gallery. Rado estimated he had only a handful of minutes before the Brethren returned.

* * * * *

Thorn floated above the floor like a dark cloud. Her head hung back, mouth open and jaw slack. Rado grinned when he saw her. He wished he could preserve this scene for her to see later. Her mortification would be delightful.

He loosened the center rope and lowered her to the floor. The chair twisted as it descended. Thorn's head lolled from side to side. Rado's amusement vanished. Was he too late? Was she dead? If she was, it was not by the Fact's orders.

Using a shard of broken glass he found on the floor, Rado slit the leather cuffs that held Thorn to the chair. He never expected the knee that snapped up and connected with his chin. He blundered backward, losing the bit of glass. Thorn sprang on him, turning him over as she locked an arm around his neck and plunged a knee into his kidneys. She held him like that, taut as a bow, and said, "Now you die, Fact!"

"No—*uh*—no!" Rado gurgled. "It's me, Rado!"

"How do I know that?"

"How does an ignorant bitch like you know anything?" The insult convinced her where no persuasive words would have. She unlocked her grip. Rado sat up, rubbing his neck. "I should've known you were laying for me."

"Truth, I didn't wake up until the chair bumped the floor," said Thorn. "How did you get here?" He related his experiences of the past few hours. "So you rooked the Fact, eh? Not much of a god, fooled by an itinerant swordsman and petty gambler."

"Sharp words from one who was just trussed up like a market-day pigeon. Can we discuss our shortcomings later? The Brethren are on their way."

Thorn got up hobbling. Her legs were cramping from being bound and hanging so long. "I don't suppose you've got my stiletto, have you?"

"No, and it's hardly the time to go searching for it. Come! Let's take our leave of this spirit island," he said.

They ran up the gallery to the stairs. A plan of the sanctuary rippled through Rado's head. He made every turn with certainty, knew where every unlocked door was. Thorn was surprised by his preciseness.

"When did you learn the fortress so well?" she asked.

"When I communed with the Fact, I learned a great many things," he replied. He jolted to a stop. "That way." They weaved through a large, vault-ceilinged room divided by free-standing wooden partitions.

"Where are we going?" Thorn demanded.

"To the bat-batteries." He stumbled on the word. "The room where the Brethren keep the spirits captive who do all the magic here." He skidded past a pair of metal doors. "This is it. Help me." They each spun a heavy screw that held the massive door bolts in place. The doors swung ponderously inward.

The room, another converted cistern like the one where Thorn had been held, was lined from floor to ceiling with wooden scaffolds. On the shelves were rank upon rank of cubic glass containers filled with yellow-green liquid. Plates of dull lead and copper were immersed in each cube, and a mare's nest of wiring fell from the scaffolding to a pair of copper rods buried in the center of the ceiling.

"They capture sunbeams," Rado recited, "and feed them to the spirits that move their machines."

"You mean if we smash these glass bowls, all their machines will stop?" He nodded, and Thorn kicked around under the scaffolding until she found a short balk of timber. Clutching the timber in both hands, she raised it high, ready to smash the closest container.

"No!" Rado shouted. "The water inside would burn your arm off. There's a better way." Fragments of Fact knowledge churned inside him. He turned aimlessly in a circle. "Metal . . . we need something metal."

Thorn dropped the timber and rooted around. Finally she found a length of iron chain. "Will this do?"

"Yes, but be careful the spirits don't strike you dead." A roar of voices echoed through the corridors outside. The guardians were back, searching for them.

"Spirits be damned," Thorn said. She hurled the chain at the farthest bank of containers. The iron links only cracked the thick glass bowls, but when the chain hit the wires, they stuck fast. A thunderclap blasted across the room, and lightning lashed from the ceiling rods to the floor, melting a deep gouge in the slate.

"Now you've done it! Now they're loose!" Rado yelled. Glass cases exploded, showering corrosive liquid everywhere. As the pair fled, more lightning erupted from the smoking, glowing wires, and the spirit boxes burst apart like eggs under a hammer.

Halfway back through the partitioned room, Thorn and Rado were confronted by eight men, four of whom were guardians armed with wooden staves. Thorn shouted a challenge at them and attacked. Rado had little choice but to follow.

She stormed in, kicking over furniture to impede the guardians' progress. One of them swung his club at her and missed. Thorn grabbed his outstretched arm and threw him forward. He hit a partition headfirst, fell, and didn't get back up. Thorn took his baton and broke it over her knee. She kept the piece with the sharp, splintered end.

The first guardian was lucky; the second man Thorn met tried to spar with his baton. She feinted under his attack and rammed the broken stave into his heart.

Rado bombarded the others with jars and boxes he snatched off tables close by. The unarmed Brethren gave ground until he was alongside Thorn. One box he snatched up rattled. He flipped the lid open. Cutlery.

"Give me that," Thorn said, digging her hand into

the open box. She came out with a bone-handled, two-tined fork. Tossing it to her right hand, she charged for the door. One brother stooped to retrieve a dropped stave. No sooner was it in his hand than she spiked it to the floor with the fork. His screams disheartened his comrades, who fled.

Rado threw the box of cutlery after them. "Thorn, listen," he said. "No matter what happens, keep going *up*. Understand? The way out of here is up, so if I'm knocked down, keep going. Find any stairs you can and keep going up."

She palmed the sweat from her forehead. "Who were you calling an ignorant bitch?" she asked coldly.

"That? I just wanted to let you know it was me." More commotion in the hall. "Blood, I'd give my right arm for a sword!"

"What would you wield it in? Your teeth?"

From the shouts and screams outside, it sounded to Rado like the Brethren really meant to have their heads. He'd never heard such caterwauling from men. He and Thorn ran along the passage toward the next set of stairs. The dazzle lamps on the walls flickered and went out.

Thorn crossed in front of him. "Tell me where to go," she said.

"Another twenty steps, and the stairs will be to the right," Rado said. She took his hand and led him through the black hallway. He felt an odd sense of relief at her touch.

Footsteps clattered on the bare stone floor.

"Guardians!" she barked. "Lie down, Rado, and don't move."

He dropped on his belly close to the wall. Thorn went on like a ghost in the night. The guardians were babbling insanely for some reason. Rado heard one chanting, "Butter, butter, tub of butter," over and over. One by one their voices were stilled. Rado tried not to think about Thorn moving among them, that ugly fork striking with impunity. The guardians didn't seem at all alarmed by their diminishing numbers; indeed, the last man spouted on about butter until Thorn silenced him forever.

She tapped Rado on the head. He flinched. "Rise, Count," she said.

"What was the matter with them? They sounded like they were drunk."

"Drunk or mad. Something's amiss with the Brethren, Rado. Those men could hardly walk, much less fight."

He tried to dredge some clue from his Fact memories. There was nothing there. He realized with dismay that his entire store of the Fact's knowledge was fading. Haltingly he confessed as much to Thorn.

"No matter," she said. "We keep going up, yes?"

On they went, ignored or missed by Brethren who blundered around the darkened fortress raving utter nonsense. They slipped by scores of guardians who shouted and pounded the walls with their batons in vain.

They entered a short passage with carpet on the

floor and tapestries on the walls. This meant they
were high up in the sanctuary, in the prelates' quarters.

"Where next?" asked Thorn. "Where are the
stairs?"

"I don't know," Rado stammered. He groped along
the cloth-covered wall. "I don't remember. . . ."

His hand closed around a cold metal handle. A
doorknob. Rado pushed down, and the door swung
in. The room beyond was richly furnished and lit by a
soft red glow coming from the ceiling.

Thorn barged past him to the source of the light.
"It's an atrium," she said. "We can get on the roof
from here." She dragged a thickly upholstered chair
away from a desk, positioning it under the skylight.
Rado picked up a roll of vellum from the desk.

"This is Goss's room," he muttered. A dying em-
ber of Fact memory flared briefly in his mind's eye.
The polished barthwood cabinet behind the desk
broke easily under the blows of his booted foot.

"What are you doing? Give a hand here!" Thorn
demanded. Even standing on the chair, she couldn't
reach the skylight.

"Here," he said, tossing her temple stiletto butt-
first to her. Thorn caught it. Rado reached into the
shattered cabinet and took out his dueling sword.
With the buckle snapped and the baldric settled on
his shoulder, he felt himself again.

He stood on the chair with Thorn and laced his fingers together. She planted a foot in his hands and

stood up. Thorn's head bumped the lattice covering the atrium. Rado heard her grunt, and the lattice toppled aside.

The red glow was the sunset. It warmed the black peak of Mt. Prios and tinted the white fortress a delicate pink. Rado threw a leg over the skylight rim and rolled out onto the roof.

The summit pyramid over the Fact's vault was far away, across a tile-covered plain. The flat roof was empty save for some iron rings set in the terra-cotta tiles and a few coils of heavy rope.

"Now what?" Thorn asked. "We're up as far as we can go. What now, my lord?"

"We should be here." He didn't remember why. "We should be here," Rado repeated.

Hoarse shouting and the sounds of general mayhem surrounded them. Thorn's gaze flicked uncertainly at the open skylight. The roof was too open, too exposed. If the guardians came after them in force . . . "Why didn't we go to the harbor?" she asked heatedly. "How do you expect to get off an island without a boat?"

The answer came swimming out of the sparse ruby clouds. Rado suddenly understood his compulsion to go up—a compulsion he'd gotten from the Fact. The flying ship was coming.

"See? This must be where it roosts," he said. The whale-shaped vessel put its blunt gray nose down and sank toward them. Shade claimed the underbelly of the craft, but they could see what looked like a small pinnace slung below the flying ship by means of ropes. A face appeared, peering over the pinnace's side, white against the dark gray hull.

The spinning wheel behind the small boat slowed, and Rado saw it was shaped like the huge bronze "flower" he'd seen in the streets of Miyesti. The word *propeller* came to mind, but it didn't mean anything to him.

"Follow me!" he said, running for the descending ship.

"Where are you going?" she shouted.

"To fly! To fly! Come on if you don't want to be left behind!"

The propeller stopped, then reversed direction. The flying ship drifted forward slowly, then began to retreat. The man in the pinnace saw Rado and Thorn running at him. He threw out some heavy-looking bags, and the wheel reversed again.

Rado leaped, and his hands caught the rail of the pinnace. Thorn jumped harder and bent her belly over the side of the boat. The flying sailor threw out more bags, and the ship lifted higher into the air.

By the time Rado was safe inside the pinnace, Thorn had the sailor down and the stiletto at his chin. "Don't," Rado warned. "We need him to work the ship." She jerked the frightened man to his feet.

"Please," he said, "can you tell me what to do? Every time I try to call the prelate, all I get is gibberish from the speaking box."

"You don't wear a headband," Thorn noted.

"Not when I'm flying," the man replied. "I have to keep a clear head."

"Turn this thing around and take us to Miyesti," said Rado.

"Oh, I cannot! I am forbidden to fly over the city before the tenth hour of night."

Thorn pricked him below the ear. "Take us to Miyesti," she said quietly. Wide-eyed, the sailor agreed.

He went to the small brass ship's wheel mounted at the fore end of the pinnace. He spun it hard to port, and the flying ship's nose came around. From their present height, they could already see the highest spires of the colleges on Banner Street.

Rado put his face into the wind. "Faster!" he shouted. The sailor pulled a long lever farther back. The propeller hummed louder, and the stream blew harder against Rado's grinning face.

Thorn was pale. "Do you like it?" Rado asked.

"Flying is for hawks, not people," she said. He laughed.

The sun dipped below Mt. Prios, and the crimson-washed sky turned purple. The sailor pushed a lever down, and a large dazzle lamp hanging from the pinnace's bowsprit blazed. The beam cut a swath across the wind-scoured strait. Rado yelled and pointed when the lamp picked out a cavorting dolphin.

The sky ship quivered. The hum of the whirling wheel changed pitch, and the sailor hurriedly worked his levers. "The spirits are failing," he cried. "I feared this! I was due to take on new spirits on Prios—"

"Will we fall?" asked Thorn, alarmed.

"Worse. We shall drift out to sea with the wind. Without food and water, we'll die!"

The dazzle declined from brilliant white to warm yellow. The sailor raised the forked lever and put out the lamp. The propeller recovered a bit but slowed again before long.

"Harbor Town!" Rado cried. He leaned over the side and shouted, "Ahoy, Harbor Town! Ahoy!"

Thorn said nothing but watched the weakening propeller. The sailor put the helm to starboard. His usual landing place was in the hills on the Kurukish mainland. The flying ship was a secret, he said, so the Brethren didn't dare keep it in the city.

They sailed over Harbor Town as the first stars were born in the new night sky. Torches and chimney fires winked below, and Rado shouted himself hoarse at people he couldn't even see.

"Be still, Rado," Thorn said. "Look, there are fires in the town!"

She was right. Several patches of orange and red pulsed beneath them. Strands of smoke drifted through the air. The sky sailor put the wheel over still farther to starboard to avoid the violent eddies. Flames were running up the sides of tall buildings and spilling out of the highest windows.

And then the propeller quit.

The metal spokes creaked and stopped. The sailor looked back in terror. "The spirits have gone," he gasped. "I've no control!" Already the offshore wind was pushing the sky ship back toward the harbor.

"What keeps us in the air?" asked Rado, still surveying the fires below.

"The bag holds in the god's breath," said the pale-faced sailor. "Being divine, it rises to heaven and lifts the ship with it. . . . We're going to die; we're going to die!"

Thorn squinted up at the bulging silk bag. "God's breath," she muttered. "I'll get us down!" She pulled Rado's sword from its sheath, raised the keen blade in both hands, and slashed into the hull over their heads. Rado and the sailor shouted for her to stop, too late. The pleated gray fabric split loudly, and a gust of cold, sulfurous air gushed out. The sky ship lurched, throwing them all to the bottom of the pinnace.

"You've killed us!" screamed the sailor.

"At least we won't starve," commented Rado.

The noxious air drained rapidly from the center of the ship. The hull buckled, pitching the pinnace back on its transom. The three tumbled to the stern, one atop the other. Nose and tail of the flying ship rose as the center bowed. They were falling at a rapid rate.

Rado clasped the pinnace's rail and hauled himself up. One of the taller Miyestan towers roared by, fire belching from the windows and molten lead running from the rainspouts. The heat singed his face as they passed. They skimmed over streets thick with people, all battling and screaming in full riot.

But there was no time to worry about the Miyestans; the flying ship was about to crash. The keel of the pinnace struck a rooftop and rebounded. Thorn was almost tossed overboard, but Rado snagged her legs and held on. The sailor, sick with fear, scrambled forward on hands and knees. He kicked a latch on the bottom of the boat, and a trapdoor fell open. As the ship bounced across the rooftops, the sailor gauged their speed and threw himself out. He hit the roof of one of the houses and flopped like a broken puppet.

The fins on the tail snagged a row of chimneys, slowing the deflated bag. They drifted over a burning house. Heat and smoke lifted the ship over a cluster of spiky metal towers covered with Fact symbols. Once past the towers, the ship sank on an even keel into a square north of Cormoring Way. Thorn and Rado jumped from the pinnace just before the collapsing hull could engulf them.

Solid ground was scarcely comforting. For some unknown reason, all of Miyesti seemed bent on ruin and murder this night. Rado and Thorn caught their breath in a sheltered doorway and watched mobs rage up and down the street, attacking anyone not part of their gang. These weren't thugs and criminals, but ordinary men and women—and children, too— howling hatred and madness to the sky. The only thing the mobs had in common was that they were led by headband-wearing Brethren.

"Do you see?" asked Rado, pointing to the marauding mobs. "The Prios insanity has spread."

Thorn picked up a guardian's lost baton from the

street and hefted it. "Then we shall fight our way to safety," she said.

Harbor Town was the logical place to go. It was freer of the influence of the Fact, and they could get a ship there. When a lull opened between the rampaging hordes, Rado and Thorn started down the hill toward the sea.

Everywhere were signs of chaos. Windows were shattered, doors battered down, petty valuables scattered in the street. Go-abouts smashed into houses, each other, and unfortunate citizens. Here and there the sick, the injured, and the dead lay untended. Those still living pleaded for help, but there was no help forthcoming. They passed a wounded brother gnawing the pavement in an unfathomable rage.

Thorn and Rado were within sight of the city walls when a crowd of crazed Miyestans appeared in their path. Thorn's belly tightened when she saw that some of them carried crossbows. Much of the large-scale destruction was the work of thunderbolts.

Thorn and the count turned and started up the block, but a mass of equally deranged people barred the way. No alleys offered escape. The two mobs spied each other and roared utter hatred.

"What about the houses?" asked Rado, eyeing the blank doors. "We could barricade ourselves inside."

"No," Thorn said firmly. "They'd topple the walls down around us." She readied herself, stave in her left hand, stiletto in her right. "Keep to my back, Rado, and we'll carve these lunatics apart!"

He stepped back until he felt her bump against him. He looped the tip of his sword in wide circles. A knot swelled in his throat. Rado swallowed, trying to force it down his gullet.

The two mobs rushed together. Rado felt as if he were standing between two collapsing houses. Thorn shouted and tore into them, cracking skulls right and left. Their attackers were the same folk who, a day earlier, had been models of decorum. Now they were ravening wolves. When the crude weapons were struck from their hands, the Miyestans tore up the paving stones for bludgeons. The press of the rear ranks often overcame those in front. Trodden to the ground, the Miyestans still continued to fight.

No one paid Rado or Thorn any special attention. They were submerged in a river of total anarchy, raw bloodlust set free. Working together, Thorn and Rado were able to hew a path to the edge of the street. Backs to a stout stone wall, they held off the rioters with some success. Soon the dead and the insensible made such a bulwark around them that some of the Miyestans turned to other, easier foes.

"How long does this go on?" asked Rado.

"Until they're dead or we are," Thorn replied.

Fatigue assailed them more surely than any of the rioters. Rado's sword arm took on the weight of lead. In time, he could only parry. Thorn wasn't doing much better. The baton broke, leaving her with the stiletto, a close-in weapon that exposed her to side and back blows.

She had just finished off a man brandishing a cleaver, when the man behind him struck her with a broken table leg. Thorn fell to her knees. A trio of women showered her with cobblestones, and Thorn went facedown on the bloody street.

Rado bellowed and advanced into the melee. He stood over his fallen partner, slashing and thrusting. A cobble hit him in the chest. He ran a smoke-stained guardian through. The sword felt so heavy now he had to use both hands just to keep it on guard.

Somewhere far off in the throng, someone blew a hunting horn. The flat notes echoed far and wide off the stone dwellings. The mob drew away from Rado. He used the opportunity to drag Thorn back to the wall. Standing over her, he leaned his blade on his shoulder. Blood ran down the blade so thickly the cup hilt was coated with gore.

A forest of pikes and halberds appeared in the lower end of the street. The Hunter's horn sounded again, nearer this time. For the first time, indecision appeared on the faces of the rioters. Some began to run. As the mob was thus distracted, Rado set Thorn up against the wall. She had a fine goose-egg bruise over her left eye, but she was breathing normally.

The pikes swung down level. The horn blared, and the traditional chase cry of "Blood and boot! Blood and boot!" erupted from the pikemen, who charged the mob. The few Miyestans who stood their ground were cut to pieces. The great mass of rioters recovered their senses enough to flee for their lives.

Rado strained to see who was clearing the streets. Kuruks? Landed corsairs?

Riding behind the front ranks of pikemen was Princess Sverna. She spied Rado slumped against the wall and turned her dappled gray gelding in his direction. The pikemen continued on up the street, putting the last Miyestans to rout. A guard of halberdiers escorted the princess, and a motley company of bowmen followed close on their heels.

"Count Rado," said Sverna. "Are you well?"

"I'll live."

"And the Sentinel?"

"She's had a nasty whack, but she'll live, too."

"I rejoice. The hour of destiny has come, my lord. The Goddess has thrown down the infidels, and the city is in her hands once more."

"Who are these men?" Rado asked. He could barely see, he was so tired.

"The men of Harbor Town answered my call to arms. When the madness struck the Brethren, the guardians abandoned the gates. We entered at four points and fought our way here."

The sword fell from Rado's fingers, ringing dully on the sticky pavement. "When did the madness strike?" he murmured.

"Why, two hours before sunset," said Sverna. Or shortly after Rado broke the vial of the Goddess's Tears over the image of the Fact.

XVI

Violence persisted throughout the night. By the rising of the sun, a pained and suffering silence hovered over Miyesti.

Sverna and the army of Harbor Town won the streets, but they were too few to occupy every house in the city. The common folk awoke that first morning feeling shattered and betrayed. The Brethren had promised them peace and plenty. Now the Brethren were dead in the streets or raving in chains after capture by Sverna's army.

The princess rode to the College of Peace, and from a balcony overlooking Banner Street declared the Fact and its worship outlawed. No one cheered. Few were thinking of spiritual matters that morning.

Without the constant stream of knowledge flowing into their heads, the Brethren and guardians lost everything. Dazzle lamps and go-abouts no longer worked. Moving rooms and talking boxes became useless blocks of wood and metal. The Brethren's galleots and feluccas beached themselves and were burned by laughing Harbor Town boatmen.

A hospital was organized in the College of Health. The wards soon overflowed with burned and injured citizens. The healers from Harbor Town couldn't cope with the swell, and many Miyestans died of basically minor wounds. Sadness spread like a plague, and the western gates of the city were thereafter clogged with people leaving for the inland country of the Kuruks.

Rado, rested but not restored, rode with Thorn to Sverna's palace. And who should greet them there but Geffrin, the Emerald duelist and gambler. He was acting as chamberlain to the princess.

"The streets are being cleared of the dead," Geffrin reported. "Pyres have been built on the plain to consume them. No one knows for certain, but the healers estimate perhaps a hundred thousand men, women, and children died in the riots and fires."

"There are more dead on Prios," said Rado. "Has anyone gone there yet?"

"I believe that's what Her Highness wants to discuss with you," said Geffrin. Outside the door to the princess's chamber, Geffrin paused and offered a hand to Rado. "You've done the world a great service," he said. "You've saved it from a consuming evil."

Rado shook his hand, but it was a hollow gesture. All he could think of were the hundred thousand dead Miyestans.

Sverna received them like a queen. She had a tall chair set on a platform, and armed Harbor Towners formed an honor guard along the wall.

"Greetings, my lord! Greetings, Sentinel! I am pleased to see you," she said.

Rado bowed and replied, "Thank you, Highness. We came as quickly as we could." Thorn remained stonily silent.

"The work repairing the city goes apace. It's a prodigious job, but the Miyestans are beginning to recover from their delusions and are joining in. In six weeks, Miyesti will be a civilized port again." She paused and looked thoughtful. "I called you here to give you a mission." Rado and Thorn exchanged glances. "I want you to go to Prios."

"For what?" asked Thorn bluntly.

"I want you to bring back the dead carcass of the Fact. I intend to display it to the world. I want no rumors to resurrect it in the future."

"We accept the charge," said Thorn.

"We?" muttered Rado.

"Excellent. I have mustered a company of men to escort you, in case the Brethren on Prios decide to fight. The madness seems to have spent itself, but there's no sense taking unnecessary risks," said Sverna. "The lugger *Tryfon* awaits you at Half Moon Dock. Good luck, and may the Goddess go with you."

She held out her hand. Rado bowed his head to it. Thorn merely sniffed and turned her back to leave.

* * * * *

Tryfon tacked across the strait, fighting a steady landward breeze. The lugger took three hours to reach Prios, much longer than the oared *Promicon* had. It was just past noon when *Tryfon* approached the Prios mole.

The first thing they noticed was the felucca, capsized at its moorings. The portside oars stuck in the air like the legs of a crushed spider. Sailors on the lugger ran out a plank to the mole, and Thorn was the first across. The twenty marines Sverna sent included the *Tryfon*'s crew, so Thorn ordered four men to stay by the boat with a signal horn. If they had trouble, a trumpet call would bring the others back.

The mole was clear. Thorn, Rado, and the armed sailors patrolled both sides carefully and saw no one. Thorn waved for them to follow her, and they went up the causeway to the silent sanctuary.

Gulls flew up, squawking. Where the causeway steps began there were bodies, four or five of them, and the seabirds had been feasting. Thorn studied the remains.

"What are you looking for?" asked Rado.

"Goss or the prelator," she said. By their equipment, the dead men were probably guardians. They continued on.

The main doors were wide open. Blood stained the marble steps. It was dark inside the windowless corridors, too dark, so the sailors smashed furniture for torches. Rado knew the interior best, so he took the lead.

The stillness was profound. Nothing stirred within the fortress except them. Here and there they found the corpse of a brother, usually battered to death. The sailors closed in together, fearful to be in this den of magic and madness.

They kicked open a few doors and found strange workshops. Here were made the spirit boxes that moved the go-abouts, the glass globes for the dazzle lamps, and the intricate interior parts that went in the talking boxes. The workshops were untouched. Every tool lay where the last man had left it; nothing was broken. Whatever the contagion had been among the Brethren, it hadn't possessed them to smash the birthplace of the Fact's marvels.

The higher in the sanctuary they went, the more corpses they found. They began to find them in groups, beaten and strangled by each other. Windows on the highest levels were broken out by a regular procession of Brethren who leaped from the heights to the tiled roofs below. By the time the expedition reached the vault of the Fact, not one living brother had been found.

Rado reached for the door at the top of the stairs. Beyond lay the vault. The sailors hung back. He said to Thorn, "Do you want to see it? It will surprise you."

She followed him. The thick metal door creaked back and stopped.

The Fact was gone.

The pedestals were there, supporting nothing; the

snaking wires hung limply from the smaller metal cases. Rado swore.

"It was here! Right here, standing on those glass rods! It was a diamond-shaped thing, all gold, as big as I am. Just like the symbols, only solid."

"Could it move itself?" asked Thorn.

"No—that is, I don't think so."

"Then the Brethren must have moved it."

"I don't see how! It was too large to fit through the door. I think they built the vault around it so no one could ever steal it."

Thorn slapped a loose bundle of hanging wire. "Well, it's gone. Maybe it went back to wherever it came from."

"Sverna isn't going to like this."

"Well, I don't like it either, and neither will the One Who Commands."

The sailors were suitably awed when Rado told them the Fact had disappeared. Some fingered amulets of their favorite gods. Others made the sign of the Goddess to ward off evil.

"What shall we do now, lady?" asked the *Tryfon's* master.

"Go back to Miyesti," Thorn said.

On the causeway, Rado happened to look to the north end of the anchorage. The black hull of the *Oribos* no longer stood in its stocks on the beach. He urged the others to investigate.

False ribs of wood stood inside the thick scaffolding. The hull of the *Oribos* had been assembled in this frame. The shape was square and high. The keel had gouged a broad gully in the sand. *Oribos* had been launched.

A sailor rapped his knuckles on a pile of black plates eight hands square. "These are iron!" he exclaimed.

The plates had rows of holes along parallel edges. The sailors stood one upright. "Do you think they built that ship of these?" said Rado.

"Nay," said the lugger's captain. "Iron don't float."

Thorn noticed a long row of wooden casks. She sniffed the bung of one. "Jodra oil," she said. This was a common edible oil among the Kuruks, who pressed it from fist-sized jodra nuts.

"I guess they oiled the plates to keep them from rusting," Rado said.

The oil gave Thorn an idea. They rolled forty casks up the causeway to the sanctuary. There Thorn stove in lid after lid and dumped the contents in the corridors. The white fortress reeked of jodra nuts.

"Get me a torch and stand clear," Thorn said. She whirled a torch around her head, whipping the flames to red heat. Then she flung the torch into the puddled oil. Instantly smoky flames filled the passages.

The sailors cheered. Fire was a solution they understood. They admired the flames so much they ran back to the beach and set the ribs and scaffolding afire. Every structure on Prios was burning by the time they returned to the *Tryfon*.

"Raise sail, master," Thorn said as soon as they boarded.

"Is this truly the end of the Fact?" the man asked.

"The Fact is dead," said Thorn.

"Dead and gone," added Rado. "Can't you see the funeral fires?"

Fifth: The Price Of Millennium

I am chaos. I am the substance from which your artists and scientists build rhythms. I am the spirit with which your children and clowns laugh in happy anarchy. I am chaos. I am alive, and I tell you that you are free.

Malaclypse the Younger,
Principia Discordia

XVII

Weeks escaped into the past, and the terrors of the night the Fact died began to fade. The life of Harbor Town seeped through the city wall and infected Miyesti. The people adapted quickly to the return of horses, candles, and the old pantheon of deities. Taverns appeared on many corners, none of them lacking in patronage. Brothels opened. They did well, too. Trade by single craftsmen, suppressed by the Brethren in favor of their magic workshop goods, resumed with verve. The clean streets acquired a lively coat of grime, and the impossibly tall buildings were abandoned. Within a few weeks, the upper stories vanished as masons plundered them for their stone. It was an eerie sight against the dawn or dusk sky—the skeletons of timber and iron picked clean of marble. As the moon grew round again, even that disappeared into the hands of the insatiable scavengers.

"A year from now you won't be able to tell Miyesti from Harbor Town," Rado declared to Thorn. "There won't be any difference."

They had audiences with the princess every day.

Thorn was the de facto chief of the new City Guard, and Rado lent his expertise by advising Sverna on the licensing of taverns and the taxation of pleasure houses. With his help, a generous treasury accumulated in the halls of the former College of Light.

Two months to the day after Thorn and Rado first entered Miyesti, Princess Sverna presented them with a ring of keys.

"What's this, Highness?" asked Thorn.

"These are the keys to the once princely houses, seven in all. The families of Miyesti's ancient nobility forfeited their rank and property when they gave their allegiance to the Brethren. Now they belong to me. As a reward for your very great services, I offer you your choice. Choose a key and choose a house."

Rado was beside himself. "Any one I want?"

"Yes, my lord. Establish the House of Hapmark in Miyesti. It is your right," Sverna said.

Rado took the ring. Some of the keys were old and worn from long use. One or two were fairly new. He chose the newest and straightest key. The princess was amused. "Why that one, my lord?"

"A new key means a well-tended lock, and a well-tended lock means a sound house," answered Rado.

"And rich furnishings," Thorn added dryly.

Sverna took the ring and offered it to Thorn. "Will you not take residence with us, Sentinel? I have sent envoys to Pazoa, to the great temple, and asked them to send a priestess endowed to begin a new temple in Miyesti. You can be First Sentinel of our temple if you desire."

The ring hung from the princess's creamy fingers. Thorn did not move to accept them.

"I thank Your Highness, but I cannot. I am not worthy to be First Sentinel of any temple."

"You are too modest! Your deeds will be sung forever. Women from here to the Homelands will honor you for your courage and daring."

Thorn cast her eyes down. "I cannot accept. I have not yet fulfilled every part of my charge. By the time of the autumn equinox, I must complete my last task and then take ship for home."

Rado caught her arm. "What task remains?"

"It's none of your concern. Your debt is discharged. For me, the hardest task still remains," she said.

Rado looked from Thorn to the puzzled princess. Sverna could only shrug her shoulders as Thorn bowed her head and left. Rado closed his fist hard around his new house key. "I never have understood that woman," he said.

"She seems pale to me. Has she been ill?" asked the princess.

"I do not know, Highness. Since our second return from Prios, the Sentinel and I have kept to separate quarters. I can inquire about it if you like."

Sverna reclined on her plush throne. "Oh, do not bother her. The strain of recent days would tax the strongest of men. Go in peace, Count Rado, and give the Sentinel my regards."

* * * * *

The mansion Rado chose formerly belonged to the princes Zodram, who for many years had controlled the resin concession with the inland Kurukish growers. Not only did Rado gain a magnificent new home, but he also discovered a cellar bursting with the finest and rarest smoking resins in the world.

"The queer thing is," he confided to Thorn, "I haven't wanted a pipe in weeks. I have a lot of catching up to do!"

Thorn divided her days between Sverna's palace, the erstwhile College of Peace, and Rado's new home. The princess formed a privy council to assist her in ruling Miyesti, and once the council was firmly established, Thorn found less and less to do. She turned over command of the City Guard to an ex-soldier named Phedrico, whom Sverna favored. That done, she took to spending her days on the broad, elevated veranda at the new House of Hapmark. Rado instructed his corps of servants to wait on her hand and foot. Thorn made few demands—a cup of cool water, a plate of fruit. In the midst of his new and exalted position, Rado took notice of her increasing withdrawal from the quickening pace of life in the city.

"What ails you?" he demanded, finding her alone on the veranda one sunny afternoon. "One would think you were mourning for the Fact."

"Your humor is as genuine as your title, Count," she said sourly. Despite the warm, bathing rays of the sun, Thorn did indeed seem rather pale.

"You're avoiding the question," he replied. "What's the matter with you?"

"Do you ever have doubts, Rado? I am beset with them, and I have only a short time to master them if I am to succeed."

"What sort of doubts? Can I help?"

"No one can help me, my lord."

He laughed a bit. "Merry, that's the first time you've called me that in weeks, and for the first time, it's true." She didn't hear him. Already her eyes were focused on some distant, unseen horizon.

He left her there. Inside the great house, he almost collided with the maidservant he'd assigned to tend to Thorn. The young Miyestan girl's arms were laden with clothing.

"Selling your mistress's clothes?"

The girl blushed. "No, my lord! I was just obeying milady's orders," she blurted. Rado lifted a few items off the top of the heap. Tunic, vest, pants . . . Thorn's entire wardrobe was here.

"What orders?" he snapped.

"I'm to get rid of these," the girl said.

"Nonsense. What's Thorn to do, run naked in the halls?" The maid blushed anew.

"Milady gave me money to buy her new clothes. I sent the coachman this morning to fetch them from the seamstress. They're in her room now."

This Rado had to see. He sent the girl on her way and ran upstairs to Thorn's rooms. He'd given her an entire wing of the Zodram palace, but she never used any room except the large open salon. Laid out on the hard couch where Thorn slept were dresses and small-clothes such as any woman Thorn's age might wear. Not extravagant gowns, to be sure; all were simple, sturdy, and ordinary. But that a Sentinel of the Temple should be clad in such normal female array was to Rado mildly astonishing. He sank down on a gilt-legged ottoman and pondered the meaning behind this odd development.

Then Rado had a startling idea.

Thorn had pledged her life to the success of their mission, to destroy the Fact. The Fact was dead, so Thorn was free, he realized. She had no reason to re-main a priestess! That had to be it. Thorn was giving up her stiletto, but the notion of living a life beyond the austerity of temple order frightened her. Maybe he could help after all. No one knew how to enjoy life more than Rado of Hapmark!

He went to the writing table and took out two sheets of fine vellum that still bore the Zodram coat-of-arms. He wrote a short note rapidly on the first sheet but took his time with the second, longer letter. When he was done, he sprinkled powder over the pages to dry the ink and rang for the butler. A young footman, his collar askew, ran in with coattails flap-ping. Rado sighed and gave him the letters.

"Do you know where these places are?" he asked, tapping a finger on the addresses. The Miyestan could read, and told Rado so. "Then deliver these as fast as you can." The boy was almost out the door before Rado finished his instructions. "And wait for a reply!" he shouted after him.

He slapped his palms on the table. What an idea! Why hadn't he thought of it sooner?

XVIII

Rado knocked on the door to Thorn's suite. He could see lamplight shining under the door, so he knew she was inside and awake.

"May I enter?" he asked.

"Come."

The high-ceilinged salon was awash in rose light. The sun had set half a bell earlier, and its fading light was bolstered feebly by a guttering lamp beside Thorn's couch. The Sentinel sat on the couch with her knees drawn up, facing the crimson-stained sky in the west windows. Her legs were covered by a woolen lap blanket. Rado looked over her shoulder and saw Thorn had an old-fashioned wax-covered writing board propped on her legs. She seemed to be ciphering long columns of numbers.

"Are you busy?" he asked.

"No," she answered, without looking up.

"I have something for you."

"Not now, Rado. . . ."

"It's a gift," he said, his tone growing firmer. He wasn't going to be put off. "I have it right here."

She set the board aside and dropped her feet to the floor. Rado snapped his fingers, and the unkempt young footman marched in bearing a dazzling sky-blue gown of finest silk. The wide neckline met at the shoulders a standing arc collar, six fingers tall in the center—the very height of Pazoan fashion. The clasps were all carved from native blue sapphires, and the hem swept the floor with deep, full pleats.

Thorn's face was blank. "What's this?"

"A dress, you fool. It's for you," Rado said proudly.

"Why would you imagine that I would wear such a thing?"

His expression rapidly darkened. "Because I thought you might like to dress like a real woman for a change! I saw the serving girl taking your boy's rags away, and I thought—"

"You think too much, my lord. In two days, the equinox will occur. At that time, I must return to the temple. I sent for simple clothing to travel in because I am tired of being Count Rado's valet. That's all."

Rado snatched the gown from the footman and gruffly ordered him out. When they were alone, he flung the elegant dress on the floor at her feet and said, "Leave then, and let me be rid of you once and for all."

He stalked to the door and flung it wide. The sounds of a large crowd filtered upstairs. Over the drone of talk and the sharp punctuation of laughter, Rado said, "I'm entertaining tonight. Join us or not, as you choose." The door shut with a hollow boom.

Thorn stared at the carved sagerwood door panels.
Her gaze drifted down to the crumpled silk gown lying at her feet. Slowly she reached out her hand to the
web-soft material.

The crowd in the great hall hushed when she appeared at the top of the stairs. Rado couldn't help but
smile when he saw her. The dress fit like a scabbard,
and Thorn made a strange and striking figure, with
her cropped hair and freckled shoulders showing in
the wide neck of the Pazoan gown. Rado mounted
the steps until he stood just one below her.

"What's the meaning of all this?" she asked.

"It's a celebration. For you," he said. "You've been
so pensive the past few weeks, I thought a little revelry would cheer you and perhaps lighten the burden
you seem to be carrying."

"You did this for me?"

Color invaded his cheeks. He chewed his mustache.
"Yes . . . well, any excuse to drink and dance is welcome." Rado held out his hand. When she took it,
the crowd let out a roar of approbation. The sound
struck Thorn like a slap in the face, and she dropped
Rado's hand. Without another word, he stepped
briskly down the stairs. Music squealed, and the
crowd engulfed Rado.

Thorn descended slowly, her heels clunking on the
stone risers. One of the Zodram servants appeared
with a tray of cut-glass goblets, brimming with gold-
en liquid. "Mead, milady?" asked the servant.

Distractedly Thorn took a glass. "What is it?" she

asked.

"Mead," the fellow repeated. "It's traditional in Miyesti to serve mead from Equinox Eve until the first ale is tapped on the winter solstice."

Equinox Eve. The Miyestans reckoned days by sunset, so it was already the day before the day of sacred balance.

She stepped into a swirl of people, all strangers. Rado had simply emptied taverns wholesale and transported the clientele here. They had the look of Harbor Towners—that is, rough and lively. As she wandered through the room, Thorn caught a shrill giggle rising above the chatter and pipe music. There was Rado, wedged between a painted Kuruk woman and a redheaded fancy girl. He said something in the Kuruk's ear, and she shrieked with laughter.

A hand came down on her shoulder. She flinched and turned sharply on one heel, poised to strike.

"Many greetings!" said a swarthy, smiling man. "You remember me, no?"

"You are familiar," said Thorn, relaxing.

The man lifted his arms and did a fast shuffle with his feet. "Indolel! Ishaf Indolel. Do you remember?"

"Oh, yes . . . the dancer from the Wild Bull."

"Exactly so! How kind it is you recall me. You are the servant of his lordship. A generous man, his lordship. But you are not what you seemed, no? Imagine, a woman who can fight as you do—"

Thorn made a dismissive gesture. The gown clung to her, pressing in unfamiliar places. Indolel bowed and retreated. She drifted on until she came to a fairly quiet spot in the corner below the staircase. A wave of nausea stirred in her belly. Gripping a stone baluster, Thorn called another servant over.

"Would you care for another glass, lady?" It wasn't until then she realized she'd drunk the first one.

"Why not?" She gave him the empty goblet and took a fresh, full one. The mead was very sweet and warm. It flowed easily down her throat and pooled gently in her stomach. Thorn had never tasted spirits before. The regimen she followed as a Sentinel did not prohibit imbibing; it was just that she had always held herself above common drunkenness.

"That's the way!" Rado shouted. Thorn opened her eyes. He waved an empty glass over his head. "Drink! Enjoy!" he shouted.

Why not? "Why not?" she said aloud. The people nearest her stared. Thorn pushed through a sea of shoulders to where Indolel stood talking in rapid Kurukish to some of his compatriots. Thorn dropped a heavy hand on his arm and spun him around.

"Dance," she demanded.

"Pardon, lady, but the music is not right," said Indolel.

"I'll fix that."

She went to the band, hired as a group from the Wild Bull, and said, "Play for him so he can dance." The piper knew Ishaf, so he struck up a vigorous Kurukish tune.

A circle cleared around Indolel. He made a sweep-

ing bow to the band and flipped his hand in salute to
Thorn. Then he lifted one leg and began to whirl in
tight circles, with sudden flings of his hands up or
down, in and out. The revelers applauded and fell to
clapping in time with the drumbeat.

A Kuruk woman gave a wild shout and leaped into
the circle. She stood back to back with Indolel, and
they competed to see who could do a step the other
couldn't duplicate. Indolel leaped and kicked, one
leg, then the other, bowed and swung his feet in
loops high over his head. The woman kept up for a
while, then ran out of strength. She staggered back
into the crowd. Indolel strutted around with his knees
deeply bent, squatting and kicking at the same time.

Thorn drained her fourth—or was it fifth?—
measure of mead and flung the goblet over her shoulder. She knocked a kissing couple apart and stood on
the edge of the circle, watching the Kuruk dancer
show off.

Indolel was having a grand time. He smiled at the
women as he passed, and many smiled back. Perhaps
he would be lucky tonight. Perhaps one of them
would seek his favor after such a magnificent per-
formance.

The cheers and clapping increased, and Indolel became aware it was not all for him. The eyes of the
crowd trailed behind him. He leaned around on his
hands, never letting his legs stop moving.

Thorn was behind him, imitating his every move,
down to the little toss of his head that Indolel gave

the ladies. The Kuruk stood and did an especially hard rolling spin. Thorn mimicked him perfectly, the blue gown sweeping up around her like an opening blossom. Indolel did a squat kick while dancing backward, and she followed step for step. Indolel was getting tired. Sweat sheened his face, and he no longer smiled. He moved in and took Thorn by the hand and waist, and together they brought the crowd up on its toes with delight. Then Thorn reversed their hands' positions and *led* Indolel through the very same routine.

The musicians broke first and quit playing. Thorn and the Kuruk stepped apart, panting. The crowd surrounded them, shaking and pounding on the dancers' backs. Rado wiggled through the throng to Thorn.

"Amazing! Damndest thing I ever saw!" he said. "I didn't know you could dance!"

"I can't," she replied. "I can only imitate Indolel."

A tray of mead floated by, and Thorn grabbed two goblets. Rado grinned as she drained them both, but his amusement vanished when she hurled the heavy glasses across the room.

"You've had enough," he said, close to her ear. "Come with me."

Holding her by an elbow, Rado ushered Thorn up the stairs. Men cheered and whistled as they went. Some offered dangerous advice. Rado waved nervously and shouted, "Not tonight, my friends! There are many ladies here, and as host, I should not be selfish with my attentions!" Massed laughter followed them up the steps.

He shoved Thorn into her room. "I wanted you to have a good time," he said. "I should have known you can't drink. That would be fine and princely, wouldn't it, to have you assault one of my guests because you're drunk? Well, stay here and sleep it off!"

Thorn said nothing. She walked swiftly to the couch and lowered herself to the cushions.

"Are you well?" asked Rado.

"Oh, yes," she said.

He returned to the celebration. Thorn lay in the dark for hours. No flying ship added its dazzle lamp to the fitful light of the quarter moon. Mead coursed through her veins. She rode on it, as she would a wild horse. Sweat chilled on her face. Her doubts fled, banished by the heat of drink and dancing. Tomorrow was the day. She would fulfill the last act of her destiny.

Thorn caught the front of the Pazoan gown in her fingers. The muscles in her arm tightened, and she tore the blue silk down to her waist.

XIX

The great house was still at last. Raucous revelers had inhabited the old Zodram palace for two nights and a day, singing, fighting, drinking, eating in total joyous frenzy, like a wildfire fed by servants bearing trays of mead and platters of meat. In the square outside the palace, curious cityfolk gathered, drawn by tales of the riotous merrymaking going on inside.

Through all the happy mayhem, Thorn's suite remained an island of guarded peace. Now and then a pixilated couple in the throes of romance would burst in, searching for a quiet room to occupy, only to be repelled by Thorn's stern frown and glittering stiletto. She did not harm anyone. No one came near enough for that. One look at the naked Sentinel, seated cross-legged on the floor, honing her weapon with a chip of oilstone, was enough to convince the most stupefied lovers to go elsewhere.

By nightfall of the second day of the revel, the house had settled into an exhausted silence. The servants went to their quarters and fell dead asleep across their narrow beds. The city bells tolled as equal day met equal night.

Thorn prepared herself. She had eaten nothing since the mead had worn off twenty-four hours ago. From a giant pitcher standing in the corner, she poured cold water into a basin. She dipped a cloth in the water and pressed it dripping to her face, her neck, and breasts. She washed completely, even to the soles of her feet.

From her small travel case, the one she'd brought all the way from Pazoa without opening, Thorn removed her last clean garments, a gray clerical robe and a silk vest of bright scarlet. The vest hung almost to her knees. She combed her hair with a silver comb once used by the princesses of the House of Zodram. In the past six weeks, her hair had grown out enough to cover her neck again.

She walked upstairs, making no sound at all. Sodden men and women lay on the floor or sprawled in unlikely, and uncomfortable, positions on the furniture. Thorn didn't look at them. Her feet fell lightly on the ancient carpets. Eyes closed, she counted with precision the number of steps to Rado's room.

The handle of his chamber door turned easily. Inside, she heard the noisy breathing of more than one sleeper. Which one had he picked? Nearer the bed, she opened her eyes and saw two contrasting heads of hair, one black, one red. The fancy girl and the Kuruk both had made it to Rado's bed.

But where was Rado?

Thorn spied a pair of feet with knobby white toes

protruding from under a blanket. Rado had pushed
two couches together and was sleeping there. She put
her hand over his mouth.

His eyes sprang open, and a lost word vibrated
against her palm. "Say nothing," she whispered.
"Rise and walk with me."

Disheveled and confused, Rado followed Thorn
out into the corridor. "What's this all about? Why are
you dressed that way?"

She paused a few paces ahead of him, framed by
dozing drunkards. "I'm leaving," she said.

"What, now? You woke me to tell me that?"

Thorn didn't answer but continued along the passage until she reached the door to her suite. She beckoned to Rado to follow her. Yawning and scratching
the belly of his mead-stained shirt, he stumped down
the hall. When he entered her room, Thorn was lighting a candle. "Close the door, Rado," she said. He
pushed the elaborately carved panel shut.

"So you're leaving," he said, hands on hips.
"What do you want from me? Money? I can give you
as much as you need; Sverna has been very liberal
with the privy purse."

"I don't want your money, Rado. There's something I have to tell you." She held her hand near the
candle flame, as Sentinel Oriath did with the old
priestess Kapthys long ago. "I am with child, Rado,"
she said.

A single eyebrow—his left one—twitched. "Mine?
Of course it's mine." He sat down shakily. "Are you

certain?"

Thorn pressed a hand to her lower belly. "I am. I've known for several weeks."

"So that's why you were acting so strange—why you gave up your boy's clothing! Why didn't you tell me?" he said sharply.

"What difference would it have made? I am no farm girl, dreaming of a dashing husband. And you no more want me for your wife than I want you as a husband, so don't pretend you care about me now."

He cupped his face in his hands. "I never meant this to happen." She shrugged. "I will help you," he went on. "There are healers, wise women who know how to end things . . . certain potions . . ."

"That's not a choice," Thorn said. "I am an initiate of the temple. The life I carry already belongs to the Goddess. I cannot shed it like some soiled garment."

Rado made a sudden long step toward her. "Then stay here in Miyesti. Stay at least until the child is born. Hunter's blood, I know what kind of man I am and what sort of woman you are, but I've got a place here. This house, my title. We're not the good father and mother of hearth legend, but I daresay we can bring the child up right."

She turned away and went to the veiled windows. Thorn looked through the gauze curtains. The square was white with mild moonlight, and the veil seemed to cast a mist over the houses.

Rado clasped her arms from behind gently. "I want a son. Bear the child here, and leave him to me, if you must. I'll pay back all the gold I owe the temple."

Twisting out of his grasp, she dashed across the room. Her face bore a hunted look, something Rado had never seen there before. "You don't understand," said Thorn quickly. "None of us act by our own will. The Goddess has chosen our fates, Rado. Neither you nor I can deny them."

"Oh, rot! Haven't you learned anything? We killed a god, didn't we? These gods and goddesses are no more to us than we are to a rabbit in the forest— bigger, yes, and they may know more than us, but they're not all-powerful. We *give* them their power over us." Rado was nearly shouting. He mustered his calm and lowered his voice. "I want my child. You can't take him from me," he said.

Thorn faced him. There was no pretense of love in their expressions. She crossed her arms under her vest. The moment of weakness was gone.

"The child belongs to the temple. I go back to Pazoa on the morning tide. It must be so, Rado, if the world is to remain free of the Fact," she said.

"What are you saying? What has the Fact got to do with our child?"

"The world has survived another thousand years. Tonight is the Millennium. In order to prepare for the next cycle, there must be one last act of contrition. The seed of the Godkiller must be preserved after his death."

In whatever instant that passes between knowledge and ignorance, Rado realized the truth. By reflex, his

hand went to his hip—for nothing. His sword hung
on the bedpost in his room. Thorn's hands dropped
to her side. The stiletto caught the single candle's
flame.

He ran to the door. Even as his hand closed over the
handle, he heard her bare feet whisper on the floor
and knew she was behind him. Rado threw himself
aside. The stiletto scored a chip out of the fine sagerwood panel. Rado blundered against an elegant side
table and reeled away, into the center of the salon.
Thorn didn't come after him directly. He saw her
standing by the candle. She licked her thumb and
forefinger and snuffed out the flame.

A heavy pall of darkness fell over Rado. He knew
she could see in the dark like a cat. His only chance
was the window; like the spy Ferengasso, taking the
time to open the door would only earn him a blade in
the back.

Moonlight silvered the shaft of the stiletto. Rado
caught her wrist in both hands, turned, and threw
Thorn against the closed windows. The frames
cracked, and a single pane fell out on the balcony but
did not break. He could see half her face—one eye,
one cheek, a swatch of unruly yellow hair. Rado might
have cried out and aroused the house to his defense,
but no one could have saved him. He knew it, and so
did she.

Lightning fast, Thorn flicked her wrist and tossed
the stiletto from one hand to the other. Rado could
not block the thrust of her free hand. The polished

steel point touched his heart. She felt his last breath
shudder through the shaft into her reaching hand.

"Godkiller," said Rado, and died.

The stiletto came out as easily as it had gone in. So
small was the wound, no blood clung to the slim
spike. Thorn dropped the weapon and bore Rado silently to the floor. His eyes were open. She closed
them.

Utter calm prevailed in the House of Hapmark.
Thorn covered Rado with the scarlet vest. Whoever
found him in the morning would have to look hard to
see the blood.

She recovered her stiletto, put on her shoes, and
closed the salon door quietly behind her.

XX

From the sea, Pazoa was unchanged. The timber houses, made gray by years of salt air, flowed up the hills to the middle town, the merchants' quarter, with its false marble columns and brown stucco walls. Overtopping these, at opposite ends of the city, were the royal palace and the great dome of the temple. Thorn came ashore in a skiff with the pilot who had guided her ship to safe anchorage. No one paid any special heed to her coming. No cheering multitude greeted her on the dock. The pilot, a leather-faced oldster with a grimy black cap and permanently squinting eyes, helped the pregnant woman up the ladder from the boat. Thorn stepped onto Homeland soil five months after leaving it.

She walked all the way to the temple, declining offers from several dray masters to give her a ride to her destination. Though her feet were sore and her back ached, she wanted very much to traverse the streets of Pazoa on foot, to immerse herself in the life she had almost forgotten.

The streets were full of farmers' wagons bringing

produce to the fall market festival. Ragged girls and boys trailed after groaning apple carts, waiting for a ripe present to fall into their hands. Thorn smiled at a tiny girl who had won such a prize. Eridé had once been an orphan of the street, and she remembered how sweet the apples of chance could be.

"Hello," she said. The girl clutched her apple in both hands, close to her thin chest. Her skinny fingers could scarcely encompass the hearty fruit. Thorn smiled and tried to look as unthreatening as possible, but the girl bolted anyway. A pack of jeering children trailed after her, trying to steal her prize.

Between the harbor houses and the merchants' quarter stood a ring of trees that encircled the center of Pazoa like a living moat. The oaks and maples were losing their leaves; already horses and men's feet had trodden the fallen leaves to yellow powder. The smell of crushed dry leaves was sharp in Thorn's nose, like incense.

Streets in the merchants' quarter were wider, but no less clogged with traffic. People made way for the pregnant woman. A cooper halted his pushcart in front of Thorn and presented her with an ash staff to lean on. She accepted it gratefully. It would be very useful in climbing the terraced lanes to the temple precinct.

The massive dome cast a wide shadow over the lower town, and when Thorn entered the shaded area, a chill crept into her limbs. She missed the warm sun of the seaside already. Climbing steadily up the irregular cobbles, she spied the outer wall of the sacred precinct. No one stood watch at the gates. That was a good sign. When times were bad, armed Sentinels stood guard to prevent the plundering of the temple's gardens. That the gate was untended meant Pazoa was placid and happy in the waxing days of autumn.

Thorn kissed the sacred glyph by the gate as she had done a thousand times. The gate stood back hard against the brick wall, held open by a stake pounded into the mossy earth. Thorn leaned her staff against the wall and dipped a gourd into the woman-sized stone jar that stood inside the gate. Even the rainwater in Pazoa tasted sweet.

She heard voices and saw two temple sisters pruning dead limbs from plum trees that lined the path to the Inner Temple. "Hello, Aridane," she called to the plump older woman bracing the ladder.

The priestess squinted. Aridane still hadn't gotten her spectacles. "Who are you? This is sacred soil. Do you have business here?"

"Don't you recognize me, Dani?"

She closed the gap between them to a scant three paces. Aridane's face brightened. "Eridé! Mother save my eyes! Kilowe, it's Eridé!"

The gray-haired sister atop the ladder set aside her bowsaw. "So it is," she remarked without much enthusiasm. "Is that any reason to let go of the ladder?"

Aridane hastily resumed leaning on the ladder. "We've been counting the days till your return," she said. "Why didn't you let us know you were coming? We would have met the ship."

"Oh, I wanted to come home quietly."

"Stop shaking the ladder!" commanded Kilowe.

Aridane turned around and sat on the most convenient rung. Kilowe raised the saw and lopped off a dead branch. "You've had quite an adventure, haven't you?" asked the sister from her lofty perch.

"Indeed. Enough for a lifetime."

Aridane took her hand. "You look so wan. Was it a hard voyage?" The priestess didn't notice Thorn's swelling belly, covered in the loose folds of a seaman's coat. From above, however, Kilowe could see Thorn's condition clearly.

"Don't keep her standing there all day, Dani," she chided her nearsighted friend. "Eridé must be exhausted."

"I must see the One Who Commands," Thorn said. She asked the two priestesses if they knew where the high priestess was.

"At this hour, she would be in the hearth room," said Aridane. Thorn moved on. She was almost to the inner wall when Aridane called out, "You did a magnificent thing, Eridé! Magnificent!"

The inner courtyard was piled high with firewood, and some artisan sisters were whetting axes on a grindstone. On the roof of the public shrine, girls from the foundling school were sewing thatch in place over thin spots. Everywhere she looked, Thorn saw the signs of winter's coming.

Thorn ritually washed her hands and feet from another rain basin. She left her shoes outside the door of the Inner Temple. It was warm within, and incense spiced the air. Somehow the aroma pleased her less than the smell of crushed oak leaves. The galleries were empty this time of day, as the priestesses were about their work. Thorn was grateful for that. Much as she loved her sisters, Kilowe, Aridane, and all the others, she was not ready yet to deal with their stares and scowls when they recognized her gravid state.

It was too warm for the seaman's coat, so she shucked it off and let it trail on the floor behind her. The Inner Temple was a single vast room, walled by shadow and partitioned by ritual. In the very center, under the great dome, was the hearth. It was the only light permitted inside the Inner Temple, the only flame. Thorn was drawn to it as surely as a moth to a candle.

There was someone seated on the wide hearth. Against the ever-burning fire, the priestess's gray robe looked black.

"Mother, may I warm myself at your fire?"

The hooded head rose. "It is not the hour for adoration—Eridé? Is that you?"

"Yes, Mother."

The gray-draped figure stirred. The high priestess, looking much older and thinner than Thorn remembered, beckoned her. Thorn came forward, and the One Who Commands kissed her on each cheek.

"I rejoice to see you," she said. "Here, sit with me

by the fire and tell me of your time away from us. I had a very florid missive from Princess Sverna, so I know the Brethren were overthrown, but what of the remainder of your charge?"

"It has all been done, Mother. The Godkiller died on the equinox as the book prescribed."

They sat, and the high priestess held Thorn's hand. "You don't know yet what a great thing it is you've done. By fulfilling the ritual of the Millennium Book, you have insured the peace and proper order of the world for a thousand years."

Thorn looked hard at her mentor. "Have I? All I really did was kill a man."

The elder woman's face creased with concern. "You feel remorse for your deed? Why is this? Did he not mistreat you? Did he not use you for his pleasure during the journey?"

"Yes, Mother."

"Did he not bear complicity in the death of our sister Ariaph?"

"He did, Mother."

The high priestess softly slapped her thin thigh. "Then why do you have this sorrow for him?"

"I don't, Mother. You chose me for this task because you knew I would carry it out no matter what happened," said Thorn.

The old woman frowned. "You never were a graceful liar. When I was First Sentinel and your teacher, I could always tell when you spoke an untruth." She who had been Nandra squeezed Thorn's hand. "I chose you not because you're some heartless slayer, but because of all the Sentinels of this temple, only you had the stubbornness and will to persevere with the true object of your charge. I knew you would accept that cockerel Rado's humiliation and transform it into unbending resolve. Any other Sentinel would have slain him long before reaching Miyesti."

"And not borne his child." Thorn scrubbed her face with her dry hands. "He was a brave man, for all his insolence. He met the Fact face to face and felt its power, and still he killed it."

"That is in the book, too. 'The doubting man shall not believe, yet if he could, the world would grieve.' "

"Was everything preordained by the Goddess? Were Rado's and my paths so irrevocable? It sounds as if there was no chance of failure."

"No," said the high priestess firmly. "Only the course of the ritual was set down by the ancients, not the final outcome."

Thorn gazed into the fire. "In a thousand years, will the Fact return?"

"In some form or another. It is the way the heavens turn. The Goddess has always defeated the Machine, but in some future millennium, she may suffer defeat. The Machine will triumph."

"That's a terrible thought, Mother."

"It's a thought to be guarded against, child. Have you ever heard of the Mirror Schism?" asked the priestess. Thorn shook her head. "It happened long ago. A group of priestesses who served the temple in

Held came under the delusion that there are many worlds, not just this one. The Mirrorists claimed that people just like us lived on these other worlds, and that every event we faced, they faced as well." The elderly woman frowned deeply. "The Homelands were in chaos in those days, and it was hard for my ancestor to exercise close authority over the sisters in Held. Then, when they began to spread the notion that the Great Goddess might not be supreme in all of these 'mirror worlds,' the Sentinels were sent against them."

"They were punished," said Thorn flatly.

"Aye, as all schismatics must be. That is why we here in Pazoa must keep the Millennium Book safe and pass along its warning to every new generation that enters the sisterhood of the temple."

Nandra stood. She walked away in a slow shuffle. Her joints were very stiff, a legacy of old injuries incurred as a Sentinel. "Sherdy is making suet pie. Will you join us for supper?"

"I'd like to stay here awhile," Thorn said.

"Yes, it is a good fire." The high priestess leaned against a soaring column. "Has his seed taken fair root?" she asked.

Thorn instinctively laid a hand on her belly. Barely aloud, she whispered, "Yes."

"It is a ponderous burden for you, child, but the seed of the Godkiller must be carried. In forty generations, the world will need him again. I will ask the Goddess to bring you a sound babe. Be at peace,

Eridé." Her softly scraping footsteps were quickly covered by the crackling of the flames.

Thorn reached into her pack. Under the dirty clothes, her last wrapped morsel of cheese, and her spare shoes, was the stiletto. She held it up. How different she felt about it now—it was no longer her comfort and strength. It seemed tainted now, and she didn't understand why.

The slim steel spike was black against the glare of the fire. Thorn threw the stiletto into the flames, and Eridé left the room.

HOUSTON, TEXAS (USA)—OFFICIALS OF THE FACT OF GOD FELLOWSHIP RELIGIOUS TV NETWORK ADMITTED TODAY THE LOSS OF THEIR NEWEST COMMUNICATIONS SATELLITE. F. MORTON PREDDY, PRODUCTION HEAD OF THE NETWORK, SAID NO TRACE OF THE FIFTY-MILLION-DOLLAR DEVICE HAS BEEN FOUND.

BUILT BY MATSUSHITA K.K. OF JAPAN AND LAUNCHED FROM CAPE CANAVERAL IN AUGUST OF LAST YEAR, THE SATELLITE, LISTED AS *SIGNO VINCES 2128* IN THE INTERNATIONAL CATALOG OF ORBITAL DEVICES, WAS ONE OF THE FIRST OF ITS KIND TO INCORPORATE A HEWLETT-PACKARD SERIES II ARTIFICIAL INTELLIGENCE. SERIES II COMPUTERS HAVE BEEN ORBITED IN MILITARY HUNTER/KILLER SATELLITES AND S.D.I. PLATFORMS SINCE THE BEGINNING OF THE DECADE. ACCORDING TO PREDDY, *SIGNO VINCES* WAS INTENDED TO TRANSMIT ORIGINAL SERMONS AND RELIGIOUS PROGRAMMING IN FIFTEEN

LANGUAGES TO EARTH-BASED RECEIVERS. THE COMPUTER WAS PROGRAMMED AT THE HOUSTON HEADQUARTERS OF THE FACT OF GOD FELLOWSHIP.

THE FELLOWSHIP IS STILL DIRECTED BY ITS FOUNDER, JOHN EDWARD MOSELEY, 56. MOSELEY, A CONTROVERSIAL FIGURE REGARDED WITH SUSPICION BY MOST MAINSTREAM THEOLOGIANS, HAS ATTRACTED A LARGE FOLLOWING WITH HIS CALL FOR A WORLD GOVERNMENT BASED UPON A PATRIARCHAL THEOCRACY.

WHEN ASKED TO COMMENT ON THE LOSS OF *SV-2128*, MOSELEY RESPONDED, "I RECKON GOD ADMIRED THAT SATELLITE SO MUCH HE CALLED IT AWAY TO HEAVEN."

THE EUROPEAN SPACE AGENCY REPORTS HAVING *SV-2128* ON TRACKING RADAR WHILE IT WAS IN A HIGH TRANSPOLAR ORBIT. WHEN GROUND CONTROL IN HOUSTON ATTEMPTED TO REDIRECT THE SATELLITE INTO A LOWER ORBIT, *SV-2128* VANISHED FROM E.S.A. SCREENS. "THE SATELLITE DID NOT FALL TO EARTH," SAID E.S.A.'s WALTHER RABB.

THE FELLOWSHIP SAYS THE SATELLITE WAS INSURED.

𝕶ingslayer
L. Dean James

In this sequel to *Sorcerer's Stone*, young Gaylon Reysson, the new king of Wynnamyr, must learn to use the magical sword Kingslayer. Will he capture a glorious victory for his people—or destroy himself and the world he hopes to save? Available May 1992.

𝕿he 𝕹ine 𝕲ates
Phillip Brugalette

Gopal, the prince of Goloka, sees his teacher burst into flames, then the many-armed Virabhadra go on a rampage. Gopal decides he must perform a sacred test but needs help from a centuries-old mystic to survive. Available August 1992.

𝕳alf-𝕷ight
Denise Vitola

Commander Ariann Centuri's betrothed is killed by the bat-faced Benar, and she is stricken with a terminal mind-bending disease. Suddenly she finds herself wedded to the Viceroy of the Galactic Consortium of Planets . . . and fighting for her life. Available December 1992.

DragonLance® Saga

Tales II Trilogy

The Reign of Istar
& The Cataclysm
On sale now
The War of the Lance
On sale November 1992

Margaret Weis and Tracy Hickman,
Michael Williams,
and Richard A. Knaak,
among others,
return to the DRAGONLANCE® World
in this trilogy of anthologies.

IT'S A WHOLE NEW EXPERIENCE IN COMPUTER FANTASY GAMING!

SHADOW SORCERER combines elements of role-playing with strategy, exploration and animated action. Control four characters at the same time, even during fully-animated real-time combat! All in 3-D isometric perspective!

Select your party from 16 different heroes, each with pre-made attributes. You've got big troubles ahead: hundreds of refugees to protect. Strange monsters in a vast wilderness. An army of draconians led by a red dragon!

And when the spells and weapons start flying, you'll appreciate the "point-and-click" interface!

Available for: IBM and AMIGA.
Visit your retailer or call 1-800-245-4525, in USA & Canada, for VISA /MC orders. To receive SSI's complete catalog, send $1.00 to:

STRATEGIC SIMULATIONS, INC.®
675 Almanor Avenue, Suite 201
Sunnyvale, CA 94086

THE FINAL CHAPTER IN THE GREATEST
AD&D® COMPUTER FRP SERIES EVER!

POOL OF RADIANCE, CURSE OF THE AZURE BONDS
and *SECRET OF THE SILVER BLADES:* together these
incredible games have sold more than *600,000*
copies so far! And now *POOLS OF DARKNESS* –
the final chapter – propels you into alternate
dimensions on an enormous quest.

Battle monsters never before encountered.
Cast powerful new spells. Achieve character
levels well above the 25TH level! Transfer your
characters from *SECRET OF THE SILVER BLADES*

intact, or create new ones! Either way, you'll
love this true <u>masterpiece</u> of the gaming art!

Available for: IBM and AMIGA.
Visit your retailer or call 1-800-245-4525, in
USA & Canada, for VISA /MC orders. To
receive SSI's complete catalog, send \$1.00 to:

STRATEGIC SIMULATIONS, INC.™
675 Almanor Avenue, Suite 201
Sunnyvale, CA 94086

Invaders of Charon Series
A New Dimension in
Outer Space Adventure!

The Genesis Web Book One
C. M. Brennan

Follow the adventures of Black Barney, from his birth in a RAM laboratory to his daring escape from his evil creators and beyond, into a world of danger and intrigue.

Nomads of the Sky Book Two
William H. Keith, Jr.

The mysterious, dreaded Space Nomads take Vincent Perelli prisoner, forcing him to fight a ritual battle for survival before he can seek the Device, a missing RAM artifact that may save the life of Buck Rogers. On sale November 1992.